Ozark Flats

Bob Williams

Ozark Flats

By
Bob Williams

JAMES D. THUESON, PUBLISHER
Minneapolis

OZARK FLATS, copyright©1983, by Robert K. Williams, is a work of the imagination based on historical facts. The story contains both real and fictional characters, some of whom were introduced in the author's novel EXCELSIOR. Minor license was exercised in the timing of events. Manufactured in the United States of America. All rights reserved. ISBN: 0-911596-16-0.

JAMES D. THUESON, PUBLISHER
Box 14474 University Station
Minneapolis, MN 55414

DEDICATED TO NELL

who, over fifty years ago, took me on my first streetcar ride and lovingly introduced this young boy to downtown Minneapolis; let me ride the city's first escalator at the Leader department store; bought me my school knickers at Kaplan's on Franklin avenue; and treated me to a performance on the stage of the new Minnesota Theater where appearing in person was the idol of all young boys, Tom Mix and his horse, Tony.

Prologue

IT IS THE TIME known as *The Gay Nineties.* It is a period of elegant fashions, mustaches, gambling, electric streetcars, and beautiful women in tightly-laced corsets. Grover Cleveland has become the first president to lose an election and then come back to be elected to a second term four years later. It is 1894 and while the rest of the country is suffering from a depression, Minneapolis is flourishing as the center of the flour-milling industry and as the railroad's gateway to the Northwest. The city is only forty years old and is already boasting about its seventy-million bushels of grain processed this year, the twelve million barrels of flour, and of Minnesota's lumber industry which produced over five hundred million feet of lumber in a year. Over a hundred and thirty-five passenger trains arrive and depart every twenty-four hours, and the University of Minnesota ranks second in the nation in attendance with nearly four thousand students. And in 1894, an exclusive apartment building on Thirteenth and Hennepin, known as the *Ozark Flats*, is about to become infamous!

Nicollet Avenue
Horses and sleighs moved along popular Nicollet avenue in downtown Minneapolis during the holiday season where Catherine Ging and Hillary Markham did their Christmas shopping in the story of *Ozark Flats*. The scene is from Fifth street looking toward the Mississippi River.

Photo, courtesy Minnesota Historical Society

The Old City Hall

The Minneapolis City Hall was located at the foot of Hennepin and Nicollet avenues between First and Second streets. The building was constructed in 1874. In the story of *Ozark Flats* in 1894, the office of the mayor, the Hon. William H. Eustis, was located on the second floor.

Photo, courtesy Minnesota Historical Society

The West Hotel

The West Hotel, located at Fifth and Hennepin, held its formal opening on November 19, 1884. One of the most elegant hotels in the nation, it was built at a cost of two million dollars, and hosted a long list of famous guests over the years—including President Grover Cleveland, Edwin Booth and Sarah Bernhardt.

Photo, courtesy Minnesota Historical Society

Grand Stairway, West Hotel
The *Grand Stairway* in Minneapolis' famous *West Hotel* was made of white marble and faced a lobby area that could easily hold a thousand guests. The stairway led to the grand dining room on the second floor as well as other elegant dining rooms, and was the scene of memorable reunions in the story of *Ozark Flats*.

Photo, courtesy Minnesota Historical Society

The Lake Harriet Streetcar
The *Lake Harriet Streetcar* is shown lumbering down Hennepin avenue's boulevard at about Colfax avenue. It would pass the *Ozark Flats* on its way to downtown Minneapolis. The last of the horse-drawn streetcars had been converted to electricity by 1892.

Photo, courtesy Minnesota Historical Society

Newspaper Row
Newspapers and printing firms lined Fourth street between Nicollet and First avenue in the area that would become known as *Newspaper Row*. Thousands and thousands of words would be printed here surrounding the events and activities of the residents of the *Ozark Flats*.
Photo, courtesy Minnesota Historical Society

The New City Hall and Court House
The *New City Hall* and *Court House* construction began in 1889 and was completed in 1895. Although not officially occupied until 1896, some portions of the building were in use in 1894.

Photo, courtesy Minnesota Historical Society

The Syndicate Building
The Syndicate Building was one of the centers of attraction in downtown Minneapolis in 1894. Kitty Ging's dressmaking shop was located in the *Syndicate Block* shown here in a view from Sixth street looking north on Nicollet avenue.
Photo, courtesy Minnesota Historical Society

The Grand Opera House
Some residents of the *Ozark Flats* attended the lavish *Grand Opera House* in downtown Minneapolis to see the original company of Charles Hale Hoyt's musical, *A Trip To Chinatown*, on a cold December night that ended in murder!
Photo, courtesy Minnesota Historical Society

Lockup Alley
Members of the Minneapolis Police Department lined up for this photograph in front of the Central Police Station in downtown Minneapolis in the area known as *Lockup Alley*.

Photo, courtesy Minnesota Historical Society

Union Station
Minneapolis' *Union Station* was the hub of the maze of passenger trains carrying businessmen, visitors and residents in and out of the city. Families would be reunited, lovers would part, and criminals would avoid police here during the story of *Ozark Flats*.
Photo, courtesy Minnesota Historical Society

Wintertime at Excelsior
In sharp contrast to summertime when the Lake Minnetonka area would become one of the most popular resorts west of Saratoga, Excelsior reverted to a quiet wintertime haven and *home* to some who resided at the *Ozark Flats*.

Photo, courtesy Excelsior Historical Society

The Ozark Flats
In 1892, a splendid new apartment house was built at the corner of Thirteenth and Hennepin in Minneapolis. It was called the *Ozark Flats* and although it was known for its elegance, it became famous because of the people who lived there in 1894.
Photo, courtesy Minnesota Historical Society

THE OZARK FLATS.

Ozark Flats

Tuesday, December 21, 1894

1

THE LAKE HARRIET CAR was already five minutes late according to Rex Barnett's pocket watch as he stood on the corner of Twenty-eighth and Hennepin on this December morning. The tall, handsome young man with the mustache put the watch back in his vest pocket and buttoned up his overcoat with the fur collar once more. Fortunately, it wasn't that cold for December. Probably around freezing, Rex thought, as he stood on the sidewalk of the boulevard, waiting for what should have been the 7:10 streetcar to downtown Minneapolis.

Rex was an early riser. He had already been up for sometime this morning, had taken a brisk walk down Twenty-eighth to the Lake of the Isles and back again to his second-floor apartment in the stucco duplex in the 2800 block of Humboldt avenue south, just a block away. Then he had fixed his own breakfast—he was one bachelor who did not neglect mealtime just because he was alone—and stacked the dishes before getting ready to go to work. When he left the duplex, he tucked last night's *Minneapolis Journal* under his arm. He would read it on the streetcar this morning.

Ozark Flats

Three more riders had now gathered on the corner when Rex saw the yellow streetcar appear over the bridge just a block south. The electric whine of the trolley car wound down as it came to a stop to pick up the early-morning passengers who crossed the one-way street to the boulevard of Hennepin avenue where the double set of tracks ran down the center of the thoroughfare. The tracks were almost new. Until last year, Rex had taken the streetcar route that went down Twenty-eighth to Lyndale avenue and then north to the downtown business district. As a matter of fact, the whole system was new. It had only been four years ago that the city council passed the ordinance that would electrify the street railway system and eliminate horsecars. And it had taken another two years to convert the system.

The wire gates opened at the rear of the car and the folding doors to the rear of the vestibule swung open at the same time. Rex was the last of the small group of riders to step up and inside, and he stopped to change a dollar bill. When he opened his billfold, the conductor couldn't help but see the police badge with the inscription, *Detective—Minneapolis Police Department*. Rex gave the conductor the dollar bill and asked for fifty cents in nickels. The conductor's money-changer, strapped to his belt, clicked out ten nickels and two quarters, and Rex headed for a seat. The car was crowded—mostly from passengers who had boarded at Lake and Hennepin—but there was still room, and Rex found a seat next to a window for the fifteen minute ride downtown. The seat was on the left side of the car, known as the pole side, and the outside of the windows on that side were covered with heavy wire to keep summertime passengers from reaching out and being injured by the Trolley poles in the center of the boulevard.

The young detective had an athletic look about him even as he slouched back in his seat and opened his newspaper. He had been born in Winona, Minnesota, a little over a hundred miles south of Minneapolis, and he was so small at birth that his parents decided to give him a small name—Rex—and with no middle name at all. So at age thirty-three, Rex Barnett was almost a native Minneapolitan. His father had been a Methodist minister with congregations in southern Minnesota before coming to Minneapolis where he served for twelve years at the Wesley Methodist church. The elder Barnett eventually became the District Superintendent for the Minneapolis Methodist District before he died of pneumonia in the Minnesota College Hospital. That's when Rex quit law school at the University of Minnesota and went to work for the *Minneapolis Tribune*.

He had grown up out in the Lake and Hennepin district where he had been a newsboy, and it seemed natural for him to move back to that area when he was on his own. He had been a star athlete at Minneapolis Central and, at his father's insistence, had enrolled at the University. He played a little football there and had the distinction of playing in what was considered the first intercollegiate football game for the University of Minnesota. The game had been brutal and was played at the state fairgrounds where Minnesota beat Hamline, 2-0. Rex left school that fall after his father died. It didn't take him long to learn that he was not cut out to be a journalist, however, and he started his career in the Minneapolis Police Department as a Bicycle Inspector, charged with "special duties to look after the bicycle interests in the city." The job came to entail the supervision of cycle paths and the wheelman of the city. Eight years ago he had the chance to become a full-fledged police officer, and he jumped at the opportunity.

He remembered when he and his good friend and fellow patrolman, John Morrissey, had been called into the Central Police Station a year and a half ago by Police Superintendent Vern Smith.

"You wanted to see us, sir?" Morrissey had asked.

"Where the hell have you two been?" the chief bellowed.

"It took us longer than we thought to come in from the Calhoun Station," Rex explained.

"All right, all right!" The chief got up from his desk and stepped over to the window to look out into the alley. "It's that goddamned newspaper again." He shook his head. "They're listing more unsolved cases everyday and now they're putting the pressure on the mayor. Bill is telling me that we've got to do something about it."

The two young policeman nodded in agreement.

"So we're adding two more detectives to the force. I've been watching you two work and I liked the way you handled the Benson case and the Holmes burglary last week. And you've been recommended by Charlie Gustavson. So go report to Captain Walton." The chief turned from the window and smiled. "I know you guys will do a good job."

Ozark Flats

The two patrolmen left the second floor office of the Central Station and ran down the stairs, skipping two or three steps at a time, and yelling, "Whooooooo .... eeeeeeee!"

Rex Barnett smiled as he gazed out the streetcar window and reminisced. Things hadn't changed, he thought. *The Journal* is still listing unsolved crimes. Then he stopped daydreaming and opened up last evening's paper to see if there were anymore stories about the police department. Fortunately, there were none. Then he turned to the want ads. He felt he could always keep in touch with the community by reading the want ads—especially the personals. Who knows what he might find there.

HELP WANTED—A good girl for general housework. German preferred. 802 Eighth Ave. So.

PERSONALS—K.G. will pick up the money. H. H.

WANTED—Salesman in every county. $75 a month can be made and will prove it. We furnish sample free. Write us. We will explain. Address Box 8006, Boston, Mass.

PERSONAL—R.W.E.T. Come home at once. Your mother is very sick.

PERSONALS—K.G. The insurance money is coming. H. H.

MAGNETIC AND MASSAGE BATHS—Miss Gertie Lewis has opened new bath and massage parlors at 241 Third Ave. N.

Rex smiled. Marvelous Gertie. He hadn't seen her for awhile. He'd call her today. Then, as he folded up the newspaper, he spotted a headline and story on an inside page. Representatives from the University of Minnesota and Purdue University were getting together to see what could be done about the violence in collegiate

football. There were simply too many ringers who weren't in school who were now playing on college teams, according to the story. Rex simply smiled.

The yellow streetcar with the white trim had now roared past the mansions at the top of Lowry Hill and down the hill past Loring Park. When the Lake Harriet car rolled to a noisy stop at Thirteenth and Hennepin, Emmett Markham boarded the car and dropped his nickel into the coin box. He had been waiting on the steps of the Ozark Flats, the new, elegant apartment building facing Hennepin avenue. He passed the crowded seats, including the one occupied by Rex Barnett, and continued up the aisle to an empty cane seat.

Emmett was new at this business of riding streetcars. He and his wife Hillary and their son, Jamie, had moved into Minneapolis and the Ozark Flats from their home in Excelsior at Lake Minnetonka just last fall. For the last five years he had been a weekly newspaper publisher in Excelsior where he owned *The Minnetonka News*. He had edited the publication for his father for four years before that, coming to Excelsior after being graduated from Brown University. In his undergraduate days, Emmett had edited the weekly publication each summer during the resort season at Excelsior, and then he would head back east to Fall River, Massachussetts, in the fall with his dad to the family newspaper and printing plant. After that, it was off to college again. He had married Hillary Blair Stockton in December of 1887 and they had settled in their year-round home in Excelsior.

Emmett was raised by his father and hung around the print shop all his life. He loved the weekly newspaper business, and when his father died in Fall River two years ago, he went back east to settle his father's affairs and eventually sell the newspaper operation there. He had earned such a good reputation as a Minnesota newspaper editor and publisher over the next few years that Lucian Swift, the manager of *The Minneapolis Journal*, offered him a managing editor's job with the city's evening daily, working for editor J.S. McLain.

Ozark Flats

The Markham family had continued to live in Excelsior during the past summer while Emmett commuted on early morning and late evening trains. With the advent of autumn, however, it was clear that they would have to move to Minneapolis—at least for the winter.

Emmett hadn't taken on the job with *The Journal* for the money. It simply didn't pay that well. He had been successful with his weekly newspaper and printing plant at Excelsior, and he had done well financially in selling his father's business in Fall River. Hillary's father had also offered some financial help to the young family. But it wasn't the money that interested Emmett. It was the opportunity to take on a new, big-city challenge—an experience that he didn't want to miss. So he hired an editor/acting publisher to run his *Minnetonka News* at Excelsior and once a month, Emmett would pay a business visit to Excelsior to go over the books and be brought up to date by his editor, George O'Brien. The monthly visit also gave Emmett a chance to have coffee with his old main street business friends and to check on the Markham home which had been closed up for the winter.

The transition from the weekly newspaper business to a daily newspaper editor had not come easy for Emmett. He could somehow cope with some of his co-workers down at *The Journal* who subtly suggested that he had too much money to be a working newsman. But those long summer hours away from Excelsior didn't get any shorter with the move to the city, and Emmett was still putting in long hours, missing meals and getting home late at night. And although Hillary was a big city girl herself, growing up in St. Louis, she had come to love the small town life and Excelsior, and this whole change in their lifestyle had been difficult for her, as well as for Emmett. As a result, there had been a series of confrontations and unpleasant words, even as late as this morning.

"But Emmett, how could you have forgotten the musical tonight?"

"I don't know, honey. It just slipped my mind."

"I already have Mrs. Blixt coming up to take care of Jamie. I thought we could stop and have dinner before the performance."

"I think we can still do that, Hillary. I'll stop and pick up the tickets over the lunch hour today. It's not that far away—I can walk over from the office."

"It's not just the tickets or your forgetting about tonight, Emmett.

She walked away from him and stared out the front window. "You've been gone so many evenings lately and I . . . I miss you when I go to bed alone. I need you to touch me."

"Oh, come on, Hillary. I've tried. But you're always sound asleep when I get home. Even this morning . . ."

"I wish we were back in Excelsior," she interrupted. "We had more time then—everything wasn't so rushed."

Emmett threw up his arms in despair. "We can't go back, now, dear. And I promise you, things will get better. I'm going out to the lake tomorrow to open up the house for Christmas and we'll all feel better after we've spent the long weekend there at home."

The Lake Harriet car had already passed the new Minneapolis Public Library on Tenth street and Emmett realized they were approaching the West Hotel and the Lumber Exchange at Fifth. Yes, he'd get the tickets for tonight's performance at noon. And he'd find time to shop for a gift for their wedding anniversary, just three days away. Things will be different after this weekend, he assured himself.

"Fourth street," barked the conductor in the rear of the car and Emmett headed for the front gates, buttoning his plaid overcoat. The gates opened and the good-looking newspaperman with the heavy eyebrows and square jaw stepped down, off the car and headed up the street towards Newspaper Row.

Two blocks later, the streetcar purred to a stop at Washington avenue and Detective Rex Barnett put his newspaper under his arm and stepped from the car, heading for the old Central Police Station and Lockup Alley. He thought again about the want ads and decided he would call Gertie this afternoon. Maybe they could have dinner together tonight.

Mayor William H. Eustis was looking out the second-story window of his office as the Lake Harriet car whined past the pie-shaped City Hall building where Hennepin and Nicollet avenues merged. The streets in the heart of the business district, were already busy with traffic—streetcars, horses and buggies, drayline wagons, and pedestrians. The mayor was holding the base of the telephone in one hand and the receiver in the other, propped near his right ear.

"I haven't seen anything in the past couple of days," the mayor said into the mouthpiece, "but that damned newspaper has already caused a stir. And now, even *The Trib* is beginning to make noises about the police department." He paused while he listened to the voice of the Superintendent of Police at the other end of the line. Then he added in agreement. "Well I appreciate your coming over this morning, Vern. Make it about eleven. That's when I've got that editor from *The Journal* coming in." The mayor paused again. "Yes. His name is . . . ." The mayor shuffled some papers on his large desk and found what he was looking for in the clutter. "It's Markham, Emmett B. Markham."

2

IT SEEMED INCREDIBLE that it had only been twenty-one years since Minneapolis merged with the Village of St. Anthoney to become the *City of Minneapolis* through the action of the state legislature. It had only had electricity for the past twelve or fourteen years, and what had been a frontier town not so long ago, was now a thriving metropolis with trade, industry and commerce that was unbelievable. With the growth and success came a bustling downtown business district, and it followed that it wouldn't be long before the city's wealth showed up in nearby residential areas—close to the action, but just far enough away from the heart of the city.

While New York had its Fifth avenue, and Cleveland its Euclid, a number of areas of Minneapolis were being compared to such famous streets. There were the magnificent homes on Kenwood Parkway, Portland and Park avenues, and Lowry Hill. With big cities came apartments, too, and all the talk these days was about such new exclusive apartment buildings as the Colonial Flats on Park avenue and the Arlington Flats over on Clinton.

Ozark Flats

On the outskirts of the business community, but still a little too close for the more affluent business and professional class, was a new and elegant apartment building on the corner of Thirteenth and Hennepin, one of the two main thoroughfares connecting the southwestern outskirts of the city with its downtown areas. The beautiful red brick structure had been completed in 1892 and was the most prestigious undertaking so close to the heart of the city. It was known as the Ozark Flats.

The impressive five-story structure faced west on Hennepin avenue. Rising above the massive entrance of special Minnesota stone, and inset into the building, were small balconies that looked out over the avenue. The apartments on the south side of the building were more spacious, and those on the fourth floor were the most expensive with large windows, arched at the top, at both the front of the apartment and on the south side facing thirteenth street where another set of balconies led to a black iron fire escape ladder. There were picture windows with arched tops in every northside apartment, providing a view of the downtown area of Minneapolis. From the rear of the building it was evident that the Ozark Flats was somewhat in the shape of an "H" with another set of small balconies looking out on to a back court.

A small store occupied the front lower half of the first floor with a corner entrance from the street. Another side entrance led to a rear apartment used as offices by the owners, and to a basement apartment. The owners were already planning some remodeling of the building even though it was only two years old. What they had in mind was a small pub to be located on the north side of the first-floor entrance which would cater not only to residents of the Ozark Flats, but to other home-owners of the area and residents of other apartments now springing up year by year. Six massive steps under a colorful canopy led to a large archway over the glass doors at the front entrance of the Ozark Flats. Inside, a large foyer was topped by a circular brass chandelier which lighted a magnificent stained glass window over a second set of glass doors leading to the first-floor hallway, the stairs and an elevator. Beautiful dark-wood wainscoting in the foyer extended down the main hallway to the elevator and also up the four-foot-wide staircase with the massive handrailing.

The largest of the fourth-floor apartments was occupied by the owner of the building, William W. Hayward and his wife, known to all as Lil. Their two sons also had apartments in the new building. Adry, the oldest, and his wife, Charlotte, had living quarters on the first floor while his younger bachelor brother, the debonair Harry T. Hayward, resided in a third-floor apartment, the same floor on which Mr. and Mrs. Henry Goosman lived. Mr. Goosman owned the Palace Liver Stable nearby. Francis Gorden Kelly, a short, red-headed lawyer, had the smallest of the second-floor apartments and was busy these days, furnishing it before his wedding in January. the other second fourth-floor flat was the home of Roger and Florence Wilhelm, the first tenants to move into the Ozark Flats when the building was completed in the fall of 1892. Mr. Wilhelm was an executive with the Pillsbury-Washburn Flour Mills, and the couple had no children. Roger Wilhelm was in his mid-forties but his premature gray hair made him look ten years older. His wife, however, was about forty but looked even younger.

In the northside apartment on the top floor, Catherine Ging was sipping a cup of coffee and looking out over the business section of the city on this December morning. She could see nearby private homes with barns out back, a smattering of apartment buildings, and smoke curling up from the chimneys of the new Public Library three blocks away, and disappearing into the morning sky. In the distance, flags could be seen flying atop the West Hotel and the new City Hall building still under construction.

Kitty Ging was a woman of extraordinary beauty. She was twenty-nine years old and was taller than most women, standing five-foot seven. She was a striking figure and those who met her for the first time were taken by her luxurious growth of beautiful brown hair and her blue eyes. A successful seamstress, she always dressed to attract attention and although breakfasting alone this December morning, she looked beautiful in a peach-colored satin housecoat and slippers. She had only been a resident of the Ozark Flats since the first of November when she and her seventeen-year-old niece, Louise Ireland, moved into the fifth-floor apartment. She had moved to the new apartment building on the urging of Harry Hayward whom she met at the Olson Boarding House across the street on Thirteenth. Many residents from the Ozark Flats could be found, regularly, eating dinner at the Olson place. And Kitty Ging and Harry Hayward discovered they had many things in common. They were both twenty-nine years old, unmarried, attractive—and they both had a yearning to have a lot of money.

Kitty and her twin sister, Julia, were born in Auburn, New York, in 1865 where they grew up in a family of workers with two more sisters and two brothers. The family never had much money and one of her brothers died at an early age. When she was seventeen years old, she left her family and went to Syracuse, New York to live with a friend of the family, Mrs. Florence Unkless, where she learned the art of dressmaking from the lady of the house. When Mrs. Unkless came to Minneapolis in 1884, she brought Kitty Ging along. Two years later, Mrs. Unkless died and the twenty-one-year-old Kitty Ging took over the dressmaking business which had been established in Minneapolis. When her father died, he left Kitty a small estate of about two thousand dollars.

Kitty had been reared a Roman Catholic and was a regular pew-holder at the Church of the Immaculate Conception in Minneapolis, even though she was not always a regular attender. She had talent—and good business sense—and by 1894 she found herself catering to an exclusive clientele. She had been engaged last year to a gentleman from neighboring St. Paul, but had broken off the engagement—and kept the ring. Then she met Harry Hayward and had been dabbling in some minor gambling during the last month. In the meantime, her dressmaking business was growing to the point where she had taken up new quarters on the third floor of the Syndicate Building on Nicollet avenue between Fifth and Sixth streets. She employed two full-time seamstresses along with her niece, Louise.

The attractive brunette moved away from the larger window and crossed the dining room and back into the kitchen of her apartment to get some fresh coffee.

When the phone rang in the dining alcove, Kitty set down her coffee cup and went to answer the call.

"Hello." There was a pause. "Oh, Harry. Yes, of course I'm up." Another pause. "No, I'm not sick. They know that I'm not coming in until this afternoon. We can't possibly take any more orders before Christmas, and the girls are working twelve hours a day to finish by Friday." She listened. "I'd like to, Harry, but I've promised my neighbor, Mrs. Markham, that we'd go to lunch today and shop a

little this afternoon." Another pause. "Well—I suppose it would be all right—that is, if you'd like to take us both to lunch." She laughed. "Fine. We'll meet at the Continental at noon. I'll tell her—and I'm sure she won't mind. —Yes, of course, Harry. At noon." Kitty hung up the phone. She'd have to go across the hall and tell Hillary Markham that there would be a third party today. Harry Hayward was going to join them for lunch.

Hillary Markham had eaten breakfast seemingly hours ago with Emmett—before they had words, and before he left for the office of *The Journal*. Since then, she had also fixed breakfast for their son, Jamie, packed a lunch for him, and sent the seven-year-old off to Douglas Grade School for the day. Then she had straightened the apartment and laid out the clothes she would wear to lunch today with her neighbor from across the hall, Kitty Ging. She didn't know her new neighbor very well, but she liked her. The attractive Kitty Ging had seemed genuinely grateful for a friendly face and an encouraging word or two from Hillary when the dressmaker had moved into the Ozark Flats. And Hillary had accepted last weekend when Kitty offered to take her to lunch and Christmas shopping today.

"I'm going to take Tuesday off," Kitty told her as they stood in the hallway Friday evening. "I'm going to sleep late and then try to do my Christmas shopping, and if you'd like, you're more than welcome to come. If we have time, we'll even stop at the Syndicate Building so you can see my shop."

"I'd like that," Hillary agreed. She needed to get out of the apartment. She had been alone most evenings while Emmett worked, and she, too, had some shopping to complete before her parents arrived on the day of Christmas Eve—this coming Friday. "Yes, I'd really like that," she told Kitty.

Hillary thought about it as she poured herself a cup of coffee in her own kitchen. A pretty blond, she was a couple of years younger than Kitty, and four years younger than her husband. This morning she was dressed in a wool, floor-length bathrobe and she had pulled the tie-belt snug at the waist. Even though she had lived in Minnesota for the past six winters, she was still a St. Louis girl at heart, and admitted being cold from the first of November until the first of April. She had met Emmett Markham when he was a young editor of *The Minnetonka News* at Excelsior some eleven years ago when she was only sixteen, and had fallen in love with him at first sight. Her father, T.J. Blair, was a vice president of the Minneapolis and St. Louis Railway at its St. Louis office, and would combine business with pleasure each summer. That's when he would bring his family along in July when he came to Excelsior to inspect the firm's resort hotel properties at Lake Minnetonka—the White House Hotel and the Lake Park Hotel.

Those first three summers had been such memorable ones for Hillary—and Emmett. That is, until she went back to St. Louis and found she was carrying Emmett's baby. Her demanding father would have never understood, and her understanding mother, Frances Blair, had finally agreed to say nothing and let Hillary marry Jim Stockton, the boy next door. Jamie had been born in May, and Tom Blair had insisted that everyone go along for the annual summer visit to Excelsior that year. It was a painful experience for Hillary and one that ended in tragedy. Emmett couldn't believe what had happened, Frances was the victim of a blackmailing scheme, and in the end, young Jim Stockton, who had an intense fear of water, drowned in a freak accident aboard the giant sidewheeler, *The Belle of Minnetonka*, on the Fourth of July. Ironically, it had been Emmett who failed in his attempt to save him.

The family went back to St. Louis, and Emmett eventually followed in the fall. They were married on Christmas Eve in the Blair home in St. Louis, and Hillary, Jamie and Emmett had come back to Excelsior to live.

Hillary thought of their beautiful home at Excelsior on the high bluffs overlooking Excelsior Bay, and those homesick feelings reminded her that her folks would arrive Friday and they would all spend the Christmas weekend at Excelsior. Perhaps that would help set things straight between Hillary and Emmett.

As she finished her coffee, her reminiscing also prompted her that she would have to buy an anniversary gift for Emmett this after-

noon. Yes, this Christmas Eve might be a very special one after all.

Claus and Julia Blixt earned free rent in their basement apartment at the Ozark Flats as part of Claus' pay as janitor and part-time elevator operator. Julia's husband had been employed at the Ozark Flats ever since it opened. They had come to Minneapolis about a year before from a small town just south of Minneapolis, Cannon Falls. Claus was thirty-seven years old now. He was born in Sweden and was about five-years-old when he came to America with his father and journeyed to Minnesota. They settled in Spring Garden in Goodhue County and Claus spoke Swedish long before he learned English. When he was twenty-one, he married Minnie Olson. They had two children before she died and he became a father three times in four years after marrying his second wife, Emma. She also died, and in 1891, he married Julia Anderson.

When he first came to Minneapolis, he worked as a bartender and as a streetcar conductor. Then he got the job as janitor at the Ozark Flats and they moved into the new apartment building. Although their apartment was small, it was still by far the best living quarters the two of them ever had. Besides his janitorial duties, lately Claus had been running errands for Harry Hayward who had assumed the duties as manager of the apartment building for his father. Julia made some additional wages by taking care of youngsters in the neighborhood. She had been particularly helpful to Hillary Markham, taking care of the Markham's seven-year-old son, Jamie, many times. In fact, today would be one of those days, and longer than usual. She would meet the young Markham boy on his return from school, fix him supper, and stay with him this evening until the Markhams returned home from a concert at the Grand Opera House. Claus didn't seem to mind. Besides, it would mean a little extra money—for a cheap bottle of whiskey.

3

REX BARNETT shared a desk with his partner, City Detective John E. Morrissey, on the second floor of the Central Police Station. The station was old and deteriorating, and would be abandoned in the near future for the new police headquarters and jail in the new Hennepin County Court House and City Hall on the block surrounded by Fourth and Fifth streets and Third and Fourth avenues. The new building was being completed now, and some city offices had moved. But the old police station was still very much in existence, located between Nicollet and First avenue on what was known as Lockup Alley, which ran between Washington avenue and Second street. It was also convenient to the mayor's office in the old City Hall at the foot of Nicollet and Hennepin, just a couple of blocks away.

John Morrissey and Rex had joined the force as patrolmen just about the time that the newly-formed Minneapolis Police Commission had taken possession of the department and announced that there would be "no more political pull" in appointing men to the Force. From then on, appointments were made on merit, education and a tough physical examination. John and Rex were the first to make the Force under the new rules which caused quite a stir within the department. Four officers had resigned and sixteen more failed the requirements. The new regime had also installed a new system of Captains, Lieutenants and Sergeants, and although the chain of command remained, the commission charter was repealed in 1888 and the ultimate power of the Police Force went back to the office of the mayor.

All of this was necessary, of course, because crime had been with the community since its inception back in the 1850's. The first burglary in Minneapolis was reported in 1855 when some $200 in goods "was purloined" from the store of William D. Babbett, followed by a $300 theft in a hotel. There were no arrests. There were no police! Then came the first Marshall (at $300 per year salary), the first murder in Hennepin County (June 11, 1856), and the first Police Chief, H.H. Brackett, who was in command of six patrolmen. They had no uniforms and their sole authority came from wearing a police star. Then, patrolmen earned $65 a month. The Chief's salary was $1,000 a year.

The Force got its first detective only twenty years ago when Michael Hoy was appointed City Detective in 1874—the same year they finally got around to getting police uniforms. Mayor William H. Eustis had named Vernon M. Smith as Superintendent of Police earlier this year, and he now led a Police Force that boasted 218 officers and men with a Headquarters detachment and five precincts. Chief Smith had come up through the ranks, was an experienced policeman and detective, and was proud of the more than 5,000 arrests his men had made this year, with fines totalling some $38,000. The entire department had cost the city $217,416 as 1894 neared its end. The mayor only had one problem. There had been a rash of robberies and assaults, many of them unsolved, in the past two or three months, and the newspapers were quick to point them out—especially *The Minneapolis Journal*. As a result, Mayor Eustis, who worked closely with the police department, had arranged a meeting this morning with the police and the newspaper.

John Morrissey had been doing some paperwork at the desk he shared with Rex Barnett. A stocky man with heavy eyebrows and a bushy mustache, he always looked uncomfortable in his suit and overcoat, as if he would rather be found in a pair of overalls out in the country. As a matter of fact, the thirty-six-year-old detective grew up on farms near Albany, New York, and Brownsville, Minnesota. He came to Minneapolis in 1881 and became a patrolman in 1886. Just last year he was assigned to the Central Station with Rex Barnett as a new detective. His wife, Mary, came from Winona, Minnesota, located along the Mississippi river in the southern part of the state, and the Morrisseys now lived on Bryant avenue in South Minneapolis with their five children.

"You're on your own, this morning, Rex," John Morrissey said to his partner as Rex walked into the large office that housed most of the detectives for the city.

"Where ya going'?" asked Rex as he took off his overcoat and hung it on a hall tree in the corner of the high-ceilinged room.

"I've got to appear in court this morning," John replied. "It's that shoplifting case from a couple of weeks ago. The one that King and Murphy were working on."

"Is that the one with the washerwoman up northeast." Rex asked.

"That's it. She'd been stealing the stuff for weeks and we were gettin' all kinds of complaints from merchants. She's a Mrs. Olson, and when we finally found her, we found just about everything you could think of—bonnets, bolts of ribbon, pocketbooks, about forty skirts, and jewelry you couldn't believe—about a thousand dollars worth of stuff! Both King and Murphy are tied up, so I'm the one who has to go to court."

Officer King was the oldest and one of the most experienced detectives on the Force. Murphy was the newest, and somehow those two hit it off, making them one of the best and most successful teams the police department had.

Chief Smith opened the translucent glass door to his office and stepped out into the main detectives' room and called to Rex. "I've got something you'll really like this morning," he told him.

"Not another shoplifting job," Rex laughed.

"No, not this time," Smith answered. "You and I are going to see the mayor this morning. Bill wants me to bring along a working detective from the department—and you're it!" He pointed his index finger directly at Rex Barnett. "And guess who we're meeting with in the mayor's office?"

Rex shrugged, already giving up.

"It's our friend from *The Journal*, Emmett Markham!"

Both Rex and John Morrissey looked at each other and their faces broke into broad grins. Rex shook his head in agreement. Maybe it wouldn't be such a dull day after all.

"I'm not sure whether I'm right or wrong, Charlie," Emmett Markham confessed over his cup of coffee. It was a mid-morning coffee break for Emmett and Charlie Strong, a feature writer and part-time editor for *The Minneapolis Journal*, who had befriended Emmett when he came to *The Journal* last summer. Charlie was about sixty years old, had kicked around Minneapolis daily newspapers for the last thirty years, and had been with *The Journal* for the last ten. He had been a weekly newspaperman in Illinois before he came to Minnesota. He loved country weeklies and always maintained that weekly newspapers were where young journalists got their start, and where big city newspapermen dreamed of getting back to in their later years. Maybe it was his country weekly background that brought him to like Emmett Markham when the young weekly newsman joined the staff of *The Journal*.

"All you can do is to stick with what you think is right, Emmett," Charlie assured him.

"Honest to God, Charlie, I really have nothing personal against the police department. God knows we depend on them. But it's a matter of record that there are simply a lot of crimes being committed here in Minneapolis—and too many of them are just not being solved. My God, Vern Smith has more men on his police force than any other town this size. And we're still in trouble."

"You may be absolutely right, Emmett," the other newsman counselled. "But don't make a crusade out of it. We may think we have our finger on the pulse of this city, Emmett," he went on. "But I doubt that we have any idea just what those guys down there at the Central Police Station face every single day." Then he added as an after-thought. "Just go down there this morning and be sympathetic.

Ozark Flats

Don't go in there with a chip on your shoulder. If anything, offer to help." Charlie sipped on his cup of coffee as the two of them sat face to face at a small table in the window of the Fourth Street Coffee House, just across from Newspaper Row. The Coffee House faced the Journal and the Tribune across the street, and was surrounded by print shops down the avenue.

"At least they've taken notice of us," Emmett consoled himself. "But you're right, Charlie. I'm not some kid with a brand clean printer's apron. I'll do what's right for them and for *The Journal*—and for me."

The two of them sat there and looked out the window as they finished their coffee. They would cross the street and then go back to the newsroom to check the first aftenoon edition of *The Journal* as it came off the press. Emmett remembered that he would have to make a trip over to the Grand Opera House during the lunch hour and get those tickets for tonight's performance of the musical, *A Trip To Chinatown*. He still had a couple of Christmas gifts to buy before the weekend, too, and something special for Hillary for their wedding anniversary on Friday. He also wondered if old Charlie might give him some advice about himself and Hillary. Charlie had been a widower for the last ten years and Emmett respected his new-found friend's common-sense approach to things. On second thought, Emmett already knew what to do—to take his job a little less seriously and to start spending more time at home with his family. After all, Hillary and Jamie were the two most important things in his life. Emmett stared out the window.

"You all right, Emmett?" Charlie asked.

Emmett returned to the moment. "Yes. Yes, of course. Let's go back to work. Then I've got to get on to the mayor's office." The two got up from their window table and started out the front door of the Coffee House. They stopped outside on the sidewalk and Emmett turned to his friend.

"Thanks, Charlie."

Ozark Flats

Adry Hayward watched out the front window of his first-floor rooms at the Ozark Flats this morning, pondering what to do. An ordinary-looking individual, Adry was not a bright person, a little slow in his thinking processes, and mostly overlooked when in the company of others. Although not always in agreement with his younger brother, the thirty-two-year-old Adry Hayward still looked up to Harry, and around the Ozark Flats, was content to be second in command in running the apartments for their father. Harry had not been particularly kind to Adry over the years, but it didn't seem to cause any hard feelings between the two brothers. Adry looked at the clock on the mantel in his living room and noticed that it was now 10:30. He had been staring out that front window since eight o'clock this morning without leaving his chair. Decisions did not come easily for him. But now he had made up his mind.

The elder Hayward brother told his wife, Charlotte, he had an errand to run, donned a muffler, his overcoat and hat, and quickly left the apartment, walking down the long hall to the front entry-way and down the steps on to the Hennepin avenue sidewalk. He was sure—at least as sure as he could be—that he had made the right decision. He was off to see an old friend of the family and Minneapolis businessman and property-owner, Levi Stewart. He hoped his brother, Harry, wouldn't be too angry with him.

Maybe he'd never find out.

Rex Barnett watched the smoke from Mayor Eustis' cigar curl upwards near the ceiling as Vern Smith spoke.

"We're not looking for a whitewash, Bill," he explained. "We'd be the first ones to admit that there's a lot going on we can't handle. There isn't a big-city police department in the whole country that has everything under control. But I think we're doing a pretty good job with the limited personnel we have."

"You've got the biggest budget in the history of the department, Vern," the mayor replied between puffs.

"Don't give me that bull," the police chief shot back. "You've got

57

the biggest budget in the history of this city, but I know damn well that you're not satisfied with everything that's going on." Vern Smith got up from his chair and paced back and forth in front of the mayor's desk as Rex sat quietly by and watched. "I've got fourteen attached to headquarters and seventy-four men downtown. Hell, I should have ninety downtown. And I'm still understaffed out in the Fifth and Lake Calhoun. I've only got eighteen men out there and that whole area is mushrooming."

"I know, Vern, I know," the mayor spoke in a calm voice. "I didn't get you—and Barnett—over here this morning to chew your ass. Hell, I'm on your side. I know what your problems are. What you have to do is to tell Markham all of this." As an after-thought he added, "And it's not just *The Journal*. Even *The Tribune* is beginning to make noises."

"Well, if he could only see these guys, see the danger they face, and see how hard they work at all of this, he'd. . . ."

There was a knock on the door. Mayor Eustis got up, crossed the room, turned the knob and opened the door.

A handsome young man in a checkered overcoat stood there, facing him. "I'm Emmett Markham," he said.

The mayor motioned to him as he spoke. "Come in, Mr. Markham. We've been expecting you."

4

IF HARRY T. HAYWARD had been born a millionaire, he would have been perfect for that kind of life in the year 1894. The twenty-nine-year-old Hayward was a dapper, man-about-town. The rosy-cheeked young man was handsome, had his hair cut a little shorter than most men of the day, sported a heavy mustache, and was always impeccably dressed in the latest men's fashions, selected from a wardrobe twice the size of most wealthy men in Minneapolis.

Managing the Ozark Flats for his father was nothing more than a hobby to Harry. He wanted—and needed—to be around a lot of people, and he was comfortable and at ease with just about everyone. He had acquired all the social graces, was attractive to women, and was liked and admired by most men. He could be the center of attraction in the lobby of the Bijou Opera House or just one of the boys in the corner saloon. He had travelled as far away as Alaska, Maine and Mexico, always seemed to have money, and didn't seem to mind spending it.

Unfortunately, Harry Hayward hadn't been born a millionaire.

He was the younger of William W. Hayward's two sons and the mere fact that Harry was not rich did not dissuade him from living the glamorous life. The problem was money—or the lack of it. That one minor problem was becoming a more serious one these days, especially for someone who considered himself a professional gambler. Young Hayward had never worked for a living and had not done too well at the gaming tables. His gambling had already forced him to sell one building given to him by his father, and he had lost all the money he acquired from an old friend of the family, successful property owner Levi M. Stewart.

If he was worried, he didn't show it. He was still the center of attraction wherever he went, and his self-confidence impressed everyone from the more sophisticated social circles to the more unsavory crowd of Minneapolis and St. Paul gambling houses. Gamblers liked him because he could change his whole being in an instant. It was his eyes. They could be warm and loving one minute and cold and calculating the next. And it was his eyes that first attracted Catherine Ging to the handsome young Hayward. They had met at the dinner table of the Olson Boarding House across the street from the Ozark Flats, and now there were all kinds of rumors about Harry and Kitty. Some thought the two were really getting serious about each other and that the attractive couple was about to make an announcement of a forthcoming marriage. Others said Harry was helping Kitty finance her dressmaking business and her new business quarters on Nicollet avenue. Still others suspected Kitty was attracted to the seemingly dangerous life which Harry led.

It was late in the morning when Harry realized that perhaps this was all a little more dangerous than he had bargained for. But it was not evident in those eyes of his as he sat across the table from the two men in a fifth-floor suite of the West Hotel.

The larger man in his shirtsleeves was gulping down a huge breakfast brought up by room service. His dark trousers were held up by wide suspenders and he was still in his stocking feet. "As I see it, Harry, we got two problems." He paused for more eggs and bacon. "The first is getting the green goods into circulation in this town and the second is getting our money back."

"I'm already working on that, Mr. Hudson," Harry assured him. "I've got nearly seven thousand already out and I would guess most of that is already in circulation. It'll just take a little time, that's all."

"That's very good, Harry," the large man replied while chewing on the bacon. The other gentleman, a smaller man who was fully dressed in a plaid double-breasted suit and still wearing his bowler hat, got up from the table and stood near the window looking out on Fifth street. He did not enter the conversation. "But what about the debts?" the large man inquired.

Harry got up from the chair across from the breakfast-eater and paced a little. "You don't have to worry, Mr. Hudson, I'm passing the goods as quickly and discreetly as I can. Those few debts will be wiped out before the month is over, I can promise you."

"You solve those two problems, Harry, and we'll do some more business after the first of the year. But in the meantime, I'd like to see some returns by the end of the week. I don't think that's asking too much."

If Harry Hayward was worried, he didn't show it. Without any hesitancy, he agreed. "By the end of the week I'll have some money for you, Mr. Hudson. You can count on it. You have my word." He looked him straight in the eyes and extended his hand to shake on it. The big man shoved his hulk of a hand across the table and shook with Harry.

"Why don't you call me about Friday. We'll setup a meeting," he told Harry.

The two men shook hands again and Harry started towards the door. He stopped and turned to the small man by the window. "Nice to see you again, Mr. Farber," he said. Then he turned and left.

"Do you believe him?" asked the smaller man.

"No, but I like his style and I know he's resourceful. He won't have it by the end of the week, but I'll bet that by January he'll turn that goddamned counterfeit money into something we can spend anywhere. Pour me some more coffee."

When the two attractive young women entered the Continental Cafe on Washington avenue shortly before noon, the manager was quick to welcome Kitty Ging and her companion, Hillary Markham. It was apparent to Hillary that Kitty Ging was a frequent diner here. The manager called her by name and had their table reserved for them. Each of the ladies would have turned the head of the men diners and most of the women who were lunching at the Continental, but to have two such lovely women entering the place at the same timed caused a stir among those dining on the first floor.

Polished hardward floors and deep walnut panelling brought a dignity to the Continental that made it one of the most popular restaurants in the city, even though the prices were higher than most places. A magnificent stairway near the entrance curved around part of the main-floor dining area to a more intimate room in the loft, lighted with gas lamps and deep green table cloths. If guests were undecided as to which dining room they wanted, headwaiters always explained that if they wanted to talk business, they should dine on the first floor. If they wanted to talk of love, they should reserve a table in the loft. But Kitty had requested a table in the main dining room where there was an air of excitement, especially during this holiday season.

The headwaiter, Raymond, helped Hillary with her coat, a fitted brown wool that matched the wool suit she had chosen for the day. Under a sealskin cloak, Kitty Ging was dressed in one of her own creations, a navy wool serge skirt and a striped shirtwaist with a navy bow at the neckline. They had no more than been seated when a waiter brought them each a glass of wine, compliments of Mr. Harry Hayward who had phoned ahead and said he would be a little late.

The two looked at each other across the table and for the first time, Hillary noticed Kitty's beautiful blue eyes. But it wasn't just the natural beauty of her eyes. Kitty had applied some kind of grey, glittering eye make-up so expertly that it looked very natural. Hillary admired that. Even though she had grown up in St. Louis and considered herself a big-city girl, Hillary had never worn that kind of make-up. Perhaps it was in deference to her conservative father whom she had always tried to please. But Kitty was beautiful this day. Perhaps she would ask her new friend about the make-up sometime. It would be fun to try it.

The two of them raised their glasses and then sipped the wine. "I don't know why we didn't do this a long time ago, Hillary. We've lived across the hall from each other for almost two months now, and this is the first time we've really had a chance to visit."

"I know," Hillary replied apologetically. "I'm afraid I haven't been very neighborly. But I'm glad that we're here today."

"Yes, and we'll have a chance to do a little Christmas shopping after lunch."

"I'm looking forward to that," Hillary agreed. "And Emmett and I are going out for dinner before we go to the Grand Opera House tonight to see *A Trip To Chinatown*."

"That sounds like a good time," Kitty said as she sipped her wine. "I've got to stop at the shop later this afternoon." She hesitated for a moment. "And I've got things to do tonight."

Hillary felt an uneasiness as Kitty seemed to stop and think of what she wanted to say—then carefully go on with the conversation. She enjoyed Kitty and was truly sorry that they hadn't planned such a day a long time ago. It was just what Hillary needed to get her mind off of her unhappiness at home and her new life in Minneapolis. She felt a certain excitement, too, about having lunch not only with Kitty, but with the dashing Harry Hayward who arrived momentarily, just in time to order lunch. If he had worries on his mind about the meeting on the fifth floor of the West Hotel this morning, it didn't show. He apologized if he had really intruded on a "girls' luncheon date" and he kept both women entertained throughout the lunch hour.

"I think we should do this again sometime soon," Harry told them, "and next time, we'll have Mr. Markham join us." They all agreed. When the check came, Harry reached for his wallet in the inside breast pocket of his suitcoat. But Kitty insisted that the lunch was her idea, and although she had kidded Harry earlier this morning about picking up the luncheon check, she would pay for it. She quickly reached into her purse and pulled her hand back clutching a fist-full of bills. Hillary's eyes widened. The bills were all twenty-dollar bills! Lots of them! She must have more than a thousand dollars in her hand, Hillary thought! Maybe two thousand!

Harry glared at Kitty. "For God's sake, put that green goods away, Kate!" he said in supressed tones.

"It's all right, Harry. I'm not going to lose any of it, at least not here," she assured him.

Ozark Flats

Harry recovered and turned to Hillary. "I just don't like to see anyone flash too much money around. You never know who's watching."

Kitty paid the bill and the threesome got up to leave. Harry said he had to meet an old friend, and Kitty and Hillary went on their way Christmas shopping. Raymond watched them go as he put the tip Kitty had left in his pocket. He had never seen so much money at one time in his whole life as Kitty pulled from her purse. Yessir, he thought. She is either a very busy dressmaker—or a very expensive one.

Harry Hayward met his old friend, Tom Waterman, at a cigar store on Washington avenue at about 2 o'clock and the two of them made the rounds of popular saloons throughout downtown Minneapolis. It was more than they could handle in one afternoon, and they took time out from their drinking spree to stop at the Dime Museum and later, at a shooting gallery over on First avenue. After a couple of more bars, the two stopped at a drug store on First avenue and Washington where they were joined by an attractive blond woman wearing a flashy red coat with a black fur collar. The three of them set off down the avenue to Fourth street where Tom Waterman and the woman left Harry at the foot of the stairs next to another drinking establishment and went up to the second floor. Harry went into the bar on the first floor and had another drink. Twenty minutes later, Harry climbed the stairs and let himself into room number 209. As he expected, Waterman was pulling his pants on. The blond was still lying on the bed, clad only in a corset and a pair of opera hose. Harry declined an invitation to join her and hustled his friend out of the room and down the stairs to the street. There was one more stop—at a jewelry store—on their way across town to the West Hotel and the billiard room. Even Harry agreed that it was time to slow down.

Ozark Flats

It was the Christmas shopping season in downtown Minneapolis. The Plymouth Clothing House at Third and Nicollet was selling men's pants for $3 and suits were on sale for $10. There was a Christmas sale going on at the Minneapolis Dry Goods store, and at the George S. Beall and Company on Nicollet avenue between Sixth and Seventh, Kid Gloves were selling for $1.67, Irish Linen Hankies at twelve cents apiece, Cloaks and Furs were priced from $6 to $12, and Muffs were $2. The store advertised "Neckwear for Gents, 48 cents"!

Kitty Ging and Hillary Markham seemed to have made just about every store in town this afternoon. They had been to Donaldson's Glass Block on Sixth and Nicollet where, like all shoppers on this day, they paid ten cents admission to the store with the admission price going to a Christmas charity. While they were there, they were treated to music by the Third U.S. Infantry Band and a concert by a black group, the Jubilee Singers. They shopped the entire length of Nicollet avenue, from R.S. Goodfellow and Company at 247 Nicollet to Dickerson's on Sixth and Nicollet where they bought towels, women's hose, and where HIllary had purchased a blanket for ninety-five cents.

When they were only a half a block from the Syndicate Building, Kitty invited Hillary to come up and see her dressmaking shop on the third floor. Two seamstresses looked busy and Kitty's niece, Louise, was doing some last-minute pressing. There were dresses and materials everywhere and Hillary wondered how they could keep track of anything at all. They only stayed a few minutes and Hillary said goodbye to Louise when they left. Kitty told her niece she'd be back before they closed. Then the two women were off to their last shop of the afternoon at the New England Furniture and Carpet Store.

"I can't thank you enough," Hillary gratefully told Kitty as they stood on the corner of Third and Hennepin. "I can't remember when I've had so much fun."

Kitty laughed. "I'm down here everyday and the town never seemed so exciting before. I think you've given me the Christmas spirit, too."

Ozark Flats

Hillary was carrying three large bundles of Christmas gifts and the two stood on the corner, waiting for a streetcar for Hillary. A minute later, the car came rattling down the center of Hennepin avenue and slowed down to their stop. The two of them stood there for a moment, as if they were saying goodbye at a train station, and then they embraced each other as best they could with the packages in the way. In much more subdued tones, Hillary thanked her again. "The lunch and the shopping with you was just what I needed. Thanks again," she smiled.

"We'll do it again, some day soon," Kitty said.

Hillary crossed to the center of the broad street and stepped up and on to the rear platform of the Hennepin-Lake streetcar. Kitty called out as an afterthought. "I'll have you and Emmett over soon for dinner!" Hillary looked back, nodded and tried to wave. But it was no use. The doors were closing.

Kitty would head back toward Nicollet avenue now, and to her own dressmaking shop where she still had some packages to mail. She also realized that it was too late to get to the bank this afternoon. She'd go in the morning. But she stood on the corner for just a few seconds longer as the streetcar pulled away. "She's living in a whole different world," she mused. "But not a bad lady. Not bad at all."

Two blocks away, young Paul Born, a messenger boy recently hired at the West Hotel, was returning from a trip to the postoffice when a grey-haired man stopped him on the corner in front of the hotel. "Do you want to make a nickel?" The gentleman asked the young messenger boy.

"Sure do!" the fifteen-year-old replied enthusiastically.

"Just take this envelope over to the Syndicate Building on Nicollet and deliver it to Miss Kitty Ging at her dressmaking shop on the third floor. You got that? Miss Kitty Ging, Third Floor, Syndicate Building."

The boy nodded and started to cross the street. Then he stopped, turned back and chased after the man with the grey hair and the mustache who was now disappearing into the crowd.

"Hey, mister," he called out. The gentleman stopped and looked around. "What's your number at the hotel?"

"Oh, I'm not staying at the hotel," he explained. "But I'll pay you now." He seemed a little flustered, but he dug into his pants pocket and gave young Paul Born the coin. "There won't be any answer."

The two parted and the messenger boy started back across the avenue. The son-of-a-bitch wasn't going to pay me anything at all, he thought.

5

WHEN THE WEST HOTEL held its formal opening on November 19, 1884, it was heralded as the finest and best hotel in the entire country. The evening was highlighted by "the most elegant banquet ever given in Minneapolis" as five-hundred gentlemen were seated in the main ballroom for a twelve-course dinner which cost $10 a plate. The evening was dedicated to the late Charles W. West and was hosted by the proprietor and owner of the magnificent hotel, Col. John T. West, who served as master of ceremonies. The 25th United States Infantry Band from Fort Snelling played for the occasion and 150 waiters in full dress greeted the guests as they entered the main room. Every famous name in Minneapolis and St. Paul was on the guest list for the opening night dinner, including George A. Pillsbury, John S. Pillsbury and William S. King. W.D. Washburn served as toastmaster for the evening and James J. Hill, president of the Great Northern Railroad, addressed the audience. When the formal opening was over, there were so many guests waiting to register at the hotel that some were not assigned rooms until two o'clock in the morning.

It had all started, of course, when Charles West purchased the site at the corner of Fifth and Hennepin back in 1881 for $45,000. The excavation began the next summer and the cornerstone was laid by Thomas Lowry in 1883. It was an impressive structure, nine stories high, and the architecture had been called a combination of Queen Anne and Colonial. The outside was Joliet Marble on the first and part of the second story and the rest was red pressed brick laid in red mortar with red terra cotta trimmings and a roof of tiles. The main entrance on Hennepin avenue was flanked by pillars of polished stone and covered with an arch some two stories high. A second entrance on the Fifth street side was even more impressive, with a massive carriage porch of solid marble extending to the curb. Colonades, oriel windows, arched recesses and a tower that reached two-hundred feet into the air, commanded attention from everyone passing by.

Inside, a huge center court extended from the first floor to the roof with a heavy glass shield protecting the lower floor from rain and snow. The hotel advertised that the court gave inner apartments light and air "not even surpassed by outside rooms." The center of attention was a grand stairway of white marble. The entire first floor was tiled in marble with mahogany woodwork everywhere.

Off the rotunda area, known as the Exchange, were reading rooms, a telegraph office and a bar and billiard room. Up on the second floor was a grand dining room, touted as the "finest beyond all question in America." The floor also housed three or four parlors, a gentleman's club room, and four suites of private rooms for bridal parties and other special guests. The dining room for the general public was located just above the billiard room, and all the flooring was marble except in the suites which had luxurious carpeting. The walls were wainscotted with marble and mahogany with ceiling panels of carved mahogany. All the floors above contained a total of four hundred and seven rooms, all with hot and cold water, and about a hundred and fifty bath rooms were scattered throughout the floors. The rooms were furnished in mahogany and cherry, and every room was connected with the main hotel office by a speaking tube.

Ozark Flats

The hotel had cost two million dollars—and rooms were three dollars a day.

Emmett and Hillary Markham had been seated in the main dining room on the second floor of the West Hotel and ordered dinner. The total tab for the evening would be less than six dollars and that would include the wine at twenty cents a glass and Emmett's bonded whiskey which he had ordered when they first arrived. He looked across the table and smiled.

"Hillary, you look absolutely lovely tonight." He raised his whiskey glass as if toasting her.

"Thank you, dear. Perhaps I look all right because I feel all right," she explained. "This has been marvelous day for me. I sent Jamie off to his last day of school before Christmas vacation, and I just about finished my Christmas shopping this afternoon." She became more excited. "And I made a new friend today!" Then she proceeded to tell Emmett all about her lunch date with Kitty Ging—and Harry Hayward—and the afternoon shopping spree with Kitty. "She showed me shops I didn't even know were there," she explained, "and I hated to see the afternoon end."

Hillary was radiant now. Her long blond hair was done in an upsweep to the top of her head and held in place by two small, beautiful combs. Her dress was a luxurious deep-wine velvet gown with a low neckline and long sleeves. Emmett was aware others had taken notice of Hillary when they came into the dining room.

"I guess you two hit it off pretty well, then?"

"Emmett, when I left her, I was so moved that I gave her a big hug. When I got on the streetcar and looked back and saw her standing there, I felt like I was boarding the train in St. Louis and saying goodbye to an old friend." She paused. "She said she'd like to have us both over for dinner some night, soon."

Emmett smiled. "I'd like that. It's about time we begin to make some new friends here in the city."

"I've been so busy telling you about *my* day that I haven't even asked how things went with you today," Hillary apologized.

"It was——" He searched for the right word. "——interesting. First I got some good advice from Charlie Strong and then I went to the meeting with the mayor that I was telling you about."

"Are you still speaking to each other?" she asked, jokingly.

"Oh yes. We didn't resolve all of our differences, but I think I have a better understanding of what the police are doing now. I not only met the mayor and the superintendent of police, but a detective the chief brought along. His name is Barnett and I was very impressed with him. Apparently he is one of three or four new detectives appointed within the past year and he seemed to know what he was talking about. I was impressed," he repeated.

There was a lull in the conversation. "I also had some time to think about us today, Hillary. And I promise, I'll honestly try to turn things around. I know I'm at fault for most of what's happened between us."

She reached across the table and took his hand and smiled. And the waiter brought the main course to the table.

When Emmett and Hillary had arrived at the West Hotel and started up the marble stairway to the dining room, Harry Hayward and Tom Waterman were just finishing their last game of billiards, and their last drink at the adjacent bar. Only five of the sixteen billiard tables were being used. Harry looked around and said it was time for him to go—that he had appointments to keep this evening. He set the empty whiskey glass down on the bar and they both left the billiard room and headed for the front entrance of the hotel.

"I wonder if you'd do me a favor," Harry asked as the two men left the hotel.

Ozark Flats

While the Markhams were enjoying their dessert, gentlemen in the lobby were taking notice of another attractive lady, dressed in a seal-skin cloak worn over a dark blue skirt. She also had on a carefree sailor hat and wore woolen gloves. Kitty Ging crossed the rotunda area and came down the steps to the carriage entrance on the Fifth street side of the hotel. She had already called the Palace Livery Stable and ordered a rig to be at the hotel at 7 p.m. It was already waiting for her under the massive canopy protecting it from the light snow now falling. She smiled as she came through the doors and saw that the buckskin mare she had asked for was there. She had used the same livery service several times because Mr. Goosman was a neighbor in the apartment, and because the service had been good. And she had asked for the same mare each time. The horse was gentle, easy to handle, and seemed to know the city without much direction.

The doorman helped her into the black two-passenger carriage with side curtains added to protect occupants from the winter weather. She thanked the doorman and drove off down Fifth street. The doorman looked at his pocket watch. It was 7:08. Another twenty minutes and he'd be through for the day.

Claus Blixt was looking out of the window of his basement apartment of the Ozark Flats and watching the light snowfall. The supper which his wife had left for him when she went upstairs to take care of the Markham boy this evening, was still on the kitchen table. In Claus' right hand was a more than half-empty bottle of cheap whiskey. He was proud of just how sober he was for having consumed so much whiskey in such a short time. He couldn't remember when he had so much to drink—maybe when he lost his job as bartender. They said he'd been stealing. Actually, he was just borrowing the money for a day or two. He had every intention of paying it all back, he told himself.

It had not been the first time he'd been fired for dishonesty. He had been let go by the Twin City Rapid Transit Company, too. Conductors simply did not steal from the company, and after having been given a second chance, he was eventually fired for taking money a second time. The janitor now looked out into the darkness and from the faint lights of the window, he could still see the snow falling.

"Förbanna!" If this kept up very long he'd have to get the coal shovel out tonight and clear the walks before morning.

Harry Hayward didn't seem to be particularly hungry as he ate supper in Olson's Boarding House across from the Ozark Flats with two regulars. Perhaps it was because he had enjoyed such a generous lunch with Kitty and Hillary Markham earlier in the day. At any rate, Harry excused himself from the dinner table earlier than usual, and headed across the street to the Ozark Flats. The dutiful son took the elevator to the fourth floor and stopped to see his parents for a few minutes, then continued up to the top floor to Kitty's apartment. Only Kitty's niece, Louise Ireland, was home, however, and the seventeen-year-old told Harry she really wasn't sure just where Kitty was this evening. He thanked her, and left, taking the elevator back down to the first floor to see his brother Adry.

"I can't stay," he told his brother. "I just stopped to see that everything was all right here in the building. I've already been down to tell Blixt to get the snow shoveled before morning."

"I wish you wouldn't go," Adry pleaded. "I feel so down, tonight." He adored his brother, and would do just about anything to please him. Right now, however, he needed to be with someone—and Harry was already there.

"Can't stay, brother," Harry told him. "I just can't stay tonight. Maybe tomorrow night."

With that, Harry left, walked down the hall and stepped outside of the front entry of the Ozark Flats and into the snowy evening.

Adry was alone. His wife had gone to visit her parents and Adry sat in the dark of his living room and looked out the front window at the snowfall. He thought back to his visit with Levi Stewart earlier in the day and although he felt good about talking to his old family friend, he was still depressed. He hated being alone here in the apartment. Perhaps he would go out for awhile—for a walk—or even rent a buggy and go for a ride. It was still early in the evening. Yes, he'd go now, and he got up and went to get his cap and coat.

Miss Mabel Bartleson opened the front door of her father's home on Douglas avenue to let Harry Hayward in. She had been expecting him and they had talked about going skating this evening. It was almost eight o'clock and Harry apologized for being late. Then he told her of a change in their plans for the evening and said he'd like to take her to the Grand Opera House to see the opening performance of *A Trip To Chinatown*.

"The curtain is at 8:15 and we're already going to be late," he told Mabel. As she rushed to get her coat, her father, Charles J. Bartleson, a well-known Minneapolis attorney, came out of his study and into the living room to see who was there.

"Why, hello, Harry."

"Good evening, Mr. Bartleson," Harry greeted him. "We're a little late and we're off to the Grand Opera House tonight to see *A Trip To Chinatown*.

"I understand it's very good," Mr. Bartleson said encouragingly.

Mabel returned. "Sorry father, but we have to run. We're already late!" They exchanged goodnights and the couple left.

The two of them walked down to Hennepin avenue and took the first streetcar that came along. When they arrived at the Opera House, Harry purchased two tickets at the boxoffice and they were seated while the performance was in progress. The curtain had gone up fifteen minutes ago.

Ozark Flats

Both Emmett and Hillary were in good spirits when they left the hotel dining room and started down the stairs to the lobby of the West Hotel. They had enjoyed a lovely dinner, exchanged accounts of their day's experiences, and agreed that this evening was exactly what they needed to ease the tension between them. Now they were both looking forward to an evening's entertainment at the Grand Opera House, and looking even further ahead to the weekend at Excelsior, to their anniversary, and to Christmas in their very own home.

As the handsome couple crossed the Exchange and headed for the main entrance, they heard someone call.

"Emmett! Emmett! Hillary! Wait a minute!"

The voice sounded familiar as the sounds came closer. "Hold on a minute, you two!"

The Markhams turned to see a familiar figure running across the Exchange toward them, dodging guests in the crowded lobby. It was Andy Ross! He flew into their arms and the three of them stood there under the rotunda, holding each other.

"Andy! What the devil are you doing here?" Emmett asked excitedly.

"I'm working here! I'm the new assistant manager! I got here yesterday and it took me until this afternoon to find out where to reach you. When I called the apartment, they said you were both out—gone for the day."

"We thought you were in New York," Hillary explained.

"I was. Then I got this letter about two weeks ago from Mr. Charles Shepherd, the manager of the hotel here. Then came a telegram, and then another. And all of a sudden I was on the train, leaving New York and heading back to Minnesota. I'm so excited to be back. I've been staying with my folks over at the Nicollet House, but I'll be moving in here as soon as they can find a god-damned room for me!"

Andy Ross was a boyhood friend of Emmett Markham's. His dad owned the Nicollet House, and in the summertime, Andy and his folks moved to Excelsior on Lake Minnetonka where he had grown up with Emmett Markham and John Stark. The three had been inseparable through those years and all had been successful young men in Excelsior. Emmett had edited his father's weekly newspaper there.

75

John Stark became the youngest steamboat pilot on the lake, had actually been in charge of *The City of St. Louis*, the second largest steamer on the lake, and eventually was the owner and captain of the third largest of the Minnetonka steamboats, *The Hattie May*.

The money to help purchase the old Hattie May had come from winnings from the Fourth-of-July race seven years ago when John Stark captained *The City of St. Louis* to a victory over its larger sister ship, *The Belle of Minnetonka*. Andy was manager of The White House at Excelsior, one of the leading summer hotels on Lake Minnetonka, and the two of them had pooled their life savings and bet on *The City* in the traditional holiday race. The older and larger *Belle* had won all of those races, but on that day, John Stark out-maneuvered *The Belle's* old curmudgeon of a captain, Lamont Loos, and *The City* won the race.

That day had also been a memorable one for Hillary. She was married to Jim Stockton then, the boy next door in St. Louis, and they had been aboard *The Belle* that day. Emmett was also on board, with Hillary's two younger brothers, Tom and Dave. Just when it was apparent tht *The City* would win, going away, Jim Stockton was swept overboard as the crowd on the top deck crushed to the side railing to watch the finish. He was caught in the giant sidewheeler's paddlewheel and thrashed underwater. Emmett made a valiant effort to save him, but it was too late. When they pulled him out of the water, Jim Stockton was dead.

All of that crossed Andy Ross' mind in an instant. He remembered giving his share of the winnings to John Stark so he could buy *The Hattie May*. He also remembered serving as best man when John Stark and Rose Fortier were married that fall. Then Andy headed for New York and the hotel business there.

The jubilation stopped short as Andy looked down at the floor.

"I was sorry to hear about John. I would have come back for the funeral if it had been possible." He looked up at both Emmett and Hillary and his face had suddenly turned sad. "I just couldn't get back."

"It's all right, Andy. We all understood. There wasn't anything that anybody could do about it. It just happened."

Emmett hadn't thought about John Stark's death in months. He had somehow put the tragic event out of his mind ever since he and Hillary and Jamie had moved into the city. The accident happened last summer. John had promised to help an old friend fix the boiler on *The Kenosha*. After working most of the day, they took the small steamboat out for a trial run and as they entered Excelsior Bay on the return trip, the boiler exploded and the whole ship went up in flames and sank! There were only three crewmen and John on board. They were all dead.

"How's Rose?" Andy asked quietly.

"We haven't seen her since last summer," Hillary explained. "I think she's gone back to Cleveland to stay with a cousin there."

There was a quiet pause in the conversation. Then Emmett brightened up and spoke. "If you can make it, Andy, why don't you come out to Excelsior for part of the Christmas holiday. We're going to open up the house for the weekend and celebrate Christmas and our anniversary! Hillary's folks are coming from St. Louis but we'll have plenty of room."

Andy grinned. "I'd like that. Maybe we can take time to look at *The White House* and stop at Fred Hawkins' saloon! I'm going to be with my folks on Christmas Eve—but I'll come out on Christmas Day and stay overnight. It'll be quiet here at the hotel over the holidays, and besides, I don't officially start work until next Monday."

"Good," Hillary beamed. "It'll be like old times. And Dad will be so happy to see you." Hillary's father gave Andy his first break as a hotel manager. Tom Blair was a vice president for the M. and St. L. Railway and still in charge of the railroad's hotel properties. He had hired Andy as manager of *The White House* and had never been sorry for it. When Andy finally resigned and left for New York, Tom Blair made some inquiries for him and helped land him a job on the staff of *The Plaza*.

"Look—we're on our way to the theater now," Emmett explained, "but it's a date for this weekend. We'll see you sometime Christmas morning." The two shook hands and Andy embraced Hillary.

"I wouldn't miss it for anything," he said gratefully.

Ozark Flats

The Grand Opera House was probably the most impressive of the downtown theaters—larger than either the Pence or the Bijou. It was located on Sixth street, between First and Second avenues, and there was a traffic jam of horses and carriages, and a long line of streetcars out in front as the curtain time for the musical neared.

The large theater billboard in front of the boxoffice read:

GRAND OPERA HOUSE

First of a Week's Engagement
Featuring Harry Conor and the
Original Company in
CHARLES HALE HOYT'S
A TRIP TO CHINATOWN
With newly added musical numbers
25¢   50¢   75¢ $1.00

COMING—
Stuart Robson in
THE INTERLOPER
COMING—
SHE STOOPS TO CONQUER
LEAP YEAR
THE HENRIETTA

Emmett had their tickets in his hand as he and Hillary passed by the large columns outside the Grand Opera House and entered the theater. It had been an eventful day, Hillary thought, and with the lovely dinner, seeing Andy Ross again, and now the musical, it would be an unforgettable evening.

She was never more right.

6

IT WAS A BLACK BUGGY, number twenty-seven, and it was enclosed for winter use with curtains. It came on to Hennepin avenue and turned south toward Lake street. The driver wore a dark shortcoat and a black cap. In a few minutes he pulled the reins and moved the horse to the right on Lake street and headed for Lake Calhoun. The woman alongside of the driver sat straight up and kept her hands under the goat-skin lap robe draped over her skirt. She was half-hidden by the winter curtains that had been added to the rig. The horse and buggy clip-clopped on around the north end of Lake Calhoun and then the horse was slowed down to a walk. Twice, the woman leaned forward to look out the side of the buggy at the swamp and the woods around Lake Calhoun, and twice, the driver turned and raised his arm as if to strike her from the back. Then she would settle back behind the protective side-curtain and he would concentrate on his driving. Most of the time they rode along in silence. She spoke only twice, and the driver answered in a few, short words.

As if she were expecting to meet someone, the woman peered out the side of the buggy a third time and at that moment, the driver pulled a revolver out from under the carriage robe, stuck it near the back of her head and pulled the trigger! The woman had just started to turn her head back to the driver when the shot rang out and her head and body lurched back toward the side-curtain. The horse bolted at the sound of the gunshot but quickly recovered and the driver pulled him up to a stop. At the same time, the woman's body fell back toward the driver and he swung the barrel of the pistol down across the head and face of the woman as if he were protecting himself. His arm came down two or three times and her body fell back into the buggy, remaining upright against the back curtain. Then there was silence as the snow continued to fall on the horse and buggy.

The horse stood still and the driver draped the carriage robe against the body and drove on past Lake Calhoun and on to Excelsior road. Then he pushed the body out of the slow-moving buggy and the right rear wheel rolled over the dead form lying in the street. He stopped the rig, climbed down and carefully placed the dead body of the woman on the lap robe. Then he quickly climbed back to the seat of the carriage and drove off toward Lake Calhoun again, now at a gallop.

Near Fifth and Hennepin in front of the West Hotel, the giant hands of the ten-foot sidewalk clock had just turned to eight o'clock.

Charles H. Hoyt's *A Trip To Chinatown* was first performed in New York on November 7, 1891. After successfully touring the country, it returned to New York in early 1894 to good reviews and then went on the road again, ending up in Minneapolis in December. The play starred Harry Conor in the original version and he was still playing the leading role when the production came to Minneapolis. Anna Boyd was the co-star in the musical that featured dancing, singing and imitations. Critics called it a 'funny play' and explained that Hoyt had taken the plot for his latest musical farce from French comedy.

"It's a raw, western American rendering of the theme of *For-*

bidden Fruit, Contempt of Court and *Americans in Paris*," said the critics. The musical was set in San Francisco and involved everyone going to a masquerade ball and the pursuit of an attractive widow. New York reviews suggested that "Mr. Hoyt is often frankly vulgar—but he is never suggestive." Then one critic added, "It's a diversion for folks who are easily pleased—and it's likely to be popular." Another critic was taken with a young woman's dance with mirrors and the kaleidoscopic colors it produced. True to the critics, this opening night production pleased its Minneapolis audience. It would be a popular show here.

At the intermission, Emmett and Hillary moved with the crowd to the outer lobby just to stretch their legs. Even in the midst of this holiday season and on a snowy night, the opening night performance was playing to a full house. A number of well-known Minneapolis businessmen and community leaders were attending this first performance tonight, and Emmett recognized Thomas Lowry and one of the Pillsburys. As they crowded into the lobby he ran right into Mayor William H. Eustis who recognized Emmett immediately.

"Hello, Markham," the mayor greeted him.

"Good evening, Mr. Mayor." Emmett shook his hand. "I'd like you to meet my wife, Hillary."

"It's a pleasure to meet you Mrs. Markham," smiled the mayor. "Your husband and I had a long and fruitful session this morning."

"Yes, Emmett was telling me about it over dinner earlier this evening. It sounded like it was helpful to both you and the police department, *and* to the newspaper."

"I think it was," the mayor added, "and I'm encouraged to think that Emmett felt it was successful, too." The mayor had recognized someone else across the lobby. "It's nice to meet you Mrs. Markham. And nice to see you again, too, Emmett." He pushed off in the direction of a friend inching toward him across the crowded lobby.

Emmett heard someone say that Senator Washburn was also there this evening, and he looked around for the United States Senator from Minnesota. The Minneapolis industrialist had also been the president of the M. and St. L. Railway long before he became a senator and had hired Hillary's father, Tom Blair, and made him a vice president of the railroad. Senator Washburn had been in the Blair home in St. Louis on several occasions and knew Hillary well.

But neither Emmett nor Hillary could see him in the crowd. On their way back into the theater someone called out to them from across the row of seats in the far aisle.

"Hello! Markhams! Hillary!"

Both Emmett and Hillary looked around and then saw the familiar face across the way. It was Harry Hayward with an attractive young lady, moving back down the aisle to their seats for the second act of the musical. The Markhams waved back.

"Two women in one day," said Hillary. "I'd say he's doing all right for himself."

The house lights went down, and the musical continued.

It was still snowing lightly when William Echard stepped off the St. Louis Park streetcar at the line's turn-around point at Thirty-first street and Excelsior road, just west of Lake Calhoun. He was an athletic-looking man with a short haircut, a square jaw and a sharp nose. He hadn't taken twenty steps up the road when he heard the clatter of galloping hoofs and he stepped back to the side of the road just in time to see the horse and buggy race by. In the darkness and the snow, he wasn't sure whether there was a driver or whether the horse was a runaway. Then the rig turned up the street, bound toward the city lights. William Echard started walking again and almost stumbled over a body sprawled in the middle of the road. The horse must have bolted, he thought, and threw her from the carriage.

"You okay, lady?" He stooped over the body which was lying face down on a carriage robe on the snowy road. He started to speak a second time, when he noticed the pool of blood on the robe. She was lying face down on her left side, her clothing was bloody, and her nose appeared to be broken. There were also bloodstains on her hair and skin behind her right ear, and then he saw it—her left eye. It was hanging out of its socket!

"Oh my God!" he whispered to himself. Then he turned and hiked back toward Lake Calhoun and the city. It was over a mile to Lake and Hennepin where he called the police from the drug store on the corner.

"A woman has been killed in a runaway accident on Excelsior road," he explained. He added what few details he had and hung up the phone. Then he turned and slouched back against the wall phone and took some deep breaths. All he could think of was that left eye!

A doctor arrived on the scene in about a half hour and pronounced the woman dead. The police patrol wagon from the Calhoun station was also summoned and arrived thirty minutes later. There was no identification on the body which was placed in the wagon and taken to the county morgue.

Officer Peter Fox was in charge of the body at the morgue this night until the County Coroner, Willis Spring, could get there. It had been a quiet couple of days for the police department and Officer Fox realized that the victim of this runaway accident was the first real police business in some time out at the Calhoun station. He not only took the body back to the county morgue but was in charge of the remains until the coroner arrived about 11:30 p.m. By this time, the body was unclothed, the corpse was measured and the pockets of the outer coat worn by the dead woman had been searched. There was no identification at all. Just fifteen cents in change and a Yale key in her pockets.

The bullet hole in the back of the ear was not discovered until Coroner Spring pushed the left eye back in place and felt a hard object with his finger. Then he found the bullet in the left eye. He removed the flattened piece of lead and held it up to the gas jet to examine it. Then he shook his head.

"This is no runaway accident, Peter. This woman has been murdered!"

The doctor examined the back of the head and found the round and ragged wound about a quarter of an inch in diameter. The wound was surrounded by blackened skin, and the hair had been burned off. The bullet had entered the back of the head, two inches behind her right ear and had crossed the skull diagonally, passing through the brain, severing the internal carotid artery and lodging in the left eyeball which had been forced out of its socket. The flattened piece of lead was heavy enough to be a thirty-eight-calibre bullet, he thought. Willis Spring knew that death had been instantaneous. But there was more. Her nose was broken, there was a cut on her lower lip, and her skull was fractured in three places.

In the meantime, Officer Fox was checking out a faint laundry mark found on the white collar of the dead woman's blouse, and had immediately called the Central Police Station to notify Lt. Thomas Coskran about the discovery of the bullet and to tell him they now had a murder on their hands.

The stable boy at the Palace Livery Stable didn't think it unusual when the horse and buggy number twenty-seven appeared back at the stable without a driver a little after nine o'clock. There didn't seem to be anything out of the ordinary about the appearance of the horse or the rig at first glance. The reins were loosely wound around the carriage whip which was stuck in its socket to the right of the driver's seat. But when he informed Mr. Goosman, they took a closer look at the buggy.

Henry Goosman could not believe his eyes. It seemed as though there was blood everywhere—as much as a quart of it. There was blood on the left side-curtain and blood had also trickled down the back curtain of the carriage and on to the back part of the carriage seat.

"What's this stuff?" the stable boy asked his boss.

"I don't honestly know," Henry Goosman replied. He was getting sick to his stomach. "It looks like—like, brains!"

The livery stable owner rushed to the telephone and called police headquarters to ask if an accident had been reported. He was told that word had been sent into headquarters that a woman had been injured in a runaway near Lake Calhoun. Henry Goosman then explained about the empty buggy returning to his livery stable and about the blood that he and the stable boy had discovered. He said he would check back in later, and hung up.

Ozark Flats

Francis Gordon Kelly had just hauled a large framed mirror home to his apartment and was struggling to put it into the elevator when Adry Hayward came up the steps and through the front door of the Ozark Flats. The older Hayward brother had to come down the hallway and turn left at the elevator to get to his first-floor apartment and as he passed the elevator, the red-headed lawyer greeted him.

"Good evening, Mr. Hayward."

Adry Hayward passed the elevator without saying a word. His dark coat and cap were covered with snow, and Francis Gordon Kelly could hear him put the key in the lock at the end of the hall. Kelly shrugged and told Joey, the elevator boy, to take him up to his apartment.

Joey was the day-time elevator operator most of the time at the Ozark Flats and shared some night duty and weekend hours on the job with Claus Blixt. Joey wasn't supposed to be working tonight but came on in when it started to snow. He knew that the janitor would have to shovel the front steps and the side entrance as well as the sidewalk. He also knew that the walks hadn't been shoveled yet—and he knew why. Claus Blixt was down in his apartment, sleeping off the effects of some pretty heavy drinking.

When it came to women, Rex Barnett had always been shy. In his younger days in high school and at the University, he could be a terror on the football field. But put him in the classroom next to a girl, or with his high school friends at the corner drug store and he became quiet and self-conscious. Being alone wasn't anything new to the young Barnett. When he was going to Whittier grade school, he had spent a lot of time alone. He would spend hours at the Minneapolis

Athenaeum library, reading American history and looking at drawings and photographs of the Civil War. As he grew older, he began to explore not only his own neighborhood, but the rest of south Minneapolis. By the time he was in high school, he knew that quarter of the city as well as any postman. But outside of athletics and an occasional hayride party out beyond Lake street, Rex Barnett was pretty much on his own. He dated occasionally and once took Winnifred White, the girl who lived down the block, to the circus.

He had met Josephine Johnson while working at *The Minneapolis Tribune* and had fallen in love with the young secretary. Their love affair had become serious after about six months, and they were beginning to talk about marriage. That's when Rex decided that he was not cut out to be a newspaperman and got his first job with the police department. That's when Josie began to have some doubts about their proposed marriage. When Rex became a full-fledged patrolman, Josie simply told him that she did not want to go through life married to a policeman and worrying about him all the time. It wasn't long after that when she took a new job in Milwaukee, Wisconsin, and Rex joined the police department. He never saw her again. He met and dated a number of young women after that, but the scars from his love for the pretty blond-haired Josie had left him too vulnerable, and he kept up a constant guard against another such occurence.

Then he met Gertie Lewis. She had been a dancer for Big Glady, a restaurant and bar owner who booked and controlled most of the work for dancing girls in both Minneapolis and St. Paul. Some of the younger patrolmen would stop in at Big Glady's place, *The Fountainhead*, when they got off duty, and drink beer and joke with the dancing girls. It seemed to be one place where Rex Barnett felt comfortable in talking with attractive young women. And Gertie seemed to be particularly easy to talk to. It was no intense love affair. But they would have dinner together once in awhile, and then it might be weeks before they would see each other again. In the meantime, Gertie quit dancing and worked as a seamstress, mostly making costumes for Big Glady's girls. Now she had opened her new Massage Baths over on Third avenue and was, herself, a businesswoman.

Rex was glad he had called Gertie earlier today. She'd been thinking about him, too, and they decided that Gertie would come over and fix supper at Rex's apartment this evening. After supper, they bundled up and went for a walk down Twenty-eighth street to the Lake of the Isles and along the path near the shoreline.

"I love to walk here," she said as she hung on his arm and leaned ever so lightly against his coat.

"I do, too," he answered. "I try to walk down here every morning before I go to work, and bike it in the summer."

"I'm glad you called today, Rex. I've been so busy with the new place that I haven't had any time for myself at all."

"I'm glad I called, too, Gert. It's just one of those times when I needed to be with someone." He hesitated. "Someone like you."

They walked on without speaking and the silence was only broken by the laughter and faint voices of skaters on the ice of the inlet.

"Do you want to stay all night?" Rex asked, almost apologetically. She just giggled and squeezed his arm.

Then they both laughed, quickened their pace and crossed the street, heading up Lagoon avenue.

Back at the apartment, Rex was already in bed when Gertie came in from the bathroom in Rex's bathrobe. Even in the dark, she turned away and let the robe slip off. Rex could still see the outline of her attractive figure and knew the smoothness of her skin. She slipped into bed and into his arms.

Afterwards, Gertie put her arms around him and caressed the back of his neck.

"Rex."

"...mmmm...hhhh...?"

"You need a haircut!"

When the phone in the hall between the living room and the bedroom rang, it was almost midnight. Rex got up and made his way down the hall to the ringing.

"Hello," he said in a sleepy voice.

Ozark Flats

"Rex, This is Tom Coskran. Sorry to bother you but you're the only one with a phone besides the lieutenant. We got something that looked like a runaway accident and it's turned out to be a murder. I've already called Lieutenant Morrissey and I'll get John Stavlo on it tomorrow. But right now, Morrissey wants you to get over to Thirteenth and Hennepin. Peter Fox has already gone out there and he'll fill you in."

There was a pause. Rex asked him to hold the phone for a minute and called to Gertie. "Dammit, Gert, I've got a case that won't wait—and I'll have to go. Wanna stay here until morning by yourself?"

"Sure, dear. I'll be here when you get back," came the voice from the darkened bedroom.

Then it was back to the phone. "Yeah, Tom."

"Sorry about the time, Rex, but you'll have to get over there right away, even though it's late. The place is called Ozark Flats. The victim is a gal—her name is Catherine Ging!"

Wednesday, December 22, 1894

The life of the ordinary patrolman is more or less filled with accident and incident, which lends a tone of interest to the daily life of the profession. During certain fixed hours he appears in his uniform at a certain locality in the city, where his very presence is an augury that law and order are in force, and that he carries in his own proper person the goodwill of law abiding citizens and may upon the slightest show of voilence or crime call to his assistance—instantly, if required—every man in the neighborhood for the maintenance of the public peace, for the arrest of law breakers or to put down with strong hand all tumultuous or riotous proceedings. And so, year after year, he walks his daily round until he becomes one of the most familiar features of the neighboring landscape. Every boy and girl of his neighborhood knows his first and his last name, and many is the harmless, though mischievous prank which is nipped in the bud by the timely appearance of the 'policeman' as he strolls leisurely along his accustomed beat.

Advancement from patrolman to the detective force has come to be justly regarded as a promotion to be worked for and sought after. All crime by its very nature is stealthy, secret and avoids publicity. It is the duty of the trained detective to penetrate the obscurity with which the artistic practitioners of crime surround themselves—to turn the searchlight of full publicity upon the dark spots of our complex social life, and correct through the authorized agency of the courts all wrongs against individual citizens, all outrages against the dignity and safety of the whole body politic.

It goes without saying that the professional life of a trained detective is full of interest, because each day is marked by its kaleidescopic incidents charted to the brim with small details, out of which must be evolved the evidence for the conviction of criminals of every degree of guilt, and for the protection of society.

—History of Fire and Police Departments
of Minneapolis, 1899.

REX BARNETT wasn't reading his newspaper this morning as he road the Lake Harriet streetcar to work. He was tired. He had been up half the night because of last night's murder and he knew today would be a busy one with new pressure on the police department. Gert Lewis had made him breakfast and he had slept so late he skipped his morning walk to the Lake of the Isles.

"I don't make breakfast at this hour very often," Gert kidded him, "so appreciate it!" Rex was too tired to laugh but he managed a smile. They finished their coffee and she helped him with his coat and muffler. Then she gave Rex a kiss and told him to be off, and that she'd clean up the breakfast dishes and let herself out.

Rex leaned against the streetcar window, half sleeping and thinking about last night's events. He wished that this streetcar had come along last night so he could have ridden down to the Ozark Flats. But there was no streetcar in sight at that hour and Rex had hiked through the snow down Hennepin avenue, the fifteen blocks to the apartment building. Practically every light in the building was on as he arrived and he remembered a small gathering of residents in the hall of the main floor. Officer Fox met him at the front door.

"She lived up on the fifth floor, Rex," the policeman told him as he reviewed the night's events. "The first call came in from a drug store at Lake and Hennepin from a—Officer Fox looked at his pad of notes—a William Echard who reported a runaway accident. But I was down at the morgue when the coroner found the bullet and the rest. It was not a pretty sight." Then he filled the detective in on the condition of the body.

"Was there a purse or anything?" Rex asked.

"Nope. All we found was fifteen cents and a Yale key in her coat pocket." Then the policeman added, "But in going over her clothing we found the name 'Ging' on the inside of the white collar of her blouse—and after that it was easy to find out who she was and where she lived."

In the meantime, Lt. John Morrissey had arrived at the Ozark Flats and the two detectives took the elevator to the fifth floor to Kitty's apartment to tell Louise Ireland what had happened. When Rex Barnett stepped off the elevator on the fifth floor, he saw Hillary Markham for the very first time. She was standing in the hall with Emmett and was still dressed in her green velvet gown which she had worn to the musical earlier in the evening. Emmett was holding her and Rex could see that she had been crying. Even with her reddened eyes, Rex thought she was beautiful.

"Detective Barnett." Emmett recognized him and was the first to speak.

"Mr. Markham," Rex smiled. "I had no idea that you lived here."

"I'd like you to meet my wife, Hillary," Emmett said. "This is Detective Rex Barnett and—" Emmett didn't know the other man who was with Rex.

"Lt. John Morrissey," Rex completed the sentence. Both detectives nodded respectfully to Hillary and John Morrissey shook hands with Emmett.

"We need someone to awaken Miss Ging's niece," John Morrissey explained. "Could you help us, Mrs. Markham?"

It was apparent that Hillary was upset, but she nodded and said she would get her up. Then she crossed the hall and kept knocking on the door to Kitty Ging's apartment until Louise Ireland opened the door slightly and peeked out. She recognized Hillary, let her slip inside, and closed the door. Louise Ireland was almost hysterical with grief when Hillary let the two detectives into the apartment to question her. No, she didn't know much about her aunt's gentlemen friends. Yes, she worked at the dressmaking shop. She had come home alone to the apartment by herself this evening and had not seen Kitty at all. She didn't know Kitty had been riding in a buggy, and her aunt never told her where she was going when she went out. They had lived here in the Ozark Flats since the first of November and she couldn't imagine that Kitty Ging had any enemies or would possibly commit suicide. The youngster had been alone in the apartment since suppertime and the only one she had talked to was Harry Hayward who stopped by to ask for Kitty early in the evening. "I told him she hadn't come home at all today," she explained to the detectives.

"So you have no idea who she was with earlier today," John Morrissey asked in a quiet voice.

"I was with her for lunch—and most of the afternoon," came a woman's voice from behind the two detectives. It was Hillary, speaking in a wavering voice and beginning to cry again.

Rex was still leaning against the streetcar window and he smiled as he remembered and admired the way John Morrissey had been so gentle with Louise Ireland. He also remembered that he hadn't been able to take his eyes off Hillary Markham. She was beautiful.

Rex also remembered that there were others who had been questioned last night at the Ozark Flats. Henry Goosman had been most cooperative, telling Rex and John Morrissey how Kitty Ging had hired rigs from his livery stable before. Once she came to the livery stable and once she ordered it to be delivered, just as she did earlier in the evening. This time, she asked for the buckskin mare, Lucy. He told the detectives how there hadn't seemed to be anything unusual in the appearance of the horse and rig—and then he told them in detail about discovering the blood and calling the police.

"When I first called the police and learned that there had been a runaway accident, I thought that Miss Ging and her companion had been near when the accident happened, and that they had taken the injured woman into their carriage and driven to some drug store. I thought the horse might have started off while the woman was being taken into the drug store. That buckskin is very gentle and I wouldn't be surprised that it could reach the stable by itself."

Rex recalled the young elevator boy and the visit with Francis Gordon Kelly, and with Mr. and Mrs. Hayward, Sr. The two detectives had also visited with Adry Hayward and Rex was struck by Adry's physical appearance. He was stylishly dressed—like his younger brother—but thick set and muscular. He wore a thick blonde mustache and had a large, full face with heavy jowls. His head above the eyes was almost too small for the rest of his massive face, and his light eyes were almost closed by the heavy swell of flesh beneath them.

Then there was Harry Hayward. Rex mulled over in his mind the questioning of Harry on the night before as the streetcar rattled along this morning, headed for downtown. Harry had explained how shocked he had been at lunch yesterday when Kitty flashed all that money. And he told about the interest that was shown by the waiter at the Continental Cafe. Harry accounted for all of his movements during the day of the murder, and other residents of the building also told the detectives what Harry had said when he first returned to the Ozark Flats, even before they were sure that she had been murdered.

"I have been expecting that they would do her up," Harry had apparently told the group of residents gathered in the hallway. "My two thousand dollars is gone to hell!" Then he added, "It is nobody but Miss Ging. She has not been hurt in any runaway accident. She has been done up for her money!"

"How can you be sure, Harry?" one of the residents asked him.

"I'm sure—I have my reasons," he replied emphatically. Then he took a revolver from his pocket. "If anyone comes to do me up, they'll get the contents of this!"

Rex also had a whole pad of notes taken the night before as Harry told him and John Morrissey how Kitty had money in the Minnesota Loan and Trust Company. He threw out such figures as $2,500 which he said he had advanced to her and which she was to pay back before he lent her another $7,000 for her business.

Harry and Henry Goosman had accompanied the two detectives down to the morgue last night, too, where they identified the body. "There's no question about it, the woman is Miss Ging," Harry told them. He identified the clothing, too, and added that "she has been killed for her money!"

Henry Goosman had also told John Morrissey that Harry kept talking about $2,000 gone to hell and had said "What a fool I've been."

Rex also thought it was interesting that Harry had apparently asked Henry Goosman whether he thought life insurance was good in case of murder. Mr. Goosman told Harry that he didn't really know.

The familiar downtown sites prompted Rex Barnett that he was almost back to work again and he knew there would be hell to pay down at the Central Station and over at City Hall this morning.

It had simply been too late last night to get statements from everyone. John would go back there this afternoon, and he expected that Vern Smith would put a lot more detectives to work on this one before the day was over. Rex also remembered that Hillary Markham was too upset to answer any questions last night, and besides, it had become too late in the evening for that. Instead, she had volunteered to stop down at the Central Station to see Rex late this morning to answer questions.

He thought about her as he stepped off the streetcar. She sure was beautiful.

8

WHEN THE FIRST ELECTION was held in 1852 in the community that was eventually to become Minneapolis, Col. James M. Goodhue, editor of the *St. Paul Pioneer* called the neighboring new town, *All Saints*. Other names were considered, too, including *Lowell* and *Winona*. The Board of Commissioners eventually decided on *Albion*. At St. Anthony, across the river, the newspaper suggested *Minneapolis*, using the Dakota word, *Minne*, meaning water, and *polis*, the Greek suffix for city. *Water City*. Before the end of that year, the people of the community had demanded that *Minneapolis* replace *Albion*, so by December of that year, *Minneapolis* boasted twelve houses, real estate and property valued at $43,605, and first-year taxes of $566.87. The first term of court was held in the city in April of the following year, and in the annual election in 1854, some 132 votes were cast.

St. Anthony and Minneapolis merged in 1872 and the Hon. Eugene Wilson became the first mayor of the newly-formed city which now considered itself "a model of Yankee energy and business ability" in such areas of industry as power, flour milling and railroads. In a couple more years, the population of Minneapolis had grown to 45,000—and so had the city's crime rate grown. There was more than $3,000 in stolen property of which all had been recovered, and court fines were now up to $8,764.

William H. Eustis was now completing his two-year term as mayor of Minneapolis. He had already made his decision months ago not to run for re-election, but he was determined to prove to his own Republican party and to the newspapers, that his had been a law and order administration for the City of Minneapolis. When the party caucuses and conventions had been held back in September, Robert Pratt was chosen to succeed Mayor Eustis as the Republican candidate for mayor. The convention had been held at Harmonia Hall and *The Tribune* had reported that "A slap at Mayor Eustis and his policy was introduced in the shape of a resolution touching the enforcement of laws."

The resolution read:

Resolved that the Republican Party is, as it always has been, the party of law and order. That we hereby require candidates of this convention to pledge themselves to enforce the laws of the city as they stand.

Mayor Eustis' name had been placed in nomination and observers were surprised at the delegate strength of the incumbent who had not allowed his friends or associates to consider him a candidate for re-election. He lost on the third ballot, but one newspaper account editorialized, "If Mayor Eustis had simply declared that if the people wanted him he would be ready to serve another term, he would have been re-nominated by acclamation!"

Robert Pratt was elected mayor in November. It had been a Republican landslide across the country.

In the meantime, William Eustis was still mayor of a city that was flexing its industrial muscles these days. It had only been three years ago that Minneapolis had received some fifty-seven million bushels of wheat and had produced nearly seven and a half million barrels of flour. Nowadays, a company like the Pillsbury-Washburn Flour Milling Company Limited, was advertising in the newspaper that it was turning out nearly ten thousand barrels of *Pillsbury's Best* flour daily, and in one week, its flour mills had produced one hundred and

twenty-two thousand, four hundred and eighty-three barrels of flour.

After yesterday's meeting with the Superintendent of Police and a representative from *The Minneapolis Journal*, Mayor Eustis had felt confident everyone would pull together and stop picking at one another about unsolved crime and any lack of police protection in the city, and of the unfair news accounts. But that was yesterday, and on this December morning, all hell had broken loose in the mayor's office with the news of the Catherine Ging murder. The mayor had already been on the phone with Chief Smith and it was decided that Vern should add more detectives to the case and that they would set up a command post at the mayor's office to coordinate the investigation. It was in this atmosphere that plans for solving the case were made and Chief Smith was quick to put his men into action.

Lt. John Morrissey was put in charge of the investigation, answerable to the Superintendent of Police and Mayor Eustis. Although he had been on the force for eight years, he had only been a detective for a little over a year. Yet he held the respect of every detective in the city and all had great confidence in his methods and approach to criminal cases. He was also unafraid. While John was still a patrolman, he and Sgt. Charles V. Gustavson made a raid on a disorderly house on First street. They were attacked by hoodlums and although they had everyone locked up by morning, John was out of action for awhile with a broken arm. He made a similar arrest last year and ended up with a near-fatal stab wound which laid him up for two months.

Last summer, Morrissey led a group of detectives, including John Stavlo, Michael Hoy and Rex Barnett, in solving a series of burglaries of residences of wealthy Minneapolis citizens. One J.E. Sutton would take on lawn jobs or solicit such work at private residences in the better part of town, and relay the information to his three partners, Al Terry, George Bishop and Swede Christofferson. The detective team soon had the four criminals in jail and the culprits eventually went to prison or the reformatory with sentences up to five years.

So this morning, John Morrissey called on the same team of detectives to take on the Ging murder case.

Detective John Stavlo was born in Trondjeim, Norway, in 1862. He went to school there and then, as a boy, had sailed with his uncle who was captain of a sailing vessel. John liked sailing but he liked people better—and he liked the idea of being in America. In 1880, he left his uncle's ship in Baltimore, worked here and there, picking up English as he moved from place to place. Finally, settling in Minneapolis in the fall, he got a room off Cedar Avenue near the fire station on Fourth street. He was young but huge and strong. He immediately found work on a construction crew and later, worked in a lumber yard and, then, for the Northern Pacific Railroad.

John loved Cedar Avenue on Saturday night. He was big and friendly and he spoke everybody's language. He had learned Norwegian and Danish in school. He picked up German aboard ship and was learning Swedish from his neighbors. His English was very good but he didn't read it well. Cedar avenue bartenders and shopkeepers liked him because he was good at stopping fights and he just generated good will. He seldom had to buy a drink. His very size had a sobering and quieting effect on quarreling drunks but also he would start saying funny things, not just jokes but hilarious remarks about everything and everybody. People told him he should go on the stage; he was just as funny as the comedians at Dania Hall. John always agreed but the very thought of standing on a stage made his legs weak. Besides John had a secret ambition—he wanted to be a policeman.

One Saturday afternoon, he was visiting, in German, with Jake Holtzermann at Holtzermann's Chicago Store. When Jake had first met him, he was shocked and deeply offended by John's coarse sailor's-German. John quickly switched to English, apologized and asked Jake for help in learning German. Jake reluctantly agreed to help but inwardly thought it was a hopeless task. To Jake's amazement, John not only learned fast but he also remembered everything Jake told him. Soon Jake began offering him jobs in the store but John always said he didn't like inside work. It was during one of those job-offers that Saturday that John disclosed to Jake his secret desire. Within a week, John received a post card inviting him to the Central Police Station for an interview.

In 1886, John Stavlo was hired as a patrolman at sixty-nine dollars a month and assigned to the Southside Station under Captain Ness, also a Norwegian. The Southside Station had just moved from the basement of the Scandia Bank across the Cedar-Riverside Square to a brand new brick building on Fourth street. John was welcomed by his fellow patrolmen, survived their practical jokes and soon was out on the beat with a new uniform and night stick. He was beside himself with joy. "It's like dying and going to heaven," he thought as he marched up the avenue to show Holtzermann.

When Professor Wraaman of Augsburg Seminary opened his South Town Academy at 514½ Cedar, John siged up for advanced English. As might be expected, he proved to be an extraordinary student and Professor Wraaman wanted him to stay on to study Latin and Greek. The idea fascinated John but he couldn't bring himself to do it.

Detectives soon learned that whenever they needed information about anything or anybody in South Town all they had to do was ask Patrolman Stavlo. After eight years in uniform, John was promoted to detective and assigned to the Central Station. He made the change with mixed feelings. He would miss wearing the uniform and making the rounds but the ninety dollars a month wasn't at all bad and, sometimes, detectives got to carry guns!

Recently, he and John Morrissey had solved a burglary that involved John Dahlgren, alias John Hanson, alias John Dalton—well-known among criminals in the area. The culprit had been stealing gold leaf and other valuables from dental offices in large cities, all the way from St. Louis to Duluth. Reports had come in from Chicago and Milwaukee and it was apparent that he was in town when dental offices were robbed in both Minneapolis and St. Paul. Then he moved his night-time operations to Mankato where he took $400 worth of valuables there.

Morrissey and Stavlo knew he'd be back, however, so they proceeded to operate a stake-out at the Medical Block in downtown Minneapolis from four to seven o'clock in the morning. Sure enough, Mr. Dahlgren-Hanson-Dalton arrived, almost as though by appointment. It turned out the burglar came from a southern Minnesota county, had a wife and two children, and was highly respected by his neighbors who attributed his wealth to his being a shrewd speculator.

Detective Michael Hoy was the oldest detective on the force, had the longest term of service, and was the city's very first detective. Born in Ireland in 1834, he came to this country in 1850 and to St. Anthony in 1855. He was a stone cutter by trade. In 1862, he enlisted in the Tenth Minnesota Volunteers and served in the Indian campaign and in the South. After the war, he served as Marshal of St. Anthony and when the two cities merged, he became Minneapolis' first detective. For his heroism in the battle of Nashville, Lieutenant Hoy was breveted to the rank of captain and was almost always called Captain Hoy by people outside of the Minneapolis Police Department.

Detective Hoy had a reputation for being an understanding police officer and he and Detective Nicholas Smith proved it when they investigated a grocery store which had been robbed of money and goods. When they talked to the two proprietors separately, they found that each one suspected the other of the thefts. The two detectives cautioned the grocery store partners that appearances could be deceiving and that they should be more careful about accusations against someone who might be innocent. In the meantime, Hoy disguised himself as a plumber and gained entry into a house where the detectives suspected the real thieves to be. Sure enough, they uncovered the missing groceries and other goods.

The same two detectives had also been assigned to a case where over five-hundred pounds of powder had been stolen from one of the powder houses in the outlying districts of the city. Hoy and Smith soon found that the thieves were youths from some of the best and most prominent families in town and had used the powder in celebrating the Fourth of July. They also sold some of it and spent the money. The kids were given a good scolding and turned back over to their parents who paid for the stolen powder, and the whole affair was dropped.

Rex Barnett already knew he had been assigned to the Ging murder case, had already started the investigation at the Ozark Flats last night, and was going to question Hillary Markham later on this morning. Although this was his first murder investigation, he had worked on solving just about every other kind of crime imaginable. Last April, Rex and John Stavlo were assigned to a robbery where two professional hold-up men robbed a William Reed of forty dollars, some rings and a gold watch. It didn't take long to locate the two professionals who were operating under the assumed names of George Van Dorset and William Hall, and during the arrest, Stavlo was slugged and nearly lost his life when Van Dorset shot at him at point blank range. But Rex grabbed the gunman from behind and the

Ozark Flats

two detectives eventually subdued the two outlaws. Each got ten-year sentences at Stillwater Prison.

This morning, John Morrissey was going over the happenings of the night before and explaining the notes that he and Rex took while at the Ozark Flats last night.

"This isn't just another case for us," he explained to the detectives as they sat around in chairs and on the edge of his desk in the main squad room of the Central Police Station. "I just came from Vern's office and he tells me that the truce they had yesterday with the newspaper won't last long if this thing drags out. In fact, it's so important to the department and to the city that Mayor Eustis has taken on part of the leadership and he and Vern will set up headquarters in the mayor's office at City Hall until we get it wrapped up."

"What else have you got for us?" John Stavlo asked.

"Not much, John," Morrissey answered, "but let's get on with what we do have." There was a pause. John Morrissey went through his notes again. He looked to Stavlo.

"John, I'd like you to go to St. Paul this morning and check out a Mr. Frederick Reed. He works at the Golden Rule Department Store over there and he was once engaged to Catherine Ging."

He turned to Michael Hoy. "I'd like you to go back to the Ozark Flats and check out some of the other tenants on this list. We simply couldn't talk to them all last night," he explained apologetically. "Then I want you to go back out to Lake Calhoun and start knocking on doors within a block of where they found the body. We might just turn up something there." Hoy nodded in agreement.

"I'm going over to check out Miss Ging's place of business and then stop at the Minnesota Loan and Trust Company to look at her bank vault," he told the small group of detectives. He turned to Rex Barnett. "I know you have that Mrs. Markham coming in this morning, and I'd like to have you meet me here this afternoon when we have Mr. Harry Hayward coming in." He added, "And check with our doctors who are looking at the body this morning."

The four detectives broke up their meeting and started to go their separate ways. Then, as an afterthought, Morrissey called to Michael Hoy. "Mike, on your way back, stop by the Palace Livery Stable and take a look at the buggy."

Ozark Flats

Hillary Markham didn't really know Louise Ireland, but she had a strong urge to go to her this morning. A Miss Cullen, a friend of Kitty Ging's, had stayed the night with Kitty's niece and was fixing breakfast in the kitchen when Hillary knocked on the door of the apartment across the hall. Louise Ireland opened the door a crack and peeked out suspiciously.

"I'm Mrs. Markham from across the hall," Hillary assured her.

"I know," said Louise. She made no attempt to open the door.

"May I come in for a few minutes?" Hillary asked.

"Yes, of course." Louise seemed embarrassed and quickly opened the door. "Come in, Mrs. Markham."

Miss Cullen heard the knock at the door and came out of the kitchen and across the dining room towards the front door of the apartment as Hillary entered.

"This is Mrs. Markham from across the hall," the young Miss Ireland explained to Miss Cullen.

"I'm Ann Cullen," she introduced herself to Hillary. "I'm an old friend of Kitty's and came over late last night after all of this had happened. I thought Lou would need someone around for the next few days."

Hillary smiled. "I thought the same thing. That's why I came over this morning."

"Lou and I are just having breakfast. Won't you join us," Miss Cullen asked.

Hillary declined, but said she'd stay and have some coffee. The three sat down in the dining room at a table near the window and Hillary looked out on a view of downtown Minneapolis she had not seen before. It was the same view Kitty Ging had seen twenty-four hours earlier.

"What a marvelous view," she exclaimed. "I've never seen the city from here before."

The three talked about the apartment, and Hillary learned how much Kitty had enjoyed living there. Miss Cullen said that the finances would be more complicated, but eventually, things would be straightened out and whatever Kitty had would surely go to Lou, although she guessed she had a sister. A Mr. Albert Connolly had been engaged as the undertaker and the funeral arrangements had been made for tomorrow at the Church of the Immaculate Conception. Miss Cullen was upset, however, because Harry Hayward had already been by this morning and offered to accompany the body back to Auburn, New York.

"I don't like that man," she told Hillary, "and I told him so." She paused. "I'm positive that he had something to do with Kitty's death—but I don't know how." She paused again. "Anyway, a Detective Hoy stopped a little while ago and, when I told him about it, he called to Police Headquarters. It wasn't very long before they called him back and he told me that Kitty's cousin, Officer Patrick Ging from the East Side, would go back to New York with Lou and the body."

Hillary found herself spending more time calming down Miss Cullen than in comforting Louise Ireland, who, for a seventeen-year-old, was holding up quite well. Actually, Hillary was having enough trouble just coping with her own feelings in losing a new-found friend. When she left, she closed the door to Kitty's apartment and stood in the hall for a moment, leaning back against the door. All of a sudden she had become sick to her stomach. All that talk in there had brought back so many unpleasant memories—Jim Stockton's death, and that long ride from Excelsior back to St. Louis for the funeral. Louise Ireland still had a long ordeal ahead of her, she thought. Then she went back to her own apartment and vomited in the kitchen sink.

John Stavlo decided to take the interurban streetcar to St. Paul, just to see what it was like. He caught the car on Washington avenue and sat on the right side as he always did on the way home. He wanted to keep an eye on the people on the sidewalk. There had been a lot of unemployed lumberjacks in town since the Hinckley and

Ozark Flats

Sandstone fires. The way the government broke the Pullman strike hadn't helped railroad labor much either. He didn't see anything amiss as he rode past all the stores on Washington avenue. At seven corners most of the passengers got off and the car moved on down to the Washington avenue bridge. At the head of the bridge where the stairs to Bohemia Flats were, all the rest got off but John and two others. Across the bridge, there were only a few houses and at Oak street Motley School stood in open country. Up the hill they went to Emerald street and on into St. Paul. The fields were white with new snow. "It's nice to get out in the country," thought John. The car picked up speed and began to sway but the motorman didn't seem to be concerned. John got used to the movement and again looked out over the countryside. It was a typical Minnesota winter day—bright white, sky blue, cloudless and bitterly cold.

At Cleveland avenue, the motorman slowed as he crossed the Transfer Railroad on a viaduct to Prior avenue. John looked at the Union Stockyards to his left. A cloud of steam rose from a huge manure pile in the nearest pen. He was glad the windows were closed. At Lake Iris, he remembered the time he took Minnie Thompsen to the dance pavilion at the Union Amusement Park. It was an unpleasant memory. He tried to think of the questions he needed to ask Reed. At Snelling avenue, one passenger got off and John looked around wondering where he could possibly go. As the car raced along, rocking from side to side, in the open country between Snelling and Dale, John decided he wouldn't tell anyone he had not taken the train.

At Dale, there began a stretch of houses and soon almost every corner had a brick building of two or three stories. Even before they got to the Wabasha turn, he could see the spires and towers of downtown St. Paul. And after the turn, the city stretched out before him. Three or four church steeples stood between him and the towers of the Capitol at Tenth street. Off to the right rose the twin spires of the German church and beyond that the grand court house. He caught a glimpse of the cathedral on St. Peter but it was hard to see. Straight ahead and slightly off to the left were more churches and the towers and chimneys of the splendid Ryan Hotel. He liked St. Paul. Its narrow streets reminded him a lot of Baltimore.

Detective Stavlo pulled himself together, got off the car at

Seventh street and made his way to the Golden Rule Department Store. It turned out to be a two-story building in the middle of the block between Minnesota and Robert streets. It went all the way through the block to Eighth street. He walked into the store and went up to the second floor where he went to the manager's office and received permission to ask some questions of one of their most highly-respected employees, Frederick I. Reed. The two men sat in a small private office that was apparently not being used these days and Stavlo listened to the man who had once been engaged to Kitty Ging tell just where he was all day yesterday and last evening.

Frederick Reed did not know of Kitty's death until the Minneapolis detective told him of the murder. The well-dressed department store man sat down and wept, and the detective gave Kitty's former boyfriend some time to compose himself so that he could go on with the questioning. John Stavlo never took a note, but such looks were deceiving. He would remember every single detail Mr. Reed was giving him. Reed explained that he and Kitty had been engaged and that he had given her a ring last year.

"It was a small diamond," Frederick Reed explained, "and although Kitty liked things to be big and flashy, she seemed to have a special liking for the ring."

Stavlo already knew the answer, but he asked the question anyway. "Did you get the ring back when the engagement was called off?"

"No." He paused and thought for a moment, as if he wasn't sure whether he should go on or not. "But even after we broke off the engagement, I would see her occasionally, and she told me that she always carried the ring in a small chamois bag pinned to her underclothes."

The two men talked some more. It was obvious to Stavlo that Mr. Reed still had a great affection for Kitty Ging. It was also clear to the detective that Fred Reed had been with friends last night who could vouch for his whereabouts. Stavlo would check out those details when he left the department store.

Did Fred Reed know of anyone who held a grudge against Kitty? John Stavlo inquired. The man couldn't think of anyone—except, perhaps Lillian Allen. He explained that she was an attractive brunette he had dated off and on for awhile. He also told Stavlo that

Lil and Kitty argued about him and that Kitty had written a note to Miss Allen's landlord and told him he had a renter of questionable morals living in his apartment house.

"Lil came across the note and was absolutely livid," he told the detective. Then he added, "But that was a year ago."

Fred Reed gave the detective the last address he had for Lillian Allen—near Eighteenth and Portland in Minneapolis.

When John was through, he thanked Reed for his cooperation and let him go back to work.

"It's the Christmas shopping season, you know," Reed explained as he left.

The Minneapolis detective walked to Mannheimer's Dry Goods Store to check on Reed's alibi and found that the assistant manager and a floorwalker had been with Reed at a gentlemen's poker game in the Dacotah flats at Selby and Western avenues. Stavlo took the names and addresses of the other players, explaining that it was unlikely that anyone would be questioned. He left and happily crossed the street to the Ryan Hotel. Walking through the ornate lobby to the cigar counter, he did not realize that the lamp shades were made by Tiffany but he did know an Oriental rug when he saw one. At the cigar counter he noticed a copy of the *Nordvestern* and started to reach for it but settled for the *Pioneer Press*. He didn't want people in the cafe to think he had just got off the boat.

In the cafe, John ordered a roast beef dinner and a glass of Glueck's.

"No Minneapolis beer, sir."

"Well, what do you have?"

"Banholzer's, Yoerg's, Stahlmann's, Excelsior on tap and St. Louis Lager and Wolf's in bottles."

"Banholzer's," said John and opened the paper.

Grover Advocates Financial Reform. President Cleveland was recommending to Congress a plan for greater issue of currency by state banks. "Good for counterfeiters," thought John. *Japanese Massacre Chinese at Port Arthur. Revolution in Salvador. Turks Slaughter Armenians.* Ah, there it is. *Bullet in Her Brain, Minneapolis Woman Found Dead, A Murder's Victim.* Three short paragraphs told of the murder and said Minneapolis police were mystified. He turned the page. *J.H. Burns Turns Himself In. Ex-County*

Auditor Says He is Tired of Trying to Find Detectives.

    Jimmie Burns reposed last night at the Ramsey county jail and will continue to spend his time there until Monday, when he will be tried on one of the old charges against him.
    Yesterday morning Mr. Burns pushed his head into the office of County Attorney Butler. He was his old insouciant self.
    "Ah, Mr. Butler," said he; "have you seen anyone looking for me?"
    "Not a soul," said Pierce, "but I hear there is a warrant for you."
    "Well," said Mr. Burns, "I wish that you would telephone the police that I am here. I am tired of looking for Meyerding and McGoiggan."
    It transpired afterwards that Burns had run across the imprint of a wooden shoe early this morning at the Seven Corners and he knew that Meyerding must be looking for him. He followed the trail to the court house. . . .

"Damned reporters," said Stavlo aloud and angrily folded up his paper. But, then, he began to laugh. Embarrassed, he composed himself and ate his roast beef dinner, grinning throughout.

Stavlo felt important, eating at the Ryan. He wished he had bought a cigar. He paid his bill, left a dime for the waiter and walked down to the station where he boarded the Milwaukee Short Line train to Minneapolis. Again, he sat on the right side although there was no need to do so. Halfway home at the Merriam Park Station, he again thought of Minnie Thompsen. Ten years ago, he had taken her to this station. The round trip was fifteen cents and admission to the amusement park was twenty-five cents. They climbed the lookout, rode the carrousel, and went to the dance pavilion. John remembered Siebert's Great Western Band and that the dancing was spirited, mostly polkas and schottisches. John was having a marvelous time drinking and dancing but after the fast part of a czardas he kept whirling around and began to throw up in the middle of the dance floor. He had staggered over to Lake Iris and washed himself off as best he could and staggered back to the dance. Minnie had friends there and was mortified. She said she never wanted to see him again and called him a *tosk* (fool). He tried to press his case but was quickly thrown out. Fortunately, the conductor allowed him to get on the train home but he had to stand in the vestibule. People rarely change but John Stavlo was going to change. He liked to be funny but he abhorred the thought of being a *tosk*. He was going to give up drinking and dancing and telling stories and he was going to church in the morning.

Detective Stavlo smiled and looked out the window. The train was slowing for the Twenty-sixth street high bridge over the Mississippi. He smiled again and remembered. He hadn't made it to church that morning or anywhere else with his hangover. He didn't quit dancing or telling stories, and he didn't quit drinking. But he never did any two at the same time from then on. He was no *tosk*.

They were out on the bridge now. The tracks on the high bridge were on top of the trusses instead of within them and many passengers shut their eyes tightly during the transit. John Stavlo, still smiling, looked down on the frozen river. He wondered what Minnie Thompsen was doing now.

In a few minutes, the train pulled into the Milwaukee depot at Washington and Fourth avenue. He got off and caught the next streetcar to Eighteenth and Portland. He found the caretaker on the first floor of the red brick building which stretched almost a block and asked for Lillian Allen. The caretaker, a short, fat little man with a mustache and a slightly balding head knew Lillian Allen all right.

"I'll say I do! No notice or nothing. She just packed her bags and a trunk and left this morning!"

MURDER!

Cold Blooded Crime Committed
In The Outskirts of the City.

Miss Catherine Ging Found
Shot to Death on the
Highway.

The Tragic Affair
Shrouded In Mystery
Yet to be Solved.

—*The Minneapolis Tribune*

FOUL MURDER!

The Body of Catherine Ging
Is Found Near Lake Calhoun

A Bullet Hole in the Head
Tells the Awful Story

Other Wounds Show That Her
Companion Did The Deed.

Harry Hayward Tells of Dead
Woman's Business Affairs.

—*The Minneapolis Journal*

9

MINNESOTANS HAD BEEN READING newspaper headlines since 1849 when the first Minnesota newspaper was published in St. Paul by James Madison Goodhue—*The Minnesota Pioneer*. The *Saint Anthony Falls Express* began publishing in the spring of 1851, but Minneapolis didn't have its very own newspaper until *The Minneapolis Chronicle* came along in 1866.

The Minneapolis Tribune was born on May 25, 1867, with Col. William S. King as publisher. *The Evening Times* came along in 1872, *The Evening Mail* in 1874 and *The Minneapolis Journal* in 1878. *The Evening Star* was a late-comer, in 1887.

Back in September, *The Minneapolis Tribune* had carried a full-page announcement to its readers:

> A great newspaper is to a more or less degree the servant of the community.
> Its duty is to chronicle, from day to day, the events of that community and the happenings of the world outside, that all

whom it serves may be brought into closer communion, the one with the other.

From its fund of information it is enabled to draw conclusions, advance ideas, destroy theories and guide general thought.

A truly great paper is a moulder of public opinion, not an angler for thoughtless applause.

Then *The Tribune* announced that beginning October 1, this par excellent newspaper of the northwest would be sold everywhere for one cent!

W.J. Murphy became the publisher of *The Tribune* in 1891. He was a North Dakota lawyer and well-known publisher of the *Grand Forks Plain Dealer*, and by 1894, he had boosted *The Tribune's* circulation to 31,000 and was publishing Sunday editions that went as high as forty pages. The newspaper had added Mergenthaler type machines this very year and also published its first cartoon just a few months ago. Subscription rates were up, too. The cost was now $5 a year with the Sunday issue alone at $2 a year. By carrier, *The Trib* was ten cents a week and the Sunday edition was twenty cents a month! On page five of today's twelve-page edition of *The Tribune*, the newspaper bragged that it had increased its circulation by 5,515 in just sixty-one days and a personal statement by W.J. Murphy told readers that "I hereby certify that the daily circulation of *The Tribune* now exceeds 30,000."

Over on the page with the Want Ads, *The Tribune* offered a Free Want Ad Page Blank for the unemployed. "Just write your ad on this blank and send to *The Tribune*."

The Minneapolis Journal was not to be outdone by its competition. "*The Journal* is newsy, readable, pure in tone, and editorially sound," wrote its editors. It also made a statement to its readers this day. "*The Evening Journal* is the best-equipped, best-established, most largely circulated, most influential, most enterprising and newsy afternoon paper northwest of Chicago. It is printed on a Hoe Web Perfecting Press of the latest pattern built expressly for *The Journal* and capable of a speed of 250 complete papers a minute, folded and ready to deliver. It employs a large, competent editorial corps and thoroughly trained men in every department. Complete *Associated Press* dispatches and full Market Reports. At 255 First

Ave. So., Minneapolis." All of this was selling at two cents a day or fifty cents a month.

Emmett Markham had too many things on his mind this morning as he pulled his notes together to go in and see his boss, J.S. McLain, the editor of *The Journal*. Emmett was concerned about Hillary. She had seemed to be in such a good frame of mind last night when they had dinner and went to the Opera House. It was the first time in weeks that they had spent an entire evening together, and it seemed even longer since they had been together for any length of time without getting into an argument. She appeared radiant last night at finding a new friend in Kitty Ging, had looked forward to Kitty having them over to her apartment for dinner soon, and began to act like her old self again—even talked about baking some Christmas cookies. That was the kind of thing that Hillary hadn't done since they moved to Minneapolis, Emmett thought.

Now all of that had changed with Kitty's death. Hillary hardly slept at all last night and she looked awful this morning. Emmett hadn't wanted to leave her, but he had to go to work. At least Jamie was home with her now. And Mrs. Blixt would come up to the apartment again and take care of their son while Hillary came down to the police station this morning to see Barnett. Thank God for Rex Barnett! Emmett was impressed with him at yesterday's meeting in the mayor's office. What a coincidence that the detective should show up at the Ozark Flats last night and be working on this particular case. Hillary would be in good hands with him.

Emmett's mind whizzed through his schedule for the day. He'd be going out to Excelsior late this afternoon to see George O'Brien at *The Minnetonka News* office, and he'd take Jamie with him on the boy's first day of school vacation. They'd help open up the house on the lake and stay overnight. Then Emmett planned to take the early-morning train back to work and Jamie would stay at the lake with Minnie Jacobs, the housekeeper, until Friday when Hillary's family would arrive. They'd all be home in Excelsior on Christmas Eve.

Ozark Flats

Emmett smiled as he thought about all of that. But there were other things to attend to, things much more immediate. He was on his way into see McLain and go over their first report of the Kitty Ging murder and make plans on how they would cover the story on a continuing basis and what kind of treatment they would give it. Emmett thought about the "truce" with the police department yesterday, and about Charlie Strong's advice. They would have to keep one eye on *The Tribune*, too, but Emmett was already confident they would do a good job with *The Journal*.

Just then, J.S. McLain stepped outside of his office and motioned to Emmett across the newsroom floor to come on in. They would look at the Ging murder stories in *The Journal* and *The Tribune*.

MURDER!

The body of Miss Catherine Ging, a dressmaker residing at the Ozark apartment house, corner of Hennepin avenue and Thirteenth street, was found on the Old Excelsior road, about a half a mile from Lake Calhoun, shortly after 9 o'clock last night, and circumstances point to a cold-blooded murder, although the police have not obtained a clue to the identity of the assassin. Death has been produced by a gunshot wound back of the right ear.

The remains were discovered by William Echard, who lives about a mile farther up the road from that point. He was homeward bound and alighted from a St. Louis Park car at the turning point, Thirty-first street and Excelsior road. He had not taken 20 steps before his attention was attracted by the clatter of a horse's hooves on the hard roadbed. He stepped aside to allow the rig to pass, and as he did so, noticed that the animal was being driven at a great speed. The night was dark, and he was unable to discern whether the buggy was occupied or not. He was inclined to the opinion that it was a runaway horse that passed him. He watched the rig and saw it turn onto the boulevard and pass under an electric light near the lake. It was bound citywards.

Continuing on his way Echard discovered the form of a woman lying almost in the middle of the road. Thinking that the horse had become unmanageable and ran away from her, throwing her from the vehicle, Echard spoke to her, but she answered him not. A hasty examination showed that she was dead. Echard hastened to a drug store at 3001 Hennepin avenue, a distance of one mile and a quarter, and notified police headquarters that a woman had been killed in a runaway accident on the Excelsior road. The patrol wagon reached the scene an hour later, and the body was removed to the county morgue where it was viewed by Coroner Spring.

THIS WOMAN WAS MURDERED. . . . MYSTERY ON EVERY SIDE. . . . BLOOD AND BRAIN MATTER. . . .

A fact which indicated that the woman may have been murdered for her money is the statement made by Harry T. Hayward, the manager of the Ozark apartments, that Miss Ging had been seen by him several times within the past few days with large amounts of money in her possession in the form of bills of large denominations. Whether or not she had any large amount of money with her last evening is not definitely known.

—The Minneapolis Tribune

MURDER HAS BEEN DONE.

A pedestrian on a lonely, dark road finds the ghastly corpse of a fair woman. By whose hand came it there in that condition?

That is the question to the solution of which the police are devoting every energy. At the morgue the battered remains of beautiful Catherine Ging lie—terrible evidence of an assassin's dastardly work.

Just why the murderer should have selected her as his victim is not entirely apparent up to this time. It is learned today that she has within a week had at least $7,000 in the safety vaults of the Minnesota Loan and Trust Company, on Nicollet avenue. Robbery may have been the motive but there are other facts in the case which tend to throw discredit upon this theory.

One of the last acts of the dead girl was to engage a single rig at Goosman's West hotel office. She drove away alone into the dark. It is known that she had lately been receiving attentions from a certain man, but seems to have exerted herself to having kept her acquaintance with this man from the knowledge of her friends. Undoubtedly this was the man who accompanied Miss Ging on her last ride. Young ladies do not take long drives at night on winter evenings alone. The supposition is that her gentleman friend was picked up soon after she drove away from the West hotel.

The police are now looking for that man.

The body itself tells an awful story. The bullet entered under the right ear, traversing the head diagonally and coming out of the left eye. The nose is broken, the blow causing the fracture having been administered from the right hand side of the face. There is a bad cut just below the mouth, evidently the result of a heavy blow which drove the lip against the teeth. This cut pierced the lip and it is a significant fact that it also is on the right hand side of the face.

When found, the body was lying in the road upon a buggy robe. This robe was saturated with blood. The girl's hair was dishpeveled, a fact in itself which tells of a terrible struggle, inasmuch as Miss Ging was always remarkably neat about her coiffure. The buggy was brought back to the livery stable by an intelligent horse, driverless, containing a pool of clotted blood and brains.

Those are the facts which the police have to work on.

Echard, the man who discovered the body, lives on the Excelsior road. He left the St. Louis car at Thirty-first street, and when a short distance from that point, was passed by a runaway horse attached to a buggy. Fifty yards further on, Echard found the remains of Miss Ging. He recognized at once that a doctor must be summoned, and at once ran to the nearest drug store, 3001 Hennepin avenue. From ths point the case was given over to the police authorities by telephone. The search for a medical man brought Dr. William Russell to the scene. The doctor was accompanied by his son, Jay Russell and a friend. The patrol wagon caught up with the medical party and carried them to the place indicated by Echard. Dr. Russell at once decided that the woman was dead. A careful search revealed nothing that could throw light on the case. It was evident that Miss Ging had been shot from behind, as shooting herself behind the ear would have been a most difficult feat.

The body was removed to the morgue and Coroner Spring summoned. Miss Ging had been attired in a closely fitting black cloth dress, sealskin sack and a hat.

Ozark Flats

> The buggy belonged to Goosman's livery stable. At the stable nothing was known except that Miss Ging engaged the rig last evening at 7 o'clock and went driving alone.
>
> *The Minneapolis Journal*

The West Hotel street clock on Hennepin avenue showed almost noon, and inside the hotel, a short little man in a checkered suit and wearing a bowler stopped at the newsstand and cigar counter, picked up the first editions of *The Tribune* and *The Journal* and headed for the elevator and the suite on the fifth floor of the hotel.

10

"I'LL HAVE A BOWL of the corn chowder, please," Hillary told the waiter with the somewhat soiled white apron. Then she handed the frayed menu back to the waiter and looked across the table to Rex Barnett who ordered the hot beef sandwich with mashed potatoes and gravy. It was listed on the menu for ten cents. The waiter thanked them and headed toward the kitchen of the New York Cafe.

Hillary looked around the dining room. It was filled with businessman and a few policemen during the noon hour. Hillary suspected that some of the men were detectives and some, perhaps, lawyers, too. There were forty or fifty there at the time and although the room was crowded, there seemed to be a feeling of privacy at each table and certainly in the booth Rex had found when they came in the corner entrance of the cafe. The room was painted an egg-shell tone with dark wood trim, dark wood booths, and matching tables and chairs. A short beige curtain with brass rings hung from a brass rod across the front window at a level that would block the view of the street outside from those sitting at a table or a booth.

Ozark Flats

Hillary slipped off her brown woolen coat. She was dressed in a long blue skirt and wore a figured blouse with colors of brown and blue predominant. A pretty beige silk scarf was tied at the neck.

"I take it that you come here often," she said.

"Yes. At least whenever I'm at the station and not out somewhere in the city." He looked around. "It's not the Continental or the West Hotel, but the food is good and it's convenient." He gave her a pleasing smile.

"I never thought I'd end up having lunch with a city detective when I got up this morning," she said, jokingly. It was true. She had known that Detective Barnett and his partner didn't have time to question everyone last night at the Ozark Flats. She also knew she was too upset last night to answer any questions, and had agreed to stop at the station this morning to see him. It was an experience, walking into the Police Station this morning. She had attracted the same kind of attention there as she and Kitty had yesterday when they entered the Continental for their luncheon date. Only this time, it was all men. She was greeted by Rex Barnett and he ushered her into the superintendent's office so they could talk in private. Vern Smith was headquartering with the mayor this morning because of the murder.

Although the police station gave her a strange—almost a brutal—feeling, she found herself quickly adjusting to the atmosphere and became even more comfortable as Rex Barnett began to visit with her about the Ozark Flats and Kitty Ging. It didn't take long for Hillary to recount that she and Emmett and Jamie had moved into the apartment on the fifth floor last fall and that she could remember when Kitty Ging became a new neighbor right around the first of November. She hadn't seen much of the dressmaker except to stop to chat for a minute or two in the hall between the two apartments or while waiting for the elevator. The murdered woman and the young niece had been model neighbors. Hillary couldn't remember seeing any gentlemen friends coming to the apartment across the hall—except for Harry Hayward.

"But she didn't go unnoticed," Hillary told Rex. "I mean, anyone who had the clothes she did and dressed with such a flair could not go unnoticed!"

Hillary continued, telling Rex about Kitty's invitation to have lunch and go shopping with her, and Rex had sensed a loneliness in Hillary's voice as she told about accepting the invitation and about yesterday's activities. Hillary thought he seemed to be particularly interested in the large amount of money Kitty had flashed in front of the waiter, and in what Harry Hayward had to say about all of that. But Hillary assured him there was nothing suspicious about Kitty's actions during their shopping spree yesterday.

"I think we both hated to see it come to an end," Hillary told him. She paused. "I felt a little sad when we said goodbye."

The interrogation of Hillary took a little longer than Rex had expected. He may have even unconsciously extended the questioning a little. But he was aware of one thing. He had been right this morning. She was beautiful!

Now Rex looked at her from across the table in the booth at the New York Cafe. "I didn't expect to be having lunch with such an attractive lady, either," he smiled, hesitatantly, as if he were not sure whether or not he was on safe ground. She smiled back. He felt better immediately. "The least I could do was to take you to lunch after keeping you so long."

"I must confess that these last two days have been the two busiest and most exciting since we moved into the Ozark Flats," Hillary told him. She felt so at ease now—almost like talking to an old friend. "Of course, these past few months have not been the most exciting for me with Jamie in school and Emmett working so much of the time at the newspaper."

"I don't know your husband very well, Mrs. Markham, but in the short time we were together yesterday at the mayor's office, I was impressed with how knowledgeable he is about the city's problems, and with his fairness."

"It's strange you should say that," Hillary broke in. "That's exactly what he said about you last night over dinner."

"I was surprised to see him again so soon when I walked into the apartment building last night. But it was a nice surprise," Rex added.

The waiter brought Hillary's soup and Rex's hot beef sandwich. Hillary was amazed—Rex's plate looked more like a dinner than a lunch.

"Are you going to eat *all* of that," she laughed.

"When you're a bachelor, you eat all you can when you sit down at the table."

Hillary was surprised to hear that such a handsome—and such a nice man was not married. She also found it easy to talk to him as they discussed Christmas plans and what each would do over the holiday weekend. She told him about her home at Excelsior, that Emmett would be going out there this afternoon to get it opened and about her family coming from St. Louis on Friday.

Rex could see the excitement in her face as she talked about Excelsior and Christmas and the Christmas Eve service at Trinity Chapel. She told him how much the little Episcopal church meant to her and her family and how important the midnight service at Trinity was to Emmett and herself. Her willingness to talk about such personal matters was infectious. He found himself talking about his childhood and his father and the endless number of church services he had sat through in congregations served by the elder Barnett. He talked about little things he remembered about his dad, things he hadn't thought about in years—his father's hands, they were always immaculate, his Bible, and the gold pocket watch with the gold cross watch fob that his father lost. He admitted to Hillary, somewhat apologetically, that he couldn't remember the last time he had been in church.

"That's what happens sometimes to kids whose dads are ministers. I think we get too much of it at too early an age, and it all becomes unpleasant." He talked about his college days at the University and without hesitation, he told Hillary about Josie and his bachelor life since then.

He sounded sad as he spoke, and Hillary wanted to reach out to him. Instead, the two simply looked at each other and in silence, without saying anything at all, they knew that each had found a new friend.

"It's getting late, and I've already taken up too much of your time,' he apologized as they got out of the booth. He helped her with her coat and started toward the front counter. Then they went out on to Washington avenue and stood there for a moment in the bright winter sunlight.

"Goodbye." Hillary extended her hand.

"Thanks again for coming downtown—and for having lunch

with me." Rex took her hand for a moment. Then Hillary turned and started toward Nicollet avenue and Rex headed for Lockup Alley with a little brighter step than usual. And he realized that he hadn't thought about Josie in years.

11

JOHN MORRISSEY never seemed to be bothered with investigating cases involving large sums of money. Such figures as ten thousand dollars seemed unreal to a city detective with a wife and five children and a salary of ninety-five dollars a month. He had gone to the third floor of the Syndicate Building to Kitty Ging's dressmaking shop where two employees and a close friend of the murdered seamstress were carrying on as best as they could to complete holiday orders. There was very little money at the shop and Morrissey obtained a list of banks where Kitty Ging had accounts.

A Miss Grace Murphy told him Kitty had talked of investing seven or eight thousand dollars in a business venture. But she added that Kitty had spoken about it in such a manner that Miss Murphy got the impression she was joking.

Mrs. Alice Murray, who handled some of Kitty's business affairs, told Lt. Morrissey she doubted Miss Ging had any large amounts of money anywhere. She had considered going into business with Kitty earlier in the fall and Kitty's entire capital at that time was less than three thousand dollars. She was also aware of some kind of business dealings between Kitty and Harry Hayward, but she wasn't sure whether the money involved was Kitty's or Mr. Hayward's.

No one at the dressmaking shop had seeen any of Kitty's gentlemen friends at the shop with the exception of Harry Hayward who stopped quite often, especially during the last month.

"But there was one caller yesterday afternoon," Mrs. Murray remembered. "I don't know whether he stopped on business or just a social call. He asked for Kitty and when we told him she wasn't here, he left."

"Did he leave a card or his name or anything?" Morrissey asked.

"No card—but when he first came up here, he introduced himself. I think his name was—Waterman. Tom Waterman."

There didn't seem to be anything else to gain at the shop in the Syndicate Building and the detective still had to make the rounds of the downtown banks. Morrissey was putting his coat back on and was about to head for the door when one of the seamstresses asked him if he wanted to see the note that somebody delivered to the shop yesterday afternoon.

"What note?" John Morrissey asked hurriedly.

"The one the messenger brought up here yesterday afternoon. When Miss Ging came, she read the note, tore it up and threw it in the waste basket."

The scraps of paper were still there in the waste basket by the desk. The detective carefully picked up all the pieces and stuffed them in his coat pocket. Then he thanked them all, and left to make the rounds of the banks where Kitty had accounts. At the Farmers and Mechanics Bank on Fourth Street, he found that Kitty had only one dollar left out of a hundred dollars that had been in her account. At the first National Bank of Minneapolis, there was still $326 in her name.

The bank officer at the Minnesota Loan and Trust Company told the detective that, according to their records, Katherine Ging had made a stop late Monday afternoon but he had no idea whether she was putting something into the safety deposit box or taking something out. He had seen her take money into the vault before. There was nothing in the vault when the two checked it out and Detective Morrissey started back to the Central Police Station. Why would she have kept large sums of money in that vault when she already had bank accounts, he asked himself. Unless, of course, it was counterfeit!

Hillary Markham waited for the elevator to come down to the main floor of the Ozark Flats and when Claus Blixt opened the elevator doors, Harry Hayward was talking to the janitor.

"And don't forget that there are leaks in the kitchen sinks in both of those apartments on the fifth floor," Mr. Hayward was telling Mr. Blixt. "When Joey comes back, you get on outside and get the rest of the walks shoveled, too. If we're gonna run a first-class apartment house, we've got to look like a first-class apartment and give our guest's first-class service. Those walks should have been shoveled last night."

"Yes, Mr. Hayward," Claus Blixt agreed. The janitor looked a little tougher than usual today, Hillary thought. In fact, he looked like he was still recovering from a hangover. Hillary stepped into the elevator as Harry came into the main hallway.

"Mrs. Markham. It's nice to see you."

"Good afternoon, Mr. Hayward," she greeted him.

"I understand that you stopped downtown at the police station for questioning this morning."

"Yes, as a matter of fact, I did. I had a long talk with Detective Barnett. I—"

It was apparent to Harry that Hillary was still not taking all of this too well and now it was difficult for her to speak.

"I'm sorry, Mrs. Markham. This whole thing has been a terrible experience for all of us. I know that this has all been difficult for you. I'm sorry. I should have realized that you didn't want to talk about it."

Hillary nodded with a faint smile. "Yes, thank you. It has not been very pleasant."

Harry started for the front door at the end of the hallway and then turned back toward the elevator and motioned Claus Blixt to come to him. "One more thing, Mr. Blixt," Hillary could hear him

say. Then the two stood at the front door and spoke for just a moment in low tones—something about money. As Mr. Blixt hurried back to the elevator, Harry called back to him. "I'm on my way to the police station. And just forget about all that talk the other day." Blixt nodded in agreement. Then he turned to Hillary as he closed the elevator doors.

"Fifth floor, Ma'am?"

Andy Ross had just left the manager's office on the first floor of the West Hotel where he now had a desk and a place to operate from. He didn't have to start work as assistant manager of the hotel until Monday, but these few days before Christmas gave him an insight into the operation of the best hotel in Minneapolis—well, at least as good as his own father's Nicollet House down the avenue. The West Hotel management was also pleased that Andy would show up for work a few days early, and because they had an assistant manager who might just turn out to be the best hotel man in the city.

Andy was on his way to the second-floor dining room where he would make sure that all of the details were being taken care of for tonight's Northwest Railway Club dinner. In his hand was the program for tonight's December meeting of the organization which met monthly, alternating between Minneapolis and St. Paul. Tonight's dinner meeting would start at 8 p.m. and would feature a paper on *Storehouse Practices and Systems* presented by S.F. Forbes, General Storekeeper for the Great Northern Railway. The Topic for Discussion would be "Boiler Coverings." None of this sounded very exciting to Andy Ross, but apparently it was an important meeting. They expected a full house for dinner.

The new assistant manager had just crossed the Exchange on the main floor and was about to start up the marble stairway when he saw her. He couldn't believe his eyes as he looked to the top of the stairs. Just starting down the stairway with two small boys was a beautiful brunette in a fur coat.

"Rose! Rose!" Andy shouted. "For God's sake, Rose, it's me!"

Ozark Flats

Rose Fortier Stark looked down the stairway and saw Andy Ross rushing up the stairs, two steps at a time, toward her. "Andy Ross!" she exclaimed.

The two embraced at the top of the stairs while the two little boys looked on in amazement. They held each other for a long time. Then Andy took her by the shoulders and held her back from him.

"My God, Rose, you're beautiful."

"You don't look so bad yourself," she smiled.

"I haven't seen you since the wedd—" Andy stopped. His grin disappeared and he bit his lip. "I'm sorry, Rose. I'm sorry about John—and I'm sorry that I couldn't get back to Excelsior for the funeral. I—"

"It's okay, Andy," she assured him. She tried to smile, but it was hard to do. Seeing Andy Ross had brought back all of those memories of Excelsior seven years ago when they were all just starting out; when John Stark had captained *The City of St. Louis* to that Fourth-of-July victory over *The Belle of Minnetonka*; and when Andy Ross had given John and Rose his share of the winnings so John could buy his own steamboat, *The Hattie May*, and John and Rose could get married. All of that whizzed through the pretty French girl's mind in a flash as she stood there looking at Andy Ross. And she knew she was indebted to him for more than just helping John financially. He had given her some much-needed advice, straight from the shoulder, that undoubtedly saved her relationship with John Stark.

"It's all right, Andy. We're getting along these days," she assured him as she looked down to her side at the two youngsters. I'd like you to meet the Stark boys," she said. "This is John Stark, Jr. and this is Andy Stark." Then she looked at Andy Ross. "Boys, this is an old friend of your father's—and an old and dear friend of mine, Mr. Andy Ross." The two kids looked up at Andy, smiled, and extended their hands.

Andy Ross smiled back and shook hands. Inside he was crying. "It's a pleasure to meet you John Stark, and you too, Andy." He looked at Rose. "I don't know what to say."

"Don't say anything," she said. There was a moment of silence. Then Andy Ross recovered.

"I thought you were in Cleveland. I saw Emmett and Hillary last night and they told me you had gone back to visit your cousin."

"That's where I've been," Rose explained. "But I got to thinking that people should be home for Christmas and we just packed up and headed back to Minnesota. We got into town this morning and we're going to stay over here at the hotel tonight and then go back out to Excelsior and home for Christmas." She looked happy again. "What are you doing here?"

"I'm a few days early to start work as the new assistant manager here," he told her. And, then, he explained how Emmett and Hillary had invited him to come out to the lake on Christmas Day. "This will make it even better," he said excitedly. "Maybe we can get together for awhile on Christmas Day. I just know that Emmett and Hillary wouldn't mind."

"I'd like that," she agreed.

"And if you're not too busy, perhaps I can treat you all to dinner tonight here at the hotel."

"We have a lot of catching up to do," she told him. "There's no better time to start than tonight at dinner."

The two stood at the top of the stairs and just smiled at each other Then they were interrupted by a tug at her hand and one of the boys reminded her of where they were going. They were on their way to Donaldson's Glass Block.

"Come on, Mom, you promised us we could see Santa Claus today!'

Detective Michael Hoy had gone back to the scene of the crime on old Excelsior Road and decided to start knocking on doors and making inquiries about the night before. It was the very first house he stopped at that a Mrs. Naegel told him of hearing shots last evening.

"You mean you heard a shot," Hoy corrected her.

"No. I mean I heard two shots," she told him. "This house isn't more than twenty yards from where she was found and I heard two shots!" She was emphatic. "Sounded like they were farther away, though."

She could add no more to the mystery so Michael Hoy thanked

her for her time and went on. There were only two or three more houses in the vicinity, and although the residents were all aware of what had happened, none could offer any information or could remember anything unusual about the previous evening.

When Michael Hoy stopped at the Palace Livery Stable, the stable boy showed him carriage number twenty-seven. There were still bloodstains on the side curtain. Detective Hoy could see the stains where the blood had trickled down the back curtain, too, and on to the back part of the buggy seat. As the detective inspected the buggy he remembered looking at the body of Kitty Ging in the morgue and the bullet hole in the right rear side of her head. Her murderer would have had to be sitting on the right side of the victim as they rode along in the buggy—the side usually taken by a man when driving with a lady.

Henry Goosman was also on the job at his Palace Livery Stable when Michael Hoy visited there and the two of them went into Mr. Goosman's office to talk some more after the detective had looked at the buggy. Hoy had three or four pages of notes as he finished his interview with the livery stable owner. Just as he was leaving, he asked Henry Goosman about Kitty ordering rigs from the Palace before.

"Yes," he answered. "Once we had a rig sent over to the Ozark Flats for her. The other time she came here to the livery stable."

"Alone?" Michael Hoy asked.

"No." He stopped to think for a moment, rubbing his chin with his right hand. "She had a gentleman with her." Then he added. "It was last Saturday—last Saturday night. They had the very same rig, number twenty-seven, and the same buckskin mare."

"Do you know who the gentleman was?" Hoy pressed him.

"Oh, yes. It was Harry Hayward.

12

POLICE CHIEF VERN SMITH had converted an adjoining office to Mayor Eustis' office into a working headquarters for the investigation of the Catherine Ging murder case, allowing the mayor to keep abreast of the progress of the case and still maintain his regular routine of work as head of the city government.

The two met in the mayor's office after lunch along with the assistant county attorney, A.H. Hall. The mayor and the chief agreed that the newspaper accounts of the murder and the start of the investigation had been reasonably accurate. But they could see by the stories that the newspapers would be highlighting the crime from day to day and not only pressing the police department for facts about the investigation, but doing a little investigating on their own, as well.

The chief already had obligations for this afternoon, but assured Mayor Eustis that Detective Morrissey was more than capable of handling the questioning of Harry Hayward this afternoon, and that he would be assisted by Detective Barnett with whom the mayor had met and been impressed yesterday. He also told the mayor that it would be perfectly all right not only to sit in on the interrogation today, but both he and the assistant county attorney could ask some questions if they wanted to. A.H. Hall had been sent over to the mayor's office this afternoon from the new and still uncompleted County Court House by Hennepin County Attorney, Frank Nye. Mr. Nye didn't think it was necessary for his office to get involved at this point, but Bill Eustis insisted that it was important that the county attorney's office be represented in the investigation of the Ging case.

The police superintendent was just leaving the mayor's office when John Morrissey and Rex Barnett knocked on the door between the temporary police headquarters room and the mayor's office. Bill Eustis opened the door.

"Excuse me, sir. I'm Detective John Morrissey and this is Detective Rex Barnett. I just wanted you to know that we're here and we'll be here most of the afternoon."

"My pleasure." The mayor extended his hand to the two policemen and spoke to Rex. "Hello Barnett."

"Good afternoon, sir," Rex greeted him.

Vern Smith followed the mayor into the headquarters room and talked to his two detectives for a few minutes. Then he left for his 1:30 appointment. In the meantime, John Morrissey brought the mayor up to date on the investigation and briefed him on the actions of the detectives that morning. Just as there was a lull in the conversation, there was a knock on the door. Rex opened the door and the three men looked at the visitor. It was Harry Hayward, impeccably dressed in a gray flannel suit and wearing a black bowler and a cape. His starched white shirt was set off by a red figured tie and when he doffed his hat, he looked even more handsome with his hair and mustache neatly trimmed. He moved into the room with a commanding grace and extended his hand to Mayor Eustis.

"I'm Harry Hayward, Mr. Mayor. It's a pleasure to meet you."

The mayor shook his hand and spoke. "Nice to meet you, Mr. Hayward. We appreciate your taking the time to come down here to answer some questions. We're hoping to clear up this whole tragic happening in as short a time as possible."

"I would agree with you, sir," Harry replied.

Then Mayor Eustis introduced Harry to Mr. Hall, who had just arrived, and the two detectives and both Harry and the policemen agreed that they had met before—last night in fact—when Morrissey and Barnett were at the Ozark Flats. Morrissey invited Harry to sit down in front of a desk near a window which looked out over Hennepin avenue. Mayor Eustis settled down in a more comfortable chair across the room, and Rex Barnett stood by the window. The attorney took the chair behind the desk. John Morrissey sat on the edge of the desk and asked Harry to tell them about his association with Catherine Ging.

Harry was more than willing to talk about Kitty. He told of meeting her while dining at Olson's Boarding House across from the Ozark Flats and how they had continued to see each other all last summer. He spoke of her as if he were talking about someone who was still alive, describing her beauty and their dinner dates, and going to the theater together. He explained that they seemed to like the same things. She was a good businesswoman and wanted to invest in even a larger business than her dressmaking shop. He told the policemen that she was fascinated by his expertise at gambling, and that he had lent her money on several occasions for gambling.

"We both like good clothes and the same social circles and she was delighted when I suggested that she move into that fifth-floor apartment at the Ozark Flats last fall."

John Morrissey asked him just what kind of relationship the two of them had and Harry answered the question head-on without hesitation. He explained that he thought she was beautiful, fun to be with, and a good friend, but that it was Kitty who had fallen in love with *him* and had wanted the two of them to get married.

Rex Barnett asked Harry to retrace his actions yesterday and Harry detailed his whereabouts throughout the day, skipping over his morning meeting in the fifth-floor rooms at the West Hotel. He went through the afternoon escapade with his friend, Tom Waterman, his dining at the boarding house, his stops at the apartment to find Kitty not there, his visit with his parents, and the brief talk with his brother Adry. He told about changing his mind and taking Mable Bartelson to the theater instead of going skating last night. He reminded the detectives that he got back to the Ozark Flats about eleven o'clock—"and you know the rest."

Ozark Flats

Mayor Eustis puffed on a cigar and watched quietly while John Morrissey continued the questioning.

"You seemed awfully nervous last night Mr. Hayward—and we have a number of people who have told us that you made some very definite statements about Miss Ging's death."

Morrissey thumbed through some papers and notes. "Last night you said to some of your neighbors: 'I have been expecting that they would do her up! My two thousand dollars is gone to hell! It is nobody but Miss Ging. She has not been hurt in any runaway accident. She has been done up for her money,' and when a patrolman asked you about that, you told him you had your reasons for it." He paused. "Who's 'they'?" the detective asked.

Harry nodded. "I was upset last night, but I was sure Kitty's death was no accident. She has been gambling heavily these past couple of months and she has been carrying large sums of money around with her. I think someone knew she had the money on her."

"You were with her at the Continental Cafe yesterday for lunch," Rex Barnett broke in. "You saw all that money. The waiter there tells me she flashed a large bank roll. Did you caution her about it?"

"I didn't want to embarrass her in front of all those people," Harry explained.

"How much do you suppose she had with her?" Morrissey asked.

"I don't know—nearly two thousand dollars, maybe."

Morrissey continued. "Last night you told Mr. Henry Goosman that someone was trying to do you up for your money. You said something about 'two thousand dollars gone to hell!' and told him 'what a fool I've been'. Was the money yours, Mr. Hayward?"

"I don't know for sure. It might have been. I've been lending her a lot of money lately."

"How much, Mr. Hayward?"

"I suppose nine thousand dollars—maybe ten," Harry replied. "She was not very successful at gambling."

The assistant county attorney broke into the conversation. "Where did you get the money, Mr. Hayward?"

Harry explained that he had been reasonably successful gambling and had originally lent the money to Kitty without question. As she needed more, however, he had asked for some promissory notes which his father now held for him. She had won some money, however, and he thought she kept most of it in a vault at the Minnesota Loan and Trust Company. "If it's not there, I've been worked," he said emphatically.

"When did she give you the promissory notes?" Morrissey asked.

"As a matter of fact, it was yesterday," Harry replied.

Rex watched intently as the questioning continued. Harry Hayward was at ease, even after a couple of hours of questioning. He seemed so sure that money was the motive, Rex thought. When Harry identified the body last night, he said she had been killed for her money. And he had told Louise Ireland last night that Kitty had "worked" him and he had given her money. According to John Morrissey, her bank accounts were practically empty—and why would she keep large sums of money in a vault instead of at her regular banks—unless she was afraid that the banks might detect the money was counterfeit. Rex kept listening—and thinking.

Harry continued fielding questions by John Morrissey, the attorney, and occasionally a question from Mayor Eustis. He admitted owning a revolver and had actually shown it to some of the residents of the Ozark Flats last night. But made it very clear that no one else had ever used the gun and no one else had access to it, not even his brother, Adry. The mayor asked Harry if he would be willing to view the body one more time and Harry, cooperating to the fullest, was agreeable. The assistant county attorney wasn't sure if it was such a good idea, but the mayor insisted. John Morrissey had no serious objections.

"Just one more thing, Mr. Hayward," asked Morrissey.

"Sure," Harry said agreeably.

"Aren't you the beneficiary of a couple of insurance policies on Kitty Ging's life?"

Harry smiled. "It's no secret. We took out the policies—two of them—so I'd have some collateral on the money she borrowed from me. I even took out a policy on myself and named Kate as the beneficiary, just to show my good faith." What he hadn't told Kitty, nor did he tell Morrissey, was that he had also let the policy on himself lapse right away.

John Morrissey already had some notes that Michael Hoy had given him from interviewing Henry Goosman earlier in the day in which Mr. Goosman talked about going to the morgue last night with

Harry Hayward. That's when Harry asked Mr. Goosman, "Do you think life insurance is good in the case of murder?"

"How much were the policies for, Mr. Hayward?" Morrissey asked.

"Ten thousand dollars!"

Morrissey stood up and thanked Harry for coming downtown. Then everyone stood up, indicating that the questioning was apparently over. As the mayor and Harry turned toward the door, Rex Barnett asked one last question.

"Who do you think the suspicion points to, Harry?"

"It points to me more than any man in the world," he answered. Then he smiled just a little. "But I can verify where I was last night."

Emmett Markham was satisfied that *The Journal* was doing its job fairly well in covering the Catherine Ging murder, and he was confident the rest of the daily operation was going along as usual. All of that made him feel better about leaving his office early this Wednesday afternoon to make his monthly visit to his weekly newspaper in nearby Excelsior. *The Minnetonka News* was the outgrowth of a long line of weekly newspapers in that small town west of the city. The community got its start in 1853 when George M. Bertram in New York had organized the Excelsior Pioneer Association which came to Minnesota and to Lake Minnetonka to settle on the south shores of the lower lake and formed the community, Excelsior. The town had grown over the years and by the mid-eighties, had become the hub of the Minnetonka summer resort area—the most popular vacation spot west of Saratoga Springs, New York.

This past summer had been one of the best for the long list of resort hotels not only in Excelsior, but throughout the Minnetonka area. Wealthy families from the south, vacationers from large cities on both coasts, and visitors from such cities as London, Paris and Tokyo, registered at the White House, the Sampson House and the LaPaul House in Excelsior; at the beautiful Lake Park Hotel in Tonka Bay; at the Hotel St. Louis, the Keewaydin and the Cottagewood in

Deephaven, and at the most popular and luxurious hotel of them all, the Hotel Lafayette at Minnetonka Beach.

Most of the hotels had been constructed or leased by the railroads, and Excelsior found its depot handling some ten trains a day during the height of the summer season. From there, many of the visitors would move down Excelsior's main street, Water street, to the municipal docks along the waterfront of Excelsior Bay, to board steamboats making regular runs to other points on the beautiful lake.

The steamboats, huge sidewheelers and sternwheelers, had been on the lake since 1855 when the steamer, *The Governor Ramsey* became Minnetonka's first steamboat. It was followed by famous fleets of boats: Captain May's fleet which included *The Hattie May*, with a capacity of 300 passengers; the Lake Minnetonka Navigation Company's fleet of steamboats; and eventually, the two largest steamboats ever to sail the lake—*The City of Saint Louis* and *The Belle of Minnetonka*. *The City*, 160 feet long, could accomodate 1500 passengers. *The Belle*, largest of all of the steamboats, was 300 feet long and was known to carry 2,500 passengers.

The little village of Excelsior grew right along with the popularity of the area, and newspapers had always been a part of that growth. *The Excelsior Enterprise* was the first newspaper in the community in 1858. Frederick W. Crosby was the first publisher, and his publication was followed by such Excelsior weeklies as *The Excelsior Cottager, The Northwestern Tourist, The Minnetonka Mirror*, and *The Minnetonka News*.

Emmett Markham would meet with George O'Brien, his editor of *The Minnetonka News*, early this evening to review the last month's operation of the community newspaper. George was an experienced weekly newspaperman and Emmett had been pleased with the successful operation of the weekly since he moved to the city. He had left the office of *The Journal* in time to stop at the Ozark Flats to pick up his son, Jamie, and head for the Union Depot.

"You two be careful now," Hillary cautioned them as they left the apartment, "and keep bundled up and stay warm. There'll be a chill in that house out there tonight."

"We'll be just fine, dear," Emmett assured her. "Minnie will have a fire going long before we get there."

"Goodbye, Jamie dear." Hillary stooped down and gave her son a long hug. "You be good for Minnie tomorrow when daddy comes back to the city. We'll all be back out there on Friday."

"Will you bring Grandpa and Grandma with you when you come?" Jamie asked excitedly.

Hillary smiled and reassured him. "Of course I will, darling. And we'll bring lots of Christmas presents with us, too."

Emmett and Hillary embraced. "I'll see you tomorrow, dear," he told her.

"Goodbye, dear." She whispered in Emmett's ear. "Remember, I love you."

Jamie took his dad's hand and they were off for the depot. They would catch the 4:30 train, one of five daily trains still scheduled for Excelsior in the dead of winter by the M. and St. L. and they would be there by a little after six o'clock. Hillary stood in the doorway of the apartment and waved again as the elevator door closed. Her smile faded to a look of despair. She wished she were going with them.

When Mayor Eustis arrived at the Connolly Funeral Parlor with Harry Hayward, A.H. Hall and Rex Barnett, he found two or three reporters standing around outside the front door. The foursome simply ignored the newspapermen and the mayor explained in curt tones that they were too busy to stop now. The four went inside and were ushered into a small room where the casket was located.

A tall, thin man, slightly balding, and wearing a black suit, greeted the foursome and closed some sliding doors to the parlor, cutting them off from the main foyer. It was quiet. No one said much, and in what little conversation there was, the men spoke in hushed tones. "Are you sure that you want to view the body?" the tall, thin man asked the mayor. "The coffin has remained closed and will undoubtedly stay that way."

Harry Hayward and the mayor nodded as they stood along side of the coffin. Rex and the attorneys stayed in the background, a few feet away. The mortician took the lid off the coffin and there was silence. Harry Hayward looked at the body with a steady gaze and did not flinch. The beautiful Catherine Ging's face was marred beyond repair and her head was turned slightly, exposing the wound where the bullet had entered the skull behind the ear. The mayor squirmed, but remained beside Harry who looked at the body for what Rex Barnett thought was a long time. Then he half turned, as if to speak to all three of the men in the room with him.

"You gentlemen think I'm guilty, don't you?" He paused. He fidgeted with his hat which he held in front of him. "God knows I am not."

The mayor nodded to the undertaker who started to close the coffin.

"Leave it open for a moment," Harry asked quietly. "I want to look at her." There was more silence, and then he spoke once more. "Oh, my God! If she could only speak!"

Harry turned away from the coffin and nodded to the mayor. As they left the room, the tall, thin man put the cover back on the casket.

The men stood in the foyer of the funeral parlor and the mayor shook Harry's hand and thanked him for coming. Harry looked toward Rex Barnett who also thanked him and told him that he was free to go. Harry said goodbye and left hastily. The other three men stood there together after he had left.

"He certainly passed the test as far as I'm concerned," said the mayor.

Mr. Hall agreed, although it was evident that he did not approve of the visit to the funeral parlor. The three men left, and outside the front door the mayor and Mr. Hall stopped long enough to visit with the reporters.

"Do you have anything more you can tell us at this time?" one reporter inquired of the mayor.

Mr. Hall seemed to think that the question was directed to him, however, and proceeded to answer. "I started out this morning with three theories," he told the reporters, "but I have abandoned them all, and at the present time, I have none whatever." The interview was over and the mayor and the assistant county attorney said goodbye and left.

Rex Barnett was still standing in front of the Connolly Funeral Parlor as the small group disbanded. He had made up his mind. As soon as he got back to the station he would recommend that John Morrissey put a tail on Mr. Harry Hayward.

13

LEVI STEWART had been a prominent attorney before he acquired such great wealth in real estate. Yet he was a man of simple tastes, lived in a small, older home on Hennepin avenue on property that was considered valuable. The fact of the matter was that Levi had refused to demolish the comfortable old home inspite of pressures from the area to do so. It had been a long day for Levi, closing a new real estate venture out past Lake Calhoun in a newly-developing area west of the city. He had been so busy he hadn't had time to sit down in his study and read the evening paper before dinner. It was already late when he arrived home, and it was well into the evening before he finished his dinner and retired to his study to read a while.

There were other headlines in *The Tribune*:

Goff At Work Again—the senate investigating committee had resumed its probe into corruption of the New York City Police Department; *Japs Preparing To Attack The Chinese Again, Tacoma, Washington Bank Liquidates, Sugar Prices Down*, and *Forty-Five Moonshiners Being Taken To Court in Kentucky*.

Levi Stewart was a businessman first, and it wasn't until he had

checked the front page of the newspaper for its business news that he glanced at the black headlines, *MURDER!* He had only to read the first sentence in the news story before he became sick to his stomach. *The body of Miss Catherine Ging, a dressmaker residing at the Ozark apartment house, corner of Hennepin avenue and Thirteenth street, was found on* . . . . . .

Levi Stewart set the newspaper down in his lap and slipped his hand up underneath his eyeglasses and rubbed his eyes with the thumb and forefinger of his right hand. My God! he thought to himself. He could not believe what he had read. He picked up the newspaper and started over from the beginning and read the entire two columns, the full lenghth of the newspaper. When he finished, he dropped the newspaper on his lap, leaned back in the overstuffed chair in his study, and rubbed his eyes again. He shook his head. He had a sort of client-attorney relationship with the boy over the years and it had only been last night that he visited with Adry Hayward, the son of his dear old friend, William, from the Ozark Flats. Now this!

The graying, middle-aged gentleman moved from his chair, across the small study to his desk where he pushed some papers around until he found the stationery he wanted. Then he removed the cork on the bottle of ink embedded in the inkwell in the upper right-hand corner of his writing desk and began to write a note:

"To the Honorable William H. Eustis. . . . . Dear Bill . . . . .

The M. and St. L. train to Excelsior was on time this December afternoon as Emmett Markham and his son, Jamie, stepped off the three-car train at the Excelsior depot at 5:46. It was already quite dark and the main street of the little village was a reflection of what all of Excelsior was like in the dead of winter—a sleepy little Minnesota town, unlike the bustling resort of summertime. The lights of the main street, Water street, came from the new street lamps in the little community, and from some of the retail stores which would be open until six o'clock when the fire siren would sound. It had already blown once today at twelve noon, and would sound again at nine o'clock tonight, just as it did everyday. At six o'clock the business district would close down for the night—with the exception of Newell's Drug Store and Fred Hawkins Hotel and Cafe. An occasional horse or team of horses and a sleigh with bells would jingle their way down Water street, and late shoppers would be heading toward home and supper at this hour.

Emmett and his son started down Water street toward the lake. Emmett carried a small travelling bag and three or four Christmas packages tied together with twine. They passed J.L. Dickinson's grocery store, went by H.F. Bullens' General Store, and Emmett could still see some shoppers in A.B. Show's grocery store across the street. Now they were in the last block before they came to the lakeshore and somehow, it seemed to get much darker. They could see the frozen Excelsior Bay, covered with snow, and as they looked out into the main lake, the snow faded away into the darkness. It was already too late in the day to see Gale's Island or Big Island, and just a few faint lights from Wayzata's main street at the north end of the lake were visible from the Excelsior shoreline.

Emmett loved this little town—even in the middle of winter—but it was far different from the Excelsior that had become famous, along with the rest of the Minnetonka area, as a summer resort. At this time in the summertime, there would be all kinds of activity. Rigs from the livery stables would be waiting in line for the dozens of passengers who would have stepped off the M. and St. L. at the Excelsior depot. And they would be transported to Excelsior hotels and boarding houses—villas was the more sophisticated term—or to Excelsior's municipal docks to catch one of fifteen steamboats bound for just about every point on both the Lower and the Upper Lake of historic Minnetonka.

Those staying on in Excelsior would find rooms at one of the three leading hotels—The White House, The Sampson House, and the LaPaul House. The White House was the oldest of the hotels, located on a large bluff at the foot of Water street, overlooking Excelsior Bay. The Sampson House was up Second street, a block away, and it too, looked out on to Lake Minnetonka from a little further distance back from the shoreline. It advertised "Electric Call Bells in Every

Room" and catered to wealthy visitors from Missouri, especially from Carleton and Jefferson City. The LaPaul House was owned by Dr. LaPaul and also looked out on Excelsior Bay. Some folks weren't quite sure of Dr. LaPaul's expertise as a physician, but no one questioned his ability to run a popular hotel. It was agreed that the LaPaul House threw some of the best parties in town during the height of the summer tourist season.

Emmett and Jamie were now standing at the corner of Water street and Lake street, looking out at the darkness of Excelsior Bay. Huge snowdrifts seemed to seal in the Blue Line Cafe which was located on the shoreline across the street from the White House. At this hour in the summer, visitors from around the world would be arriving for a summertime dinner at the Blue Line Cafe. The last of the day's fishermen would be bringing those popular Blue Line rowboats back into shore, and up in the bar, the gambling would be taking on a little more serious note.

Father and son turned west and started up the road toward the high bluff which overlooked Excelsior Bay. The old two-story house on the top of the bluff was really home to Emmett and Hillary, and to Jamie, too. And Minnie would have the house opened up and dinner on the stove for them when Emmett and Jamie arrived. After supper, Emmett would hike back down to the mainstreet to see George O'Brien and to go over the month's operation of *The Minnetonka News.*

"Come on, son, we're almost there." Emmett put his arm around the boy's shoulder and the two of them began trudging up the hill in the snow toward the flickering lights of home.

Harry Hayward had gone to bed early this evening. It had been a long day for Harry and the questioning by the police had taken over five hours. When he returned to the Ozark Flats, he stopped to see his parents and then came down one floor to his own apartment, took a couple healthy swigs of liquor from a flask, and went to bed to get some rest. It had been a long night last night, and a long a trying day today. And Harry was just plain tired.

Downstairs in the lobby, a reporter from *The Tribune* was with Mr. Hayward, Sr., who explained that the copies of the two insurance policies on Miss Ging's life were not available to the press and Mr. Hayward's attorneys had advised him not to show anyone the policies unless compelled to do so by due process of law.

In the meantime, the senior Hayward had answered almost all of the questions put to him by *The Tribune* reporter who had asked how Harry had come into so much money. Harry's father told him that he had given each of his sons eleven thousand dollars in money and real estate not so long ago, and he had disposed of some of his real estate. The reporter thanked him for his time and his cooperation and left the Ozark Flats. Mr. Hayward took the elevator back up to his apartment on the fourth floor where his wife had dinner waiting for him.

Down on the first floor, Adry Hayward had just finished eating a bowl of soup and a sandwich and was reading the evening newspaper stories about the murder. He wondered just what *did* happen to Kitty's money as he sat undisturbed in his apartment, looking out the window at the street lights on Hennepin avenue. He was alone again. Apparently no reporter had thought of asking Adry Hayward any questions at all.

Minnie Jacobs had supper all ready for Emmett and Jamie when they arrived at their Excelsior home. There was a fire in the fireplace and the big black wrought-iron range in the kitchen had been fired up, helping bring some warmth to the house that had been locked up since early fall. She still had all day tomorrow and Friday morning to get the entire house with its five bedrooms back in shape before everyone arrived on Christmas Eve for the holiday weekend. She'd do the shopping for groceries in downtown Excelsior tomorrow from a list that Hillary had sent out with Emmett. There would be beds to make, cleaning and dusting to do, and the cupboard to stock. Minnie would stay overnight tonight and again tomorrow night. Jamie was

Ozark Flats

on vacation now, and he would stay here with her tomorrow while his dad went back to work in the city in the morning. Jamie would like that. He'd have lots of neighborhood friends to play with tomorrow—the Hennessy boy down the block, Woody Smith, a Hammer boy, and the White twins.

The meeting with George O'Brien had only taken a little over an hour and Emmett was back in the big living room now with the dark mahogany beams and a blazing fire in the fireplace. He was reading the latest edition of *The Minnetonka News* from last Saturday.

"Local Jottings" comprised a long column of one-line or one-paragraph news events on the front page.

> Al. Lyman returned Monday from his hunting trip.
> And. Tharalson returned Tuesday from a trip to Sioux Falls and the vicinity.
> B.L. Perry is building on his place this winter, adjoining that of Mr. Hannon's. He expects to occupy same next spring.
> Next Wednesday afternoon, the L.A. society meets with Mrs. Lane. Transportation will be provided for all who wish to go, leaving the parsonage at 2:00 o'clock.
> The ladies of Trinity Chapel held their annual Christmas Sale on December 10 and 11, featuring the sale of fancy work and Christmas novelties. On Friday night, a baked bean supper was served and the remainder of the evening was taken up by a carefully selected literary and musical program, free to all.
> The Union Temperence meeting at the M.E. church last Sunday evening was largely attended. The speakers were the Rev. J.R. Davies, the Rev. C.L. Mears, Messrs. Beeman and Sutton.

Also included in the news columns was the familiar mark of most weekly newspapers of the day, the "reader ad," set in the same type as the news story, but obviously a paid advertisement.

> Farmers, when you come to town, don't forget to order the News. It's only $1.00 this year.
> For Rent—Six room house, three unfurnished, $3.00 a month for winter, one mile S.E. of Excelsior. Address H.L. Crane, Excelsior.

Ozark Flats

There were the ever-present Rocky Mountain Tea advertisements, too. It was only a laxative, but the ads had been so much fun to read that Newell's Drug Store had reported a run on the product.

> Makes fat, blood, and muscles more rapidly than any known remedy. It's food for the blood, brain and nerves. That's what Rocky Mountain Tea is. Ask your druggist.
>
> True beauty comes from within, instead of without. A beautiful face is the outward sign. That's why Rocky Mountain Tea makes women beautiful. Ask your druggist.

The last one for Rocky Mountain Tea read:

> If strong is the frame of the mother, the son will give laws to the land. All mothers should take Rocky Mountain Tea. Gives life and strength. 35 cents. Ask your druggist.

There were church notices for the Excelsior Congregational Church, the Excelsior Methodist Church, and Trinity Episcopal Chapel, and the officers were listed for both Excelsior Village and the outlying Excelsior Township. Old Doc Perkins was still going strong and his little front-page ad reminded Emmett that Hillary had an appointment to see him late Friday afternoon when she arrived in Excelsior. But another physician had now started practice in the community. His professional card on the front page of *The News* read:

> A.S. Whetstone, M.D., Physician and Surgeon. Graduate of the University of Michigan; post graduate course at Belview Hospital Medical College, N.Y. City, and University of Vienna, Austria, general hospital. U.S. pension examining surgeon.

One last item in the news column commented:

> LOST—The beginning of the winter, somewhere between the fall and spring. Finder please hang on until cold weather arrives.

Emmett laughed. He realized that it was the first time he had laughed out loud in a long, long time. He had enjoyed last night with

Hillary at dinner, and the musical, but with the long hours at *The Journal*, the misunderstandings at home, and now the murder, he realized he hadn't been happy. He hoped, with all his heart, that things would be different now, starting this weekend with Christmas. He loved Hillary and he would see to it that things would be different from now on. His thoughts of Hillary this night gave him a feeling of loneliness. He missed her—and he wondered what she was doing at the apartment right now. Then he whispered to himself.

"I love you, Hillary."

Shout the glad tidings, exulting sing,
Jerusalem triumphs, Messiah is King!

Hillary Markham had been playing Christmas Hymns and Carols on the upright piano in the living room of the Markham's apartment on the fifth floor of the Ozark Flats. She had already fixed supper for herself, did the dishes, and wrapped some Christmas gifts for her family and her parents. It had been a busy evening for her and she had decided she needed some relaxation before going to bed. Now she sat at the piano in a pale blue nightgown with a matching robe and closed the book of Carols and Hymns. She realized she had hardly touched the keys of a piano since they moved into Minneapolis, and she missed playing. She would have to get some sheet music down at the Glass Block after Christmas and start playing again.

She turned out the lamp alongside the piano and sat there in the dark. The small crease of light from the bedroom down the hall provided enough light for her as she sat on the piano bench, thinking of her family at the lake tonight. She missed both Emmett and Jamie tonight, although she had become used to being alone much of the time in the evenings while Emmett worked late at *The Journal*. She thought about Emmett. She needed his love. They had such a good time last night. Perhaps things would be different when they all got back to the lake and home for Christmas. Hillary stood up in the darkness and started toward the light from the bedroom down the hall. Then she heard it! A click! Like a door opening! Another click! It was coming from the kitchen! She was sure that she had closed and locked the kitchen door to the back balcony and open stairs to the rear courtyard below. She stood at the archway between the living room and dining room, frozen with a fear that crept up through her body with a cold, tingling sensation.

She placed her hand in front of her mouth as she heard a rustling in the kitchen. Someone was just inside the kitchen door in the small alcove which she and Emmett used for an informal office at home, with a desk and chair and small table lamp. Hillary dared not move. The desk light had clicked on in the alcove on the other side of the door to the kitchen. Hillary was frightened! She looked around desperately for something with which to defend herself. She backed away toward the living room and the fireplace, toward the andirons.

The swinging door to the kitchen was pushed open slightly from the kitchen side and the dark form of a man started to slide through the doorway, just as Hillary reached the fireplace. When she turned, she tripped on the rug. Her hand reached out to break her fall and the andiron rack fell over with a crash! Hillary screamed!

At that moment, there came a loud knocking at the front door of the apartment! Hillary screamed again! More pounding on the front door! The intruder ducked back into the kitchen and Hillary raced to the front door! Her fingers fumbled with the lock and the door chain as the pounding on the outside of the door continued! Hillary pulled the door open and saw Rex Barnett standing in the lighted hallway. She fell into his arms as he stepped into the apartment.

"In the kitchen!" she gasped.

Rex brushed by her and rushed through the living room and dining room toward the kitchen and burst through the swinging door! A small lamp was on at a desk in the alcove just inside the door, but the kitchen was almost dark—and empty. The detective rushed to the back door, opened it and stepped outside on to the small balcony that overlooked the rear courtyard. There was nothing but silence.

He walked back through the kitchen and found Hillary still standing by the front door.

"Whoever it was is gone!" he told her.

She stood still for a moment. Then rushed to Rex Barnett and he put his arms around her to comfort her. She was sobbing now.

"I'm so frightened."

"It's all right now. He's gone." He could feel her shiver. "Where's Emmett?"

"He and Jamie have gone to the lake tonight. He'll be back tomorrow morning."

Rex Barnett had been in situations before where he had to comfort a woman who was scared or shocked. But this was different. Now he found himself standing in the dark in the living room of her apartment, holding Hillary. He could feel the curves of her body through the nightgown and he could smell her freshness. And she was beautiful!

They stood there in the middle of the room for awhile and then he led her to the davenport in front of the fireplace and sat down with her. Hillary had gained her composure now, and explained to Rex just what had happened. He listened sympathetically, and then asked her to turn on some lights in the apartment. Then the two of them went into the kitchen. It was evident that someone had rummaged through the desk in the alcove. But Rex found no sign of any tampering with the back door latch or the lock. Either the door had not been locked—or someone had a key!

"Whoever it was, they were obviously looking for something," Rex explained. "They were going through your desk here, and when they couldn't find it, they were going to move out into the rest of the apartment." He stopped to think for a moment. "Do you keep any money here?"

"No," Hillary replied. "At least not any large sums of money. Nothing that someone would break into a house for."

The two went back into the living room and sat down on the davenport again. Hillary said she was going to fix some warm milk or cocoa for herself and she asked Rex if he would like some, too. She went out to the kitchen and left Rex sitting in the living room. My God, he thought, I haven't had cocoa in ten years! When she came back into the living room, she carried a tray with a small crockery pitcher of cocoa and two cups. She poured the cocoa and the two of them sat on the couch, sipped their warm drink, and talked.

Hillary was more relaxed now, and it showed. She talked to Rex about her home in Excelsior, how she met Emmet, about their courtship, her marriage to Jim Stockton, and all about Jamie. It was after midnight when the two of them stopped talking and Hillary said something about being tired.

"You go get some sleep, Hillary, and I'll set up camp out in the hall outside your front door," Rex told her. He realized that it was no longer "Mrs. Markham." He was now on a first-name basis with her.

"I feel much safer with you here," she told him. "but I can't let you sit out in the hall all night long. I'll get a pillow and some blankets and you can at least lie down here on the davenport."

Rex protested, but before he could finish, she was off for the bed-clothes. She was back in a minute. "Here you are." She handed him blankets and a pillow. "You just make yourself comfortable. And I'll rest a lot easier, knowing you're here."

She was off toward the hallway to the bedroom, leaving Rex standing next to the davenport holding a blanket. He shrugged, and started to spread the blanket out on the couch. Then he saw her out of the corner of his eye, standing there in the doorway in her nightgown. As he stood up, she came toward him until she was standing directly in front of him. Then she looked up and put her arms around his neck.

"Thank you, Rex," she whispered.

Then she kissed him on the mouth, and in a reflex action, his arms surrounded her waist and shoulders and he held her tight. One thought raced through his mind. Josie's shoulders were small like this.

Thursday, December 23, 1894

14

IT WAS MID-MORNING when Harry Hayward left the Ozark Flats. It was a bright sunny day and Harry decided that it was warm enough to walk downtown. He headed in the direction of the Loop at a brisk pace along Hennepin avenue. He felt refreshed after a trying day yesterday, and he had business to attend to today. The weekend was approaching too fast for him and he promised to call Mr. Hudson at the West Hotel on Friday and tell him how he was doing with the green goods. Kitty Ging's death and the investigation had put Harry a little behind schedule.

He would also stop at Mr. Arthur G. Pierce's office today and check on those insurance policies on Kitty. He was going to need that money—and soon. The money! Where the hell was Kitty's money, he thought. She had to withdraw it from the vault on Monday and Harry knew she had it with her at lunch on Tuesday. It had to be at her shop at the Syndicate Building or in her apartment. There was no place else it could be—unless, of course, she had given it to someone for safe-keeping.

Ozark Flats

Harry was so preoccupied with his plans for the day and trying to determine where Kitty's money could be that he was not aware of the small man in the checkered overcoat and wearing the bowler hat who followed him at a distance on the opposite side of the boulevard. Walter Farber had been stationed across the intersection from the Ozark Flats since eight o'clock this morning. Although it was warming up now, it had been cold out there on the street earlier in the day and once during his morning vigil he had stepped inside the vestibule of Olson's Boarding House to get warm. The smell of breakfast being served in the dining room there had tempted the small man with the mustache, but he decided that he might miss Harry Hayward if he took time out for breakfast, so he stomped his feet a few times to warm them up, and then went back to his observation post on the corner, waiting for Harry to appear. His boss seemed a little concerned yesterday when he read about the murder in the newspapers. It was then that he decided he should perhaps keep a close tab on Harry Hayward, especially after Harry's long session with the police yesterday.

Harry stopped for coffee at a small cafe on Hennepin, across the street from the new Public Library on Tenth street. Then he crossed the avenue and continued on down Hennepin to the Masonic Temple Building at Sixth street where he stopped to see his insurance man, Mr. Pierce. When he came out of the front entrance of the Masonic Temple building he felt particularly good. Mr. Pierce had assured him that the insurance benefits would be paid—and in a reasonably short time. Harry had no idea that he was being followed, not just by Walter Farber, but by a second man as well.

Detective John Stavlo wasn't too happy about "tailing" Harry Hayward this morning. Rex Barnett had asked John Morrissey late yesterday afternoon to put a tail on Harry Hayward after the long interrogation and the visit to the Connolly Funeral Home. There just were not enough detectives to go around and so John Stavlo was stuck with following Harry Hayward around during the day today. He wasn't very happy with the assignment, but it didn't take long before it had taken on a more interesting aspect. John Stavlo had actually been waiting for Harry Hayward in the foyer of the Ozark Flats and when Harry moved through the double entrance of the apartment house, Stavlo had looked busy, checking names on the

mailboxes in the front entryway. Stavlo had watched Harry go down the steps to Hennepin avenue, but before he could follow Hayward's footsteps, he noticed the short man in the bowler hat across the street move along in Harry's same direction. It hadn't taken John Stavlo more than ten seconds to determine that someone else besides the Minneapolis Police Department was interested in tailing young Mr. Hayward this morning.

Unconcerned, Harry Hayward made his way down Hennepin avenue to the end of the block to the West Hotel. It was only when he moved through the main entrance on Hennepin avenue that he had some funny feelings—like someone was following him. He had the presence of mind to stop at the cigar counter and pick up a newspaper and couldn't help but see Walter Farber, Mr. Hudson's number one henchman, come through the front entrance. At that moment, the usually suave Harry Hayward panicked and without thinking, made a swift move across the Exchange to the stairway leading to the basement. Up until then, the short Mr. Farber had been quite nonchalant about the whole thing. But when he saw Harry Hayward darting down the basement stairway, he broke into a run to follow him. He had just started his rush down the stairway when John Stavlo entered the West Hotel and saw the little man with the bowler. Now it was Stavlo's turn to take off in the direction of the stairway and he almost knocked over an elderly gentleman as he crossed the Exchange and headed for the stairs.

Andy Ross had just come out of the billiard room and bar on the main floor when he saw the action across the lobby. He had been a hotel man long enough to know when there was trouble, and he too, headed for the stairway—and the chase!

Harry hit the bottom step of the stairs on the run and headed down a wide hall with a tall ceiling covered with pipes for sewer, gas and water. He rushed past the open doorways to the storage rooms for foods and vegetables and turned the corner past the wine cellar. He could hear the staccato footsteps not far behind him as he quickly ducked through a doorway off the main hallway and found himself in the hotel laundry. Workers there, mostly black, were ironing sheets and tablecloths, and Harry barged through and out the door at the opposite side of the room. Farber was not far behind, and John Stavlo was running a close third ahead of Andy Ross. Harry turned the corner and darted through an open door that took him through the main course of the basement which served as a boiler room and housed the machinery for the hotel elevators. He could smell freshly-baked bread as he rushed down the corridor past the bakery to a dead-end. He made a quick decision to go to the left. The hall led to heavy doors leading into the freezing room where the catering department stored its fresh meat and preserved it with the latest mechanical cooling equipment. Harry could not hear the footsteps anymore and he ducked beneath the large sides of meat hanging from menacing metal hangers attached to the ceiling.

The short little Mr. Farber had lost Harry for the moment, but it was evident that he was more of an athlete than he looked. The truth of the matter was that he had been a boxer on Chicago's southside long before he took up with Hudson.

And as he approached the dead-end of the underground hallway, he became aware of someone chasing him. Farber took a quick cut to the right and pulled up short against the wall as John Stavlo came charging down the hallway. Just as Stavlo reached the dead end, the short little man, who had now lost his bowler in the chase, stepped out and gave Stavlo a terrific right to the mid-section. The unexpected blow was followed by a left to the chin which sent the stocky detective to the floor. Farber could hear other footsteps coming down the hall and decided that he'd had enough. He started back down the hall past the bakery and almost knocked Andy Ross over as he turned the corner. Andy fell against the wall but regained his balance and could see John Stavlo getting back up off the floor at the end of the hall. Stavlo identified himself and Andy called out to the receiving-room clerk to help them search the basement.

Nobody could see or find Harry Hayward. He stayed crouched in the cooler in the depths of the West Hotel for more than a half hour before he finally eased out of the freezer and moved quietly back through the maze of basement hallways, past the elevator pumps, and then to the rear of the hotel past the rooms for the employees. There he discovered the rear stairway which took him back up to the main floor and out into the back alley.

John Stavlo dismissed Andy's concern for his jaw, said he was all right, and walked back to the main floor with the new assistant manager. The he left the hotel, a little embarrassed—and mad as hell! Andy headed for his temporary office to make a phone call to Emmett Markham at *The Journal* to tell him he had just had a visit from one of his neighbors.

John Morrissey had just come back from Chief Smith's office where he received a call from J.H. Ege, the Ramsey County sherriff, who had called to tell the Minneapolis Police Department they had found Lillian Allen in a rooming house near downtown St. Paul and that she could account for all of her time on the night of the murder.

"It was just a coincidence that she moved out of her apartment over there yesterday morning," he told John Morrissey. Morrissey thanked him for his help, and hung up.

Rex was just about to suggest that the two of them take a break and go out for coffee when a patrolman from the fifth precinct came in with a handsome young man following him.

"This gentleman says he has an appointment to see you today, John," the officer informed him.

The well-dressed man introduced himself.

"I'm Tom Waterman."

John Morrissey and Rex Barnett decided that the short break for coffee could wait, and took Mr. Waterman back into the chief's office for questioning. A half-hour later, Tom Waterman emerged from the office and left, apparently none the worse for wear. He had recited the litany of the Tuesday afternoon on the town. But he had added one element that Harry Hayward seemed to have forgotten. After the two of them left the West Hotel in the late afternoon on Tuesday, Harry asked his friend to do him a favor—to stop up to Kitty Ging's dressmaking shop in the Syndicate Building and "nose around a bit" to see if he could find out whether she had any appreciable amount of money with her. But Kitty was not there when Tom Waterman paid his visit to the shop, and as a result, he had no information for Harry about any large sums of money Kitty might have had.

153

After Tom Waterman left, John turned to Rex and threw up his hands in frustration. "I didn't think there was anything there to begin with," he said to Rex, "but you never know." He thought for a moment. "But each time we cross one of these things off, we come just a little closer to the truth."

Rex agreed. But he was still uneasy about last night's break-in at Hillary's apartment and no one seemed to have a sound idea of who it might have been.

"I guess I'd like to know what some other people would also like to know," Rex said. Then he looked at John Morrissey. "Where the hell is her money?"

Andy Ross hung up the phone after talking to Emmett Markham at *The Journal* office. He told Emmett about the fracas at the hotel this morning and that it had seemed there were two men chasing Mr. Harry Hayward and that one of those men had been a Minneapolis detective. Nobody had seen Harry, but Andy was reasonably sure he had somehow left the hotel by now. Actually, Harry was still down in the freezer room when Andy talked to Emmett over the phone. The assistant manager also spoke to Emmett about the coming Christmas holiday and the fact that Rose Stark was back in town with her two children and would be back home in Excelsior for Christmas.

Andy hung up the phone and sat at his desk, thinking about Rose for a few minutes. Just before noon he would take Rose and the kids down to the Union depot to catch the M. and St. L. train for Excelsior. Rose Fortier Stark. Andy shook his head and smiled. He remembered back some seven years ago when he had discovered that the pretty young French waitress working for him in the dining room of the White House Hotel in Excelsior was submitting herself to that lecherous son-of-a-bitch, Mayor George Bertram. The mayor was absolutely no relation to one of the founders of the little community, another George Bertram, but had passed himself off as a relative. The paunchy, middle-aged lawyer had befriended Rose and her mother after her father died. Her mother had been sick for sometime and the mayor made sure they were both living comfortably and that Rose had work. Even Rose admitted that while her mother was alive, George Bertram had been a perfect gentleman, while most of the young men in town figured the dark-haired waitress was fair game. After her mother's death, however, Bertram seduced her and she remained at his beck and call even though she had fallen in love with Andy's friend, John Stark. When Andy Ross heard about it, he had called her into his office at the White House and confronted her. When she admitted the rumors about her and George Bertram were true, Andy had given her a talking to.

"What the hell are you doing playing footsie with that goddamn George Bertram for?" Andy had yelled at her. "You don't owe him that much!" he shouted. "And if John Stark ever finds out, he'll kill the bastard, Rose. That's what he'll do. And he damn well might kill you, too!"

Rose had finally faced reality. She put her face in her hands. She was crying and trying to speak at the same time. "I know, I know. And I don't know what to do about it."

Andy remembered the scene in his White House office and he remembered how Rose had promised that it would be the end of her meetings with George Bertram. It was, too. And Andy remembered always after that, he had a special feeling about Rose Fortier that he had never told John about. He was also sure that although Rose loved John Stark, she too, felt a special bond between them.

Andy noticed the large clock in the main office of the West Hotel. It was nearly eleven and it was time to see that Rose was checked out and off to the train station. They had enjoyed a wonderful evening last night at dinner and they had made plans for Andy to stop at their Excelsior home sometime during Christmas day. Andy smiled. Last night had been a very nice time. As he got up from his desk and started toward the reservation counter, he remembered who the man was who had brushed by him down the basement hall—the one who had left John Stavlo doubled up on the floor. He just realized that he hadn't recognized the little man without his bowler on. It was the little man in the fifth-floor suite!

155

A DARK MYSTERY!

Police Still Looking For A Clue
To Miss Ging's Murder

Harry Hayward Views the Corpse
He Is Given Full Freedom

Details of the Insurance Placed On
Murdered Girl's Life

—*The Minneapolis Journal*

WAS IT COUNTERFEIT?

A Theory That the Money Which Miss
Ging Had in the Vaults Was
Only Green Goods.

And She Was Killed in an Attempt to Get It Out
of Her Possession to Prevent Detection.

—*The Minneapolis Tribune*

15

MAYOR WILLIAM H. EUSTIS had spent the last hour this morning going over the Ging case with Chief Vern Smith. They had looked at the developments of yesterday and both seemed satisfied that John Morrissey was conducting a thorough investigation of the case. The mayor had suggested putting more men on the case, but Vern Smith explained that he already had four of his best detectives working full time on it and had used some others from both the Central Police Station and other precincts to help with the legwork. Morrissey and Smith had already met earlier this morning and although there was no apparent headway in solving the case, the mayor knew that a lot of work had already been accomplished in the first full day after the murder and he appreciated the effort being made by the detectives and the police force.

In the meantime, one of the clerks in the mayor's office had gone down to the drug store on Hennepin and Third and picked up the first editions of the day's city newspapers. The mayor and police chief were just finishing their review of the investigation when Miss Mag-

nuson, the mayor's secretary, brought the newspapers into the mayor's office. Bill Eustis was anxious to see how the papers covered the murder story after one day of investigation. His face flinched a little as he opened *The Journal* and read the headlines.

A Dark Mystery—Police Still Looking For a Clue
to Miss Ging's Murder.

Not A Tenable Theory—Not A Shred Of Tangible Evidence!

When the police department resumed work on the Ging murder case this morning, there was not a tenable theory in existence.

In most cases of a similar nature, there is some more or less tangible description of the murderer, and the ability to telegraph around the country after him affords a certain solace.

In this matter, however, there is absolutely nothing to show whether the murderer was a man or woman, tall or short, fat or lean. The revolver, with which the deed was committed, disappeared with the murderer. No piece of cloth or collar button, or any other such clew, as exists invariably in the most intricate detective story, is to be found in this case. There is absolutely nothing.

Harry Hayward was given entire freedom after having been under close surveillance ever since the murder.

The relations of Harry Hayward with the deceased modiate were of a rather unusual character. He lent her large sums of money, and was evidently on very familiar terms with her. Still, it was probed beyond question that Hayward spent the evening of the tragedy in another woman's company at the theater. Then, the idea of an accomplice was taken up and worked, but this theory was scarcely a good one, in view of the statement made by Goosman's man at the West.

"Be sure you do not tell Harry I have been going out in the evening," she said. "I do not want him to know it."

The liverykeeper has been closely questioned on this point, and he reasserts positively that his orders were to maintain silence as to Miss Ging's actions.

The police believed yesterday that Hayward would know more about the affair than anyone else, not directly, perhaps, but through his acquaintances with the dead woman. Yesterday, Hayward underwent what in known in the police parlance as sweating. He was asked about every conceivable phase of his acquaintance with Miss Ging, and every question was answered with deliberate coolness.

There are many members of the police department who believe that Hayward is the one man in Minneapolis aware of Catherine Ging's private history—that phase of her life which she so studiously concealed from everyone who knew her. If Hayward knows more than he has told, he is a most consummate actor. Apparently he answered every question without reservation. Stress has been laid on the fact that he took little time to frame his answers to the volley of questioning. Any man placed in a like position, knowing that every utterance is going to be weighed and sifted, would have been quite careful about his replies. Mayor Eustis was compelled to admit that Hayward was apparently telling a straight story, but many criminals have told skillful stories and the mayor has a pronounced opinion in this matter.

When the mayor finished reading *The Journal*'s account—partly to himself and partly aloud to Vern Smith, he set the newspaper down on his desk.

"I can't fault this story," he admitted to his police chief, "but they do keep the pressure on." He picked up the paper again and batted the front page with the back of his hand. "What the hell kind of headline is this?" he asked Vern Smith. "Not a tenable theory—not a shred of tangible evidence."

The Superintendent of Police smiled as he looked up from the newspaper he was reading.

"Actually, *The Tribune* carries a pretty complete story of the murder and they have obviously put some extra people on the case." Then he looked at the front page of *The Tribune* again and smiled. "Except for this opening pararaph. Listen to this."

Another day has passed into history, and the police are no nearer the solution of the mystery of the murder of Catherine Ging than they were when the body was discovered on the edge of the tamarack swamp on the lonely north shore of Lake Calhoun last Tuesday night, except that they have sifted out various rumors and have proven untenable a large number of theories which at first were thought to have been plausible.

Harry T. Hayward, who was on the rack yesterday, was

allowed to take his departure. Last night it was given out at the Ozark Flats that he was in bed securing much-needed rest, and would not be disturbed.

It need not be inferred from the fact that he has been released by the police that they are entirely satisfied with all of his explanations of his financial transactions with the murdered woman. As a matter of fact, should Mr. Hayward endeavor to leave the city he would find one of the local Hawkshaws either interposing objections to his going, or following closely on his trail in case he were allowed to depart.

With regard to Miss Ging's deposit of several thousand dollars in a safety deposit vault instead of with her regular bank, the suggestion has been made that possibly the money was counterfeit and that under some pretext or another she had been induced to keep it out of the bank in order to prevent detection of its worthlessness; that when it became apparent that she was going into business she was killed in an effort to regain possession of it. However, THE TRIBUNE said yesterday, there is only Hayward's word to show that she had such a sum.

It has been learned that the life insurance policies of $5,000 each in the New York Life and the Travelers' Companies, were taken out one week ago at the instigation of young Hayward and that the purpose was to secure for him the money he claims he had advanced to her, the total of which, according to his statement, is $9,500. He claims to hold her notes for this amount. BUT NO ONE HAS SEEN THEM.

"And the story goes on for another full column," the chief said as he put down the newspaper. "I have a feeling that they don't trust our Mr. Hayward very much."

This had not been a good morning for Emmett Markham. He almost missed the 7:20 train leaving Excelsior this morning and it was late in getting into Minneapolis. As a result, he was also late for work. When he finally got around to calling Hillary, he found that someone had broken into their apartment at the Ozark Flats and that

Hillary had been in considerable danger! Emmett was relieved when his wife recited the story of the break-in, and explained that Rex Barnett had come on the scene just as she was about to be confronted by the nighttime intruder. It had been a stroke of luck, he told Hillary, and he agreed that she had done the right thing by having Rex stay in the apartment and to sleep—or at least rest—on the front room davenport.

"When I got up and went out into the living room early this morning, he had already folded up the blankets, left them in a neat pile on the couch, and had let himself out. He was gone!" Hillary told her husband over the phone.

"Are you all right now, dear?" Emmett inquired.

"Of course I am—*now*," she told him. "But I don't want to be here alone at night again until this whole business has been resolved," she added.

"You won't be. You won't be," Emmett assured her. He went on to tell her about the trip out to Excelsior the evening before. The business meeting with George O'Brien had been successful and he and Jamie had a good time together. "And you won't believe how good Minnie has the house looking already—and she still has all day today and part of tomorrow." Hillary was pleased. But when Emmett hung up the phone in his office, he was concerned. He sat at his desk and thought about it all for a little while. Now that there had been a break-in which might very well be connected with the Ging murder, his family was involved. So he better get involved, he thought. He got up from his desk and left his office in the direction of the office of J.S. McLain. He could see through the glass door that the editor was busy, but at least he didn't have anyone else in the office with him at the moment. Emmett knocked on the door and then opened it without waiting for a response.

"Do you mind if I come in, John. I'd like to see you for a minute. It's important."

Ozark Flats

Louise Ireland and Miss Cullen had been waiting for some time for the elevator to take them down to the main entrance of the Ozark Flats. They were on their way to the Connolly Funeral Parlor and both were dressed for the occasion of the day. Miss Cullen wore a grey fitted coat with a matching hat and scarf, and Louise Ireland wore a long black overcoat and a black hat that had belonged to her aunt Kitty. When the elevator arrived at the fifth floor, Claus Blixt opened the elevator door and then took the two ladies down to the main floor On the way down, he told Miss Ireland that he would be letting himself into the apartment today to fix the leak in the kitchen sink, and that he would make sure the door was locked when he let himself out. He spoke with a slight Swedish accent and the words were clumsy, making it difficult for the two women to understand him.

When the two women stepped from the elevator and started down the hall toward the front door of the apartment house, they met Adry Hayward in the foyer. He had hardly ever spoken to anyone in the Ozark Flats, but he made it a special point to stop Louise Ireland and speak to her this morning. He explained that this was the first time he had seen her since the tragedy and he wanted to offer his condolences. He repeated several times how sorry he was for what had happened—to the point where it almost sounded as though he were personally apologizing for the murder. When the two women finally started down the front steps of the apartment house, Adry Hayward was still standing in the front door, reminding them that he would certainly be at the funeral this afternoon.

Emmett felt better after he left the office of J.S. McLain. He had explained to his editor what had happened at the Ozark Flats the night before and had pointed out that the newsroom seemed to be in excellent shape over this coming holiday weekend. He asked Mr. McLain if he couldn't possibly allow Emmett to do a little extra digging on the Ging story during this one last day before Christmas Eve.

"I know we have reporters out doing the job right now," Emmett admitted, "but since the murder victim lived right across the hall at the Ozark Flats, and since last night's break-in and threat to my wife, I feel more of a personal responsibility to help."

McLain had given him permission to go ahead and Emmett headed back to his own office at *The Journal*. He had a couple of phone calls to make. Then he would call Barnett over at the police station. Perhaps he knew something Emmett didn't know.

It was the second morning in a row that Hillary had not been feeling well. She didn't tell her husband about it over the phone. He already had enough to worry about this morning. But she didn't feel well. Yesterday had been upsetting with the thought of Louise Ireland accompanying Cathering Ging's body back to Albany, New York, by train. The memories of the long ride from Excelsior back to St. Louis with her mother after Jim Stockton had been killed, and the thought of her father bringing back her husband's body a day later, had been more than Hillary could bear. This morning was no better. The full impact of last night's burglary was just now being realized by the pretty young housewife, and the thought of Kitty Ging's funeral this afternoon had only added to that sick feeling she had this morning.

Hillary, still in her nightgown, took a cup of coffee from the kitchen, moved through the dining room into the front living room and sat down on the davenport to drink her coffee. Even sitting at the kitchen table had been uncomfortable for her and now she relaxed on the couch in the living room. She sipped her coffee and tried to relax and think of something other than Catherine Ging and all that had happened. But today's funeral kept creeping into a corner of her thoughts, and that coming even took her right back to Jim Stockton. She remembered that September day in Forrest Park eight years ago.

"Do you remember the last time you proposed to me?" she asked Jim.

"I think it was yesterday," he kidded her.

"No, I mean really. Do you remember?"

"I remember that you turned me down again."

"Do you still love me?"

"Of course, Hillary. That's a silly question for you to ask."

"If I were to say 'Yes' would you marry me?"

She remembered how Jim Stockton had looked. He realized she wasn't joking. He also sensed that something was wrong. "You know I'd marry you,' he had answered.

She remembered how ashamed she was in telling Jim about Emmett and that she had just come from the doctor and she knew she was going to have Emmett's baby. He put his arms around her and assured her no one would have to know. "It's all right," he had told her. "I love you."

Hillary thought back to the heartache of seeing Emmett that next summer. She remembered how much she had wanted him, how much she loved him. She also recalled how happy they had been over these past years—until they moved here. She sipped some more of her coffee and she rubbed her hand over part of the unbuttoned bodice of her nightgown. She realized that she was thinking of Rex. It was a pleasant feeling, a comfortable feeling. She was aware that the only time she had felt "alive" in the last few days was last night, in Rex's arms, here in this living room.

"My God!" she whispered to herself. "First I'm partly responsible for Jim Stockton's death. Now I'm wondering if I could possibly love another man. Here I am, married, with a family." Her heart and her mind were playing tug-of-war. She was resolute. "I'll have to tell Emmett. If we're going to make our marriage work, I'll have to tell him. But when?" She drank the last of the coffee. "There's a right time for everything," she told herself. "When the right time comes, I'll tell him."

She got up from the davenport and started back toward the kitchen. And she also knew that the right time might never come.

16

THERE HAD BEEN a steady stream of people in and out of the Central Police Station where John Morrissey and Rex Barnett were trying to make some sort of order out of the hodge-podge of clues and accounts given them over the last day and a half.

"There's a Mr. Wilson outside," Rex informed Morrissey. "He says that he thinks he can identify the other person in the buggy with Kitty."

"Let's talk with him right now," Morrissey said, and motioned Rex to bring Mr. Wilson into the office of Vern Smith. M.D. Wilson was in his fifties, married, with some of his children still living at home. Home was an elegant house at 1904 Kenwood Parkway. Mr. Wilson was well-known in the city as a successful liveryman, and his extensive livery service was augmented by a boarding stable for horses belonging to wealthy and prominent families in Minneapolis. The two detectives and the liveryman talked for a few minutes and then John Morrissey asked Mr. Wilson to tell them what he knew about the Ging case. Mr. Wilson sat in a chair in front of Vern

Smith's desk and explained what he had seen and heard the night before last—the night of the murder.

"I had just turned on to Kenwood parkway from Hennepin when I noticed another rig turn on to the parkway from Lyndale. We actually drove some distance side by side, and being in the business, I could tell the rig belonged to Henry Goosman. In fact, I recognized the horse—it had a particular color, and I knew it was Goosman's." Then he added, proudly, "The form of a well-known horse is as familiar to me as the form of a friend." The two detectives nodded in agreement and smiled at each other.

Mr. Wilson told the detectives he had heard the voices of two people in the rig and was sure one of the voices was that of Miss Ging. "I've rented rigs to her before and I'd know that voice anywhere."

Morrissey pressed him for more details and Mr. Wilson explained that he thought he had seen a glimpse of the other person in the rig but couldn't be sure. "But when I paid a visit to the funeral parlor yesterday, I had the feeling the man standing next to me seemed to correspond to the mental picture of the man in Miss Ging's buggy the night before."

He had no detailed description of the man, however, and had no other information to give to the detectives who thanked him for coming and said they would check the list of callers at the funeral parlor. As Mr. Wilson left the police station, he passed another gentleman heading into the police headquarters. It was Frank Farrell, who was scheduled to see Detective John Morrissey today. It all seemed like such a waste of time to the two detectives, but they both knew that sifting out material from all these people just might uncover something of substance. Mr. Farrell's information didn't seem to include "something of substance." He told the police that on the day of the murder he saw a man and a woman standing on the corner of Hennepin avenue and Sixth street engaged in a quarrel. He could not hear all of the argument but he did hear her say, "not by any means." He had even gone to the funeral parlor this morning and was sure the woman he had seen on Tuesday was Miss Ging. Then he gave the detectives a description of the man—about 45 years old, five-foot nine, with thin side-whiskers, a smooth-shaven chin, and a light mustache. "He probably weighed about a hundred and sixty pounds."

Ozark Flats

After Frank Farrell had left the police station, Morrissey and Barnett went back over all of their notes and stenographer's transcripts of those who had been interrogated over the last day and a half. Rex Barnett also looked at a report of the condition of the body which was made by two doctors from the University of Minnesota. Their findings showed the injuries to Kitty Ging's head would have been sustained after she had already been killed or there would have been even more bleeding than was evident.

The two detectives were on their way to a late lunch when Detective Michael Hoy showed up with a Mr. Harvey Axford, a gentleman friend of Catherine Ging. He had known Kitty for the past six or seven years and admitted sending notes to Kitty. While Mr. Axford was talking, John Morrissey was busy going through his notes. When the man had accounted for his whereabouts on the night of the murder, Morrissey cautioned him that just this morning they had received a description of a man who sent Kitty a note on Tuesday, from young Paul Born, the messenger boy from the West Hotel. Oddly enough, the description fitted Mr. Axford perfectly. He was about five-foot seven, grey hair, a mustache, and a ruddy complexion. Mr. Axford's complexion seemed to pale rapidly—probably more from embarrassment than from guilt. A couple of more questions and he was allowed to go.

"He's not involved," Morrissey said to Rex. "As you already know, when we pieced the note together out of Kitty's wastebasket, it read, "I cannot marry you." Morrissey got up to put his coat on.

"He was absolutely right. He couldn't marry her. He's already married!"

A phone call from Andy Ross at the West Hotel told Emmett that he had figured out who the third man was in the basement chase that morning, the man who knocked the wind out of Detective Stavlo. The culprit, according to Andy, was a short gentleman who occupied a fifth-floor suite with a Mr. Hudson. The gentleman's name was Walter Farber and they had registered at the hotel on Monday.

"Somebody in the billiard room told me they were from either Milwaukee or Chicago," Andy added. "I don't know if this is any help or not, but I thought I'd let you know."

"Thanks, Andy," Emmett said. They talked for a minute more and Andy briefly filled Emmett in on Rose Stark's return. Emmett was about to hang up the phone. "Oh, by the way, Andy, don't forget about Christmas Day at our house. We're looking forward to it. And bring Rose and the boys along. Jamie would love it."

Emmett thought some more about Harry Hayward and his reputation as a gambler and decided he was in an area he knew nothing about. But he had a friend who *did* know something about gambling. His name was George "Pinky" Wolfe and he had, at one time, been the most respected of a whole corps of gamblers that descended on Excelsior and Lake Minnetonka each summer during the tourist season. Handsome, athletic, and impeccably dressed, Pinky Wolfe had gambled with the elite of summer visitors to Excelsior—including bank presidents and railroad executives.

During his travels around the lake, he had met Jenny Chase, a wealthy and extremely beautiful widow. Her husband had died and left her childless—but with a huge estate known as Fairmount, named after the small town in North Dakota where she had been born and raised. She met Pinky Wolfe through some mutual friends at the Hotel Lafayette at a summer dinner party and their friendship grew into a much more serious affair. When Jenny thought that Pinky had put off the plans for marriage just about long enough, she simply made an unexpected trip to Excelsior on the Fourth-of-July and the next thing he knew, they were visiting with the Rev. Henry Horton, setting a date for their wedding at Trinity Episcopal Chapel in Excelsior.

There was no need for Pinky to gamble now, except socially. But Emmett was sure Pinky would have information on Minneapolis gamblers and perhaps something about Harry Hayward—maybe even information about Kitty Ging. Emmett placed the call and waited for someone to answer. The ringing stopped.

"Hello, Pinky. This is Emmett Markham. I need a favor."

Mayor William H. Eustis was not in the habit of attending funerals of people he didn't know. Such occasions were usually prompted by the dead of family, friends and some business or political associates. But the mayor had taken a personal interest in the Kitty Ging case and for reasons he could not explain, even to himself, he felt drawn to the funeral services this afternoon. There were already too many items on his daily schedule and, of course, he had taken on the additional burden of personally heading the investigation of the Kitty Ging murder with Police Superintendent Vern Smith. The mayor explained to his secretary that it might be late, but he would return to his office, even if it meant coming back this evening.

"Just leave any messages and other information on my desk and I'll look at it tonight." Then he left for the funeral.

At the end of the working day, Miss Magnuson locked up the mayor's office and left for home. She left a note reminding the mayor of a dinner meeting at the Nicollet House tonight. And in the pile of papers and notes to the mayor was an envelope which had been delivered by messenger in mid-afternoon. The return address in the upper left hand corner of the envelope read, "Levi Stewart, Kasota Building, City."

The Lord is my shepherd; I shall not want.
He maketh me to lie down in green pastures: he leadeth me beside the still waters.
He restoreth my soul: He leadeth me in the paths of righteousness for His name's sake.
Yea, though I walk through the valley of the shadow of death, I will fear no evil: for thou art with me; thy rod and thy staff they comfort me.
Thou preparest a table before me in the presence of mine enemies: thou anointest my head with oil; my cup runneth over.
Surely goodness and mercy shall follow me all the days of my life: and I will dwell in the house of the Lord for ever.
Psalm 23.

17

OVER THE LAST THREE DAYS, the body of Catherine Ging had been attended to by a number of people. Dr. William Russell was the first to examine the body of Miss Ging on that lonely road near Lake Calhoun on the night of the murder when he pronounced her dead. After the body had been taken to the county morgue, Dr. Willis Spring, the County Coroner, had discovered the bullet wound and the bullet. Two more doctors, from the University of Minnesota, had also been called in by the County Attorney's office to examine the body before it was turned over to Albert Connolly who removed it to his own home which also served as a funeral parlor.

Six pallbearers had brought the casket into the Church of the Immaculate Conception and, following the funeral mass, they would help return the casket to the funeral parlor. Among the pallbearers were Officer Patrick Ging and Francis Gordon Kelly who had strong feelings of obligation that the residents of Ozark Flats be represented in the funeral service. The young, red-haired lawyer was a Roman Catholic and was particularly fond of his church and the priest who spoke this day.

Father Keane had chosen *The Lessons of a Crime* as the subject of his homily and he spoke compassionately about Catherine Ging's character. He also had some harsh words for those who had tarnished her fair name after her death:

> *The details of that crime we all know. We are trying hard to forget them. That crime, though an individual one, stands insipid and uncommon in the community. A young woman, exceedingly beautiful, successful in business life, and successful in protecting her fair name, is foully murdered. Where are the lessons?*
>
> *The fallacy of her fame is one. Fame—it is chaff and not worthy of consideration and not worth the effort to attain it. Ambition—it is a mockery. The desire for wealth is one cause for the crime; and now view the results.*
>
> *The need of love and attachment for home is another lesson. Is all of life for the business of the world—the competition of trade? I interpose now no reflection of departed criticism on the living. The desire of notoriety displayed by some men, even in public capacities, is surprising. It is licensed by public opinion and encouraged by all who listen to the slanders that invade the sanctity of the home. Some need newspaper notoriety and insinuate basely the purity of the dead and attempt to blacken the fair name of the murdered girl. A coward could only do this; but, alas, it seems to be a national habit. Why are not they conspicuous in her favor, instead of insinuating suspicions against her? Who can undo the injuries done? No one is under obligation to protect the fair name of the dead. This is all largely endorsed by the habits of the time and because the Christian principle of charity does not prevail, and the displeasure of God Almighty is not feared.*
>
> *Let us apply ourselves that we may hold carefully, reverently, and thoughtfully revere the memory of the departed. Let it find its way into the construction of the mind. If a little child is taught that the law may be habitually violated, what is the result? Respectability is*

violated and justice is assailed. The modern school of philosophy is responsible for much of this.

Cling to the principles of Jesus Nazarene, that you may be transported into the sacredness of the truth, the sanctity of the pure, and the blessedness of the forgiven.

There would be other sermons in other pulpits in the next few weeks. And tomorrow, Louise Ireland and her aunt's cousin, Officer Ging, would accompany the body of Miss Ging to Auburn, New York. They would leave from the Union Station at the foot of Hennepin avenue tomorrow morning.

Reporters stood in the street at Third avenue north and watched as those attending the service left the church.

Mayor William H. Eustis was on his way to the West Hotel to attend a holiday reception for United States Senator William D. Washburn, home from Washington for the holidays. Tonight he had a business dinner scheduled at the Nicollet House. Then it would be back to the office before he could go home.

Frederick I. Reed had been given time off from work during this busy holiday season at the Golden Rule Department Store in St. Paul to attend the funeral of his former fiance. He would hurry back to his job by train.

Lillian Allen, who left town so suddenly yesterday morning and who was found at the Hotel Victoria in St. Paul by police, wasn't sure just why she had come—except, perhaps, her name had been linked with the murder investigation. She had satisfactorily accounted for her whereabouts on the night of the murder, but apparently wanted to show she held no hard feelings toward Kitty. She did not speak to Fred Reed.

Harry Hayward brought flowers to the funeral and was now leaving the church with his father and mother and brother Adry. Harry displayed no emotion during the short service but Adry was visibly shaken and was still drying his eyes as he left the church.

There was more than the usual number of those who attend funerals just for the sake of attending funerals. In this instance, there were many curiosity-seekers who came to see the principals in the now famous Minneapolis murder case. Reporters and strangers alike, did not recognize some of Kitty Ging's neighbors from the Ozark Flats. Francis Gordon Kelly, the red-headed lawyer from the second-floor apartment, attended the service as did the milling executive and his wife from across the hall on the second floor, the Wilhelms. Mr. and Mrs. Henry Goosman slipped out a side door of the church, unnoticed. Claus Blixt, the janitor, was on duty at the Ozark Flats, so his wife, Julia, came to the church alone.

Louise Ireland, Officer Patrick Ging, Mrs. Murray and Miss Murphy accompanied the coffin borne by the six pallbearers. Standing by and watching was Hillary Markham. Emmett could not leave work at the newspaper and she attended the funeral service alone. Standing behind her was Rex Barnett. When the hearse, drawn by a beautiful pair of shiny black horses, had left with the casket, the crowd began to disperse. Rex touched Hillary's arm and spoke.

"Hello, Hillary."

She turned, and a slight smile erased the somber look on her face. "Hello, Rex." There was a pause. "You left this morning before I had a chance to thank you."

"You already thanked me enough, Hillary," he said politely. "Are you going back to the apartment, now?" he asked. She said she was, and Rex offered to walk along with her over to Hennepin avenue. "Don't be alarmed about last night. We're working on it and we'll have someone around the building tonight," he assured her.

"I'm not worried about it, now," she replied, "Emmett's back." Then she smiled, "But I was never so glad to see anyone in my whole life as when I opened the door and saw you standing there." They crossed an intersection. It was slippery going and she took his arm. "So many things happened last night, Rex, that I forgot to ask you what you were doing there. Just *what were* you doing there?"

"I told John Morrissey that I'd stop at Olson's Boarding House across the street to ask a few more questions and as long as I was in the neighborhood, I thought I'd stop and see if everything was okay. And I'm glad I did." When they got to the corner at Hennepin they stopped. She was going to take the streetcar to the Ozark Flats. He would be heading the other way to the Central Police Station. They stood there for a moment and then both started to speak at the same time.

Ozark Flats

"I know that you're leav——," Rex was saying.

"I was wondering if I would see——," Hillary started to say. They both stopped and laughed.

Rex spoke again. "I know you're leaving tomorrow afternoon for your home at Excelsior but I was wondering if you would be free at lunchtime. I have something for you before you leave for Christmas."

Hillary looked a little embarrassed. "I guess it would be all right. I mean, I'd *love* to have lunch with you again."

Rex was elated. "I'll take you to a nicer place, Schiek's. No, we'll go to the West Hotel dining room. Would you meet me in the lobby at noon, tomorrow?" She smiled and nodded in agreement. He escorted her to the streetcar and held her arm as she stepped up. The gates closed behind her. She didn't look back but he stood there in the middle of Hennepin avenue, transfixed, until a sledge swerved by him. Its driver dropped to a crouch and yelled over his shoulder, "Get out of the road, you greenhorn!"

Mr. Hudson and Mr. Farber had stood on the front steps of the Ozark Flats and watched through the glass doors of the foyer until Joey, the elevator operator, had closed the elevator door. The two men moved through the doorway and up the stairs to the left of the hallway. When they reached the third-floor apartment of Harry Hayward, the short man with the bowler pulled out a set of keys and in an instant, the two men let themselves into Harry's apartment. Hudson looked at the clock on the mantle of the fireplace in the living room and remarked that the funeral had just started, and they would have plenty of time to look around. Walter Farber went to the rear of the apartment and began a thorough search of the kitchen. Hudson started in the living room, pulling seat cushions out of overstuffed chairs and the davenport, emptying table drawers and moving on to the dining room to continue the search. After they finished tearing Harry's bedroom apart, they took one last look at the rear balcony overlooking the court at the back of the apartment house, and checked the small balcony in the front of the apartment that over-

Ozark Flats

looked Hennepin avenue. In spite of all their efforts, they still hadn't found the money they were looking for and quietly left through the front door of the apartment and down the massive stairway. Then they left the Ozark Flats through the front door and down the front steps as if they were long-time residents of the apartment house.

When Rex Barnett arrived back at the police station, Emmett Markham was waiting for him in the outer lobby. He thanked Rex for rescuing Hillary the night before and assured him that his visit to the police station was not intended as any kind of harrassment of the police by *The Journal*.

"On the contrary," Emmett assured Rex, "we think that the investigation is going along quite smoothly, considering the complexities of this whole thing." Then he explained to Rex about his visit to the editor of *The Journal* and that he had been given the go-ahead to do some more digging on his own.

"We don't need an amateur detective," Rex said, as nicely as he could. "Reporting the news of this case is one thing. Investigating it is another."

"I know that," Emmett assured him. "But I want to help and I think I have a right to, especially after what happened—or almost happened to Hillary last night." He reached into his inside coat pocket and pulled out some papers. "And I think I have something here that might interest you." He handed the papers to Rex.

The newspaper was a *Minneapolis Journal* from last June and was turned to one of the inside pages. Sure enough, there was a short two-paragraph story of a robbery near Lake Calhoun. Two couples had been riding in a buggy and were stopped at gunpoint. The two robbers had taken the women's jewelry and money—nearly $100—but had not demanded any money from the two gentlemen in the buggy. Then the robbers left, apparently disappointed that their take hadn't been greater. The women were listed as a Miss Vedder and Miss Ging. One of the gentlemen in the buggy was Harry T. Hayward!

Rex smiled as he read the short article. Then he looked up from the newspaper.

"We've been so damn busy tracking down clues and checking out rumors that no one, to my knowledge, ever thought about checking back over our own records. How did you come on to this, Emmett?"

"Someone in our office said they remembered something about a robbery and that Kitty Ging and Harry Hayward had been two of the victims. So I went back this afternoon and looked at old issues and this is what I found."

"Everytime I turn around today, Harry Hayward's name comes up again," Rex said.

"And the newspaper isn't all, either," Emmett went on. "I had a call from Andy Ross, the new assistant manager of the West Hotel, and he tells me that the man who was tailing our friend Harry, along with one of your detectives, is a man by the name of Walter Farber who has been staying at the hotel all this week. He's the one who knocked the wind out of your detective."

"I'll check out the name," Rex told Emmett. "I have a feeling that we'll find our Mr. Walter Farber on a list from Milwaukee or Chicago—either a gambler or something to do with counterfeit money."

Then Emmett explained that he had also made a call to his old friend and former professional gambler, George "Pinky" Wolfe, who had just called him back before he came over to the police station. "And he tells me that Mr. Hayward is out of favor with a number of gambling houses here in Minneapolis. Not only that, but it is strange that you should mention counterfeit money. Harry seems to have passed some in a recent game or two." Pinky Wolfe had also told Emmett that Harry had once threatened a newspaperman for publishing an article about his gambling.

Rex Barnett was impressed. He already had his suspicions about Harry, and there were still so many different possibilities. Yes, Emmett's information seemed to fall into a pattern. Rex thanked the newspaperman for his help and suggested that they go have a cup of coffee across the street. But before they could leave the station, Rex was called to the phone. He was only gone a matter of a couple of minutes and when he returned, he motioned Emmett to come along.

"Let's go have that coffee," he said. His voice had a new bright

sound to it. "I just had a call from one of Big Glady's girls over at The Fountainhead and she tells me that Glady would like to see me tonight—that she has someone who can give me some interesting information about the Ging murder case."

"Who's Glady—and where's The Fountainhead?" Emmett asked as they stepped out on to the street and headed for coffee.

"Glady's an old friend," Rex explained. "She runs a restaurant and bar called The Fountainhead. It's a joint—but an elegant joint and it's popular, not only with gamblers but with some of the more prominent men in town. She's got dancing girls there. In fact, she books dancing girls all over Minneapolis and St. Paul, too. The whole thing looks a little shady, but she runs a clean operation—and she's helped me out a number of times when I needed information." They were at the front door of The New York Cafe and about to go inside for coffee. Rex felt that Emmett deserved something for his effort and information and to make him feel part of the investigation. He asked him, "Do you want to go along with me tonight?"

"I sure do," Emmett replied enthusiastically.

"Okay, you're on. Only I want you to know before we go that it's no Grand Opera House musical." They laughed and went inside for coffee.

18

THE NIGHT AIR was brisk and it made Emmett walk with a quickened step as he and Rex moved along First avenue in the dark, headed for The Fountainhead down by the river. Emmett felt good. He had called Hillary on the phone and she was going to stay with Louise Ireland and her friend in their apartment until Emmett got home. Hillary had not seemed upset when Emmett told her he was going along with Rex tonight. He called her, hesitatingly, because he knew that another night away from home wasn't going to set too well with her. But she encouraged him to go ahead and told him she would be waiting for him in Louise Ireland's apartment where she could be with someone. They were going to wrap some Christmas gifts and decorate some cookies with Christmas frosting. Emmett told her it would not be late.

Now the newspaperman felt a certain excitement. When he asked his boss if he could put some time in on the investigation, he never dreamed he would be accompanying a city detective on a mission that might help solve the case. He was going to see a part of the city he had never seen but only heard about—a new and mysterious side of Minneapolis. It wasn't much to look at from the outside. The Fountainhead was located in a drab, three-story building with gas lanterns at the entrance.

Inside, however, it was a different story. Although it was not luxurious, Emmett was impressed with The Fountainhead. The front doors opened into a foyer of considerable size and off to the right was a place to check coats, attended by an attractive blonde in a skimpy outfit which featured her long legs in black opera hose and not much covering her bosom which looked extremely smooth and white to Emmett. An open doorway straight ahead led to a long bar that ran straight back, almost the length of the building. A lounge adjoined the bar and was terraced, with iron railings separating the bar and the lounge and each level of the lounge which was furnished with overstuffed chairs and loveseats and small tables. There were rugs on the floor and some ornate chandeliers hanging from a high ceiling. Additional lighting came from table lamps scattered around the room, each touched off with Holly and Christmas greens. A large stairway at the right of the foyer led upstairs to two large dining areas. A second stairway at the rear of the bar and lounge also led to the upstairs restaurant.

There was an air of holiday excitement inside with red Christmas candles on every table. The place was filled with noise—the sounds of seemingly hundreds of voices, of music, smoke and the clinking of glasses. Rex was right, Emmett thought to himself. It's a joint. But a nice joint. There was a good feeling here, a friendly feeling, and Emmett knew the minute he stepped inside that people enjoyed themselves here.

Rex and Emmett checked their coats and hats and the blonde girl in the opera hose greeted Rex as if he were a regular patron.

"Glady's inside near the back," she told Rex. "She's expecting you."

Emmett followed Rex through the crowded door into the first-floor bar and lounge. Although there were people waiting behind a velvet restraining cord, a tall brunete, also in a red and black costume with the long opera hose, greeted Rex with an English accent and let him pass through. Near the rear of the lounge was a small bandstand and a small area in front of the musicians, apparently for dancing. A

Ozark Flats

trio was playing some loud, brassy marches as the two men pushed their way along the bar and up the terrace steps to the rear of the lounge.

Dominating the rear corner table next to the bandstand was Big Glady, sort of holding court over a table-full of people. When she saw Rex coming, however, she shooed away one couple to make room for Rex and Emmett. There were still two attractive young women sitting with Glady and the large woman smiled and waved to Rex as the two men approached the table. Emmett blinked. Now he knew why she was affectionately called *Big* Glady. The name was appropriate. She must weigh over 300 pounds! She was dressed in a very large black evening gown and her blonde hair was pulled up on top of her head where it was held in place by a set of combs which looked like they were studded with diamonds. Emmett blinked again! By God, they *were* diamonds! And there were more! She also wore a diamond necklace and Emmett noticed that there were a number of large rings—some with diamonds—on her chubby fingers.

Rex introduced Emmett and Glady told the two women at the table that she had some private business to conduct with Rex and asked them to come back after a while. Rex and Emmett had no more than sat down, however, when the big woman was called away from the table by a young man with a beard, apparently one of the managers of The Fountainhead. She told Rex she'd be right back and as she headed toward the back room behind the lounge and bar, Emmett noticed she was wearing bedroom slippers.

"How did you ever come to meet her?" Emmett asked incredulously.

"She's an old friend," Rex explained. "I've known her for about five years now. The first time I met her I hired two dancers from her for a policemen's stag party. We still do that about once a year. But ever since that first time, she has been a good friend." Rex went on, telling Emmett about Glady. Her husband had made some money in Minneapolis real estate and had bought and ran The Fountainhead. When he died of a heart attack six years ago, Glady simply took over the business and added some dancers. Then other places in town also wanted dancers, and before anyone realized it, Glady was booking all the dancers in town. If you were a dancer and you came to Minneapolis, you couldn't get work unless you worked for Glady. If a new booker came into town with a stable of dancing girls and got them work in a bar, Glady would simply stop by and ask the bar-owner how he'd like to have her dancers for a week at no cost. The bar-owner was delighted and the next thing the newcomer in town knew, he had four girls who were out of work and who had to be housed and fed. After a couple of weeks, he'd be off to Milwaukee or St. Louis or someplace else and Glady would go back to her regular routine.

Rex Barnett happened to like her and they got along well. He'd stop to visit her from time to time and he was grateful to her for introducing him to a lovely dancer named Gertie Lewis. Once in a great while, Rex would take Glady to lunch and they would talk about everything—except Glady's one main commodity—girls. Rex explained to Emmett that Glady had all the qualities most people looked for in a friend. She was loyal, she'd do anything for you if she liked you, she was fun to be around, and she was quick to help someone in need.

Rex had a suspicion that when Gert first quit dancing and started her own business as a seamstress, Glady probably overpaid her for the costumes she made for the girls. She probably helped finance Gert's massage parlor, too, although Gert never volunteered that information and Rex never asked. And although the big woman was good-hearted, she also ran a tight ship. All of her dancers had to look good, and they had to be on time. If they were late for a job, she'd fine them. She also insisted on no soliciting while they were working for her. What they did on their own time couldn't be helped, but she loved them all and she never forgot a birthday or failed to hold some special holiday parties just for her dancing girls and the rest of the help at The Fountainhead. Rex also knew she was a generous contributor to more than one downtown church.

Emmett believed Rex when he told him there wasn't a bartender or a waitress, a policeman or a hackie, or a politician or civic leader that didn't know this marvelous lady. In fact, Emmett recognized a member of the City Council across the room.

Glady returned to the table and after she had asked Rex and Emmett what they would like to drink and had sent a waiter off with the order, she relaxed.

"Well, Rex, I see by the papers that you still don't have the Ging murder case solved." She laughed a deep laugh. "But I'll bet you're closer to wrapping it up than the newspapers indicate." She turned to Emmett. "No offense." Then she leaned back and laughed again.

"But you've got something for me?" Rex asked.

"I've got *two* things for you," she corrected him. Then she sent the waiter upstairs and in a few minutes he brought back a woman dressed in a gypsy costume who apparently did palm readings in the dining room on the second floor. The woman's name was Emma Goodale and apparently was a popular medium. "She's known as Madam Peterson," Glady told Rex and Emmett. Then she laughed again. But what Madam Peterson had to tell Rex was no laughing matter. She explained that just last week, a man had asked her to give his lady companion some special advice on gambling—advice that he would furnish.

"My usual charge is two dollars to go back into the past," she explained, "and five dollars when the trance indicates the future." But she was suspicious of the proposal and when she asked the advice of her husband, he told her not to get involved. "The man's name was Harry Hayward," she said.

All while Madam Peterson had been visiting with Glady and Rex, Emmett noticed the lights had been dimmed around the lounge and a bright limelight was concentrated on a dancer in the middle of the dance floor in front of the bandstand. As the music continued into the second and third chorus, the dancer kept dropping her clothes in the middle of the floor. When the musical number was over, the attractive dancer was standing in the middle of the floor wearing only a black corset. Her breasts were fully exposed! Emmett was amazed. Rex kept on questioning Madam Peterson and Emmett noticed that neither Rex or Glady or Emma Goodale paid any attention at all to the stripper. At the end of the dance, the crowd applauded and Emmett realized that the near nude dancer was one of the attractive young women who had been sitting at their table just a few moments ago.

A few minutes after Glady dismissed Madam Peterson, she sent a waiter to the bar to bring back a small, middle-aged man with a large mustache who was a hack driver. The small man was Peter Valley and he sat at the table with Rex and Emmett and told how a well-dressed man had approached him last July and asked him how he would like to make some extra money. All he had to do was run his

buggy into Lake Calhoun with this woman in it and make it look like an accident!

"I told him 'no thank you' and got the hell away from his as fast as I could! I realize now, that the man was Mr. Harry Hayward, and I come to Glady with that right away!"

Rex thanked him for his help and the hackie left while Glady and the two men finished their drinks. There wasn't any doubt in Rex's mind, nor Emmett's, that Harry Hayward should be arrested and brought back to jail. He'd have a lot of explaining to do. The two thanked Glady for her help—and her hospitality—and Rex wished her a "Merry Christmas" and gave her a big, long hug. Then the detective and the newspaperman pushed through the crowd to the outer foyer to get their coats, just as the lights dimmed and another dancer appeared in the limelight. On the way back to the Central Police Station, Emmett talked about winding up his work at *The Journal* tomorrow. He still had some holiday scheduling to do for the weekend and had a couple of small problems in the Classified Ad department to iron out. At the mention of the Want Ads, Rex's mind clicked into action and he smiled as he remembered a Personal he had read on the streetcar just a couple of days ago. He knew now that Harry Hayward had placed the ad: *K.G. The insurance money is coming. H.H.* Of course it was Harry. He was just egotistical enough to do such a thing. There had been another one. What was it? *K.G. will pick up the money.* What was that all about? A ruse? He was playing a game with her to get her out by the lake. Rex quickened his step to get back to John Morrissey at the station. Emmett looked at him and picked up the pace.

At the rear table in The Fountainhead, the two attractive women returned to Glady's table where Big Glady kicked off her slippers and told the girls, "God, but my feet hurt tonight."

Bill Eustis did not get back to his office at City Hall until nearly nine o'clock in the evening. He had been at a dinner meeting at the Nicollet House nearby with some Minneapolis real estate men and an attorney representing an eastern businessman. Although the mayor and the city had no authority in the matter, as the head representative for the City of Minneapolis, the mayor was interested in the importnat real estate deal which would be completed before the first of the year.

The name of the eastern industrialist was still not known, but it appeared now that there would be a change in ownership of property located at First avenue north and Third street, now occupied by the wholesale dry goods business of Harrison, Hopgood and Company. The transaction was for a sizeable amount of money—$136,000—and it appeared that it was the first in a number of land purchases to be made in the city by the easterner. Just a few weeks ago, former Minnesota governor William Merriam had purchased the other half of the same block for $137,000. After the meeting, the attorney representing the buyer had told a reporter that the purchase showed the confidence which eastern capitalists have in the future of Minneapolis. When the meeting was over, Mayor Eustis walked the short distance down Hennepin avenue to City Hall and went up to his second-floor office.

Miss Magnuson had left a number of papers and documents on the mayor's desk and the mayor was quick to take his coat off and finish off the long day's business. He had worked his way through a half-dozen different papers and letters when he found the envelope addressed to him. It had Levi Stewart's return address in the corner. There was no stamp or post mark and the letter had obviously been delivered by messenger this afternoon while the mayor was at the funeral or at the holiday reception for Senator Washburn. Good old Levi, he thought. He hadn't seen or heard from his old friend in some time, now, but they had known each other for years, and Levi had offered some help when Bill Eustis needed it during his campaign to be elected Mayor of Minneapolis.

The mayor opened the envelope and began to read the note written on Levi's own personal stationery. "My God!" the mayor gasped as he finished reading the letter and set it down on his desk. It was two pages long and, although it was unpleasant reading, it was just what Bill Eustis had been looking for.

Ozark Flats

December 22, 1894

Dear Bill,

I have just finished reading the evening papers and have found disturbing headlines and stories in both The Minneapolis Tribune and The Minneapolis Journal about the Catherine Ging murder. The news of this tragedy is especially disturbing to me and prompts this urgent letter to you now.

Last evening, on the very night of this horrible event, the son of an old family friend paid me an unexpected call. Our two families have been friends for many years and I have known both of the sons since they were youngsters. The family which I refer to is that of William W. Hayward, and the older of his two sons, Adry, paid me a visit on this occasion, early in the evening. Although Adry is not the brightest young man in my acquaintance, he surely is not mentally retarded and I can vouch that his own personal senses can distinguish right from wrong.

His visit last evening was prompted by his sincere belief that his younger brother, Harry, was contemplating the terrible crime of murder. The young man recited, sometimes in almost hysterical tones, the fear that his brother was about to institute a plan to take the life of a female acquaintance. In a painful and sometimes almost delirious condition, young Adry expressed the sincere concern that his brother was about to commit this dreadful deed, or have it done for him by others. Although the young man who visited me did not admit it, he seemed to indicate that he, himself, might somehow be implicted in this terrible plot. And he asked for my forgiveness and advice.

Because I have known the Hayward family for so many years, I must admit that Adry's concerns and his confession to me were perhaps over-dramatic and somewhat imaginative. As a result, I tried to put his mind at ease and suggested that he return to his *apartment and seek advice and counsel from his parents who also live in the apartment house known as Ozark Flats. When he left, he thanked me for granting him the time to visit, and I had the feeling that he had been somewhat calmed and satisfied by his opportunity to talk to a trusted friend. I must confess that I considered the subject of his visit the result of his imagination and the fact that he has had far less attention and respect than his younger brother. If I thought there was the remotest possibility of such a plot, I should have advised Adry to go to the Superintendent of Police.*

After reading of the horrible crime in today's newspapers, however, I feel compelled to pass this information on to the proper authorities and I understand that you have taken a personal and active role in the investigation. I do not want you to let any person know that you received the information from me, but you can say the same as I can—that I never spoke a word to you on the subject. And I want you to burn this as soon as it is fully read. I hope this information will be helpful to you, and be equitable to those involved.

With deepest regards and friendship, I remain

Levi M. Stewart

Bill Eustis mashed out his cigar in a large ashtray on his desk and reached for the telephone to call John Morrissey at the Central Police Station. It was time to arrest Harry and Adry Hayward.

19

HILLARY MARKHAM had stayed through most of the evening with young Louise Ireland in the apartment across the hall. They had baked ten dozen sugar cookies and decorated almost all of them. They had also consumed a great number of the cookies as they busied themselves in the kitchen of the apartment. Both Mrs. Murphy and Miss Murray had also been there and would stay the night. Tomorrow, the young Miss Ireland would accompany the body of Catherine Ging back to her birthplace. It had been a long day and Hillary finally decided it was time to go back to her own apartment, even though Emmett had not returned. There was a patrolman stationed at the front entrance of the apartment house and Hillary no longer felt she was in any danger. She gave Louise Ireland one last embrace before leaving the apartment, and then returned to her own apartment across the hall on the fifth floor of the Ozark Flats.

The depression of the funeral and the emptiness of the apartment across the hall, was somehow outweighed by the feeling of anticipation of tomorrow. It would be Christmas Eve—and her folks would be arriving from St. Louis. She would join them at the Union depot and they would all take the train to Excelsior tomorrow afternoon. She realized now, that she missed Jamie, and she could hardly wait to see her young son again, even though it had only been yesterday that he made the short trip out to the lake with his father. And of course, tomorrow was the anniversary of another important event in her life. Tomorrow was her wedding anniversary and she and Emmett would be home again—really home!

Hillary wondered how much her two younger brothers had grown since she last saw them. She thought of how beautiful her mother was and hoped that her father was in good health and that he would not be too demanding during the holiday visit. As she busied herself with last-minute packing and preparations for tomorrow, she also remembered she was to have lunch with Rex tomorrow. The thought of being with him again was exciting and pleasing to her, but it also brought a note of sadness into her heart and mind this December evening. Such thoughts only confused her and she suddenly wished that Emmett were home. He would be, soon, she hoped.

Two floors down, Harry Hayward was relaxing with a glass of wine and the newspaper. It had been a long day for him, too. It had also been a trying one. He recalled the discovery of someone following him this morning, only to find it was Mr. Farber. He wasn't sure just who the second follower was but he was sure that it was either someone hired by some of his gambling acquaintances—or the police. Either way, he was a little angry with himself for losing his composure and making a run for it this morning. He even had to admit to himself that for a brief time this morning, he had been scared.

He had also been upset when he first returned home following the funeral today. The service itself, the casket, and all, would have been enough to disturb anyone, but returning to his apartment to find it had been ransacked was disconcerting to say the least. There was no mystery to Harry about it all. Obviously they were looking for the money. He only wished he knew where the hell it was. He was about to fill his wine glass for the third time when there was a knock at the front door. When Harry opened the door, he found John Morrissey standing there.

"Mr. Hayward, I must inform you that you are under arrest. Please get your coat and come along with me down to the station."

Down on the first floor of the Ozark Flats, Adry Hayward answered a knock at the living room door, only to find Detective Michael Hoy.

"Please get your coat, Mr. Hayward. You're under arrest for the murder of Catherine Ging!"

Friday, December 24, 1894

DENOUEMENT!

Harry T. Hayward and His Brother
Are Charged With Murder.

Police Believe Them Guilty of
The Assassination of Catherine Ging.

The "Green Goods" Theory A Chief Factor
In Yesterday's Developments.

—*The Minneapolis Tribune*

The developments in the Ging murder case today are mostly in the evidence against the two brothers who were arrested last evening and arraigned this morning upon the charge of murder in the first degree.

The authorities agree there will be a very strong case against Harry Hayward, but they are not so confident as to the strength of the evidence they have against Adry. The evidence that is forthcoming against the former is such that those who have conducted the investigation against the search for evidence are sure that the grand jury will return a true bill against him. The evidence they have secured cannot be got at very easily, as one of the many who have conducted the case said that they had the evidence but that it would be guarded secretly and reassured with all the vigilance possible.

This morning just before a conference was held in the office of the chief of police, and before the door had been shut, this significant sentence was overheard: "These two facts are proven without a doubt," and then followed a conversation of some length, the purport of which was known only within the office. The evidence against the two men who are now in the county jail was undoubtedly gone over and that was the two facts which had been proved beyond a doubt.

The facts which have been brought to light by the detectives have led to the adoption of this line of evidence. It is learned that the prosecution is satisfied that Harry Hayward was sort of an agent for a green goods firm in Chicago, and that he received a batch of goods amounting to $7,000 about the time he claims to have loaned Miss Ging that amount. It is also understood that he has attempted to push the goods through other parties, and in some cases succeeded. It is the theory that he gave this money to Miss Ging, and then persuaded her to rest the box in the Lord and Trust Company. His asking about the box, so that Miss Ireland would be aware of the fact that her aunt had a box, strengthens the theory that he did not want Miss Ging to place the money in a bank, and that he wanted to get possession of the $10,000 insurance, and gave the $7,000 worth of bogus money in order to get it signed over to him, and then got her to put it in the safety deposit vault so that detection would be impossible.

Today the police have discarded that look of bewilderment which has characterized their features for the past two days, and in its place is a confident look, which augurs that they are about to wind up the case of the murdered Miss Ging last Tuesday night on the old Excelsior road.

—*The Minneapolis Journal*

BOTH HARRY AND ADRY HAYWARD were in good spirits as they greeted the jailers at the Central Police Station the morning after the two brothers had spent the night in Lock-up Alley. Harry had been locked up in cell number fourteen and Adry occupied cell number forty-one during the night. Both were restless and were up long after midnight, reading last evening's newspapers, especially the stories about the Ging murder case. A little after midnight they were both served a light supper, and both had declined breakfast this morning, telling the jailers they were not hungry. They cheerfully offered "good mornings" to jailers who indicated that "they are supplied with wonderful nerves, whether they are innocent of the charge or not, for the very possibility of the charge being proven is enough to break down any man of ordinary nerve."

Mr. Hayward, senior, was the first visitor to the jail this December morning and he stayed about an hour, talking with both of his sons. Mr. W.E. Hale, a well-known criminal attorney in the Minneapolis-St. Paul area, consulted with the brothers and told them he would represent them. He had been recommended to the elder Mr. Hayward by another Minneapolis attorney, Charles J. Bartleson, the father of Mabel Bartleson, who had accompanied Harry Hayward to the Grand Opera House on the night of the murder.

At mid-morning, the two Hayward brothers and their attorney appeared in municipal court for arraignment. Harry was charged with First Degree Murder and, after the reading of the complaint, Mr. Hale stated that he was ready for an immediate examination of his clients. But Assistant County Attorney Hall explained that the grand jury was now in session and the state would like a continuance until next week. Mr. Hale made an eloquent plea for an immediate examination but the court agreed with the prosecuting attorney that it would be well to continue the case until next Monday. Brother Adry was arraigned on the same charge and the attorneys went through the same procedure. All through the court appearance, Adry looked out on the crowded courtroom with great confidence, as if he were oblivious to the seriousness of the matter at hand. When it was over, no bail was set and the prisoners were taken back to their city jail cells for a brief time. It was also announced that the grand jury would be adjourning for the holiday and would meet again on Monday morning to consider the Ging murder case.

It wasn't long before the Hayward brothers were removed from the city jail and taken to the county jail in a patrol wagon. Harry's confident manner seemed to be contagious and Adry, who would normally be intimidated easily, now showed great nerve as they climbed out of the patrol wagon and began to shove through an eager crowd. Both Haywards looked straight ahead as they walked into the county jail, flanked by two policemen. After being registered, they were assigned to cells in the East room on the third floor. They were both grateful for the spacious room, especially after spending the night in the small cells of the Central lockup. Neither man showed any emotion or fear, even after they had been left alone on the third floor. One county jailer reported that the two were talking in subdued tones when he left them, and even the jailers were not quite sure why the Haywards had been placed in the East room cage. The Harris murderers, the Barrett boys, and the notorious Phil Schieg had all been locked up in the jail's West room. Now the Hayward brothers sat in the nearly empty cells on the third floor. Later today they would be brought bedding for the iron cots. It was a far cry from the Ozark Flats.

The Christmas season always brought on a rush of business to the post office and although the main effort to mail and deliver packages had already reached its peak in such metropolitan post offices as the one in Minneapolis, smaller post offices were just now completing the Christmas mail deliveries. In the U.S. Post office on Excelsior's main street, next to August Hay's Butcher Shop, the last of the Christmas mail had been sorted and placed in the maze of small postal boxes that covered the front wall next to the two service windows which opened out onto the front lobby. Residents and businessmen in Excelsior would be stopping throughout the day to adjust the combination locks on their individual post office boxes and pick up those final letters to arrive before Christmas. There would be no mail delivery on Saturday, Christmas Day, and those expecting Christmas packages would have until six o'clock tonight to ask for them at the service windows.

The last Christmas mail delivery arrived at the Excelsior depot on the M. and St. L's evening train last night and had been hauled down the main street by hand to the Excelsior post office on a large, wooden-spoked mail wagon early this morning. The letters were sorted and the last of the packages were now stacked on a two-tiered shelf directly behind the service windows. There was no need to place any package notices in the respective post office boxes. Both J.S. Dickinson, the Excelsior postmaster, and his assistant, Ed Dyer, knew everybody in town and they would all be in to pick up their mail sometime during the day. The Wyers had a package from their son in Northfield, and there were a couple of packages for H.F. Bullens and his General Store—probably some special Christmas orders for customers. Also sitting on the second shelf behind the service window was a package wrapped in plain brown paper. It was addressed to *Mrs. Hillary Markham, Excelsior, Minnesota.* Up in the left-hand corner of the package the return address was written in a feminine hand: *309 Syndicate Building, Minneapolis, Minnesota.*

There was a lot of activity at the Central Police Station this morning. Detectives huddled in small groups to discuss the events of the past evening and this morning, and reporters were taking down statements from just about everyone from Chief Smith to the jailer, John Bradley. Vern Smith had already met with Mayor Eustis this morning and was now conferring in his office with John Morrissey and Rex Barnett.

"The mayor is pleased with what's happened," the chief told the two detectives. "He realizes we had been tailing Harry and were about to pick him up last night, even before he called about the letter from Mr. Stewart."

"The problem is that we don't have this whole thing solved, as yet," John Morrissey replied. "I hope the mayor doesn't think it's all over."

"No, of course not. But there'll be no pressure the rest of the way," the chief said. "We've got to wind this thing up reasonably soon, however."

"Well, we know Harry is guilty as hell," Rex Barnett broke in, "but we also know he didn't pull the trigger. He was smart enough to be sitting in the middle of the Grand Opera House with a few hundred witnesses when it all happened."

"And the more I question his brother, the more I am convinced that Adry is not the culprit," Morrissey added. "I'd like to go over to the county jail this morning and visit with the older brother one more time. There's got to be at least one more person involved, and I think that Adry can help us."

The chief agreed. It was obvious that Harry Hayward, who had been so cooperative during the first day of the investigation, was not going to offer any help at this point. In fact, while Harry was being arraigned this morning, more evidence was piling up against him. A Mr. Benjamin H. Gilbert, who had known Harry for years, came forward. He was an insurance man who told John Morrissey this morning that just a week ago, Harry had inquired about death due to fire.

"He asked me if a person was insured and in a building where they were burned so badly that they wouldn't be recognized, would the company pay the claim?

"I told him that the company would require absolute proof of identification of the remains."

Harry had apparently inquired further and asked if the claim would be paid on the insured if he or she was murdered."

Vern Smith agreed that John Morrissey could go back to the county jail for another visit with Adry Hayward. Michael Hoy was dispatched to check on the suspicious characters who were undoubtedly the counterfeiters from Chicago, staying at the West Hotel. Rex Barnett would remain at the station this morning to complete the paperwork on the past day's events. The meeting broke up and everyone went his own way. Rex Barnett headed back toward his desk, but his mind was not on the events connected with the Ging murder case. All this time, he was unconsciously thinking about Hillary Markham. He knew she would be leaving the city for Excelsior this afternoon and he might not see her again after today's lunch. Now he was realizing that after the murder was solved there would be no reason for him to see her again. He also admitted to himself that he was in love with her.

Ozark Flats

It was a busy morning for Hillary Markham. Emmett was off to work and Jamie was already out at Excelsior. She had no responsibilities except to herself and she was in a hurry, packing clothes for the weekend at Excelsior, putting together the last few presents which she would take with her today. It would be a busy day, however—lunch with Rex Barnett, then to the depot, and after arriving in Excelsior, a short stop at Doc Perkins' office before going home for Christmas.

She sat at the desk in the alcove of the kitchen and wrote a note to Emmett who would be back at the apartment before leaving for Excelsior late this afternoon. All he would have to worry about was bringing whatever clothes he needed for the weekend. All the presents and anything else they would need for the holiday were already taken care of. Hillary completed the note and left it on the dresser in the bedroom, propped up against a family photograph of Emmett, Hillary and Jamie.

Then she dressed for the day and asked young Joey to help her take her suitcase and packages downstairs on the elevator. As they rode down to the first floor she thought of how exhilarating Christmas could be and what a happy time of year it was. And although today was very special—Christmas Eve *and* her wedding anniversary—there was a tinge of sadness about it all. She had already lost one new-found friend this week, and now she would be separated from another—and at a time when friends are very dear. She could easily put the likes of Harry and Adry Hayward out of her mind. But somewhere in the inner depths of her heart, she was having trouble with a disquieting phrase that kept interrupting her thoughts. Those thoughts were about Rex Barnett. And she kept thinking, "I love you."

On any other Christmas Eve day, Michael Hoy would be out having a beer with other detectives and leaving work early to spend the holiday at home with his family. But there was too much going on for anyone in the department to take the day off. He had helped make last night's arrests and had escorted the Hayward brothers to court this morning. Now he was given the unpleasant task of checking out a Mr. Hudson and a Mr. Farber at the West Hotel. As he entered the Hennepin avenue door of the hotel he was greeted by John Stavlo who had already paid a visit to an insurance firm this morning to check out another phase of the Harry Hayward story. Now the two detectives approached the reservation counter in the expansive lobby and inquired about Mr. Farber and Mr. Hudson in the fifth-floor suite.

The clerk excused himself for a moment while he checked the records and was back within seconds.

"I'm sorry, sir, but the two gentlemen in suite five-ten checked out early this morning. There's no forwarding address or any information as to where they can be reached."

In a way, Michael Hoy was relieved. It was one less task they would have to perform today. John Stavlo, on the other hand, was disappointed. He would like to have gotten even with the little son-of-a-bitch in the bowler hat.

21

THEY HAD BROUGHT ADRY HAYWARD down from the third-floor East room cage of the county jail to a small, barren office on the second floor. Detective John Morrissey had been waiting for nearly a half-hour in the small room furnished only by a small library table and three chairs. John had also asked for a stenographer to record the conversation between himself and Adry Hayward. Eventually, a jailor brought Adry into the room and left him with the Minneapolis detective and the court reporter. Both Hayward brothers were usually impeccably dressed, but Adry had been wearing the same clothes that he was in when he was arrested last night and it was obvious he had slept in them. The confidence which he had shown yesterday was slowly disappearing and the seriousness of the situation was now becoming much clearer to him. He had not made a damaging statement about himself—or his brother—during the proceedings last night or in the court earlier this morning. But he seemed relieved to see John Morrissey in this unexpected visit.

The Minneapolis detective began his conversation with Adry.

Ozark Flats

Hayward talked about Catherine Ging first moving into the apartment seven weeks ago, but it was apparent that Harry had known her long before she became a resident of the Ozark Flats. And that association bothered Adry. There was an unpleasantness in Adry's voice and attitude as Morrissey took him back through last summer's events. He was still loyal to his younger brother but he was now getting a little angry because of the pressures being brought to bear on him, and he finally admitted to John Morrissey that earlier this summer, brother Harry had tried to goad him into testing his courage by shooting someone. At first, the bait was one hundred dollars. Later, Adry told the detective, the ante was raised to two thousand to kill a woman. There was still no mention of Kitty Ging, but Adry recited the suggestions made to him by Harry: he could just plain shoot her in a hack somewhere, or trump up an accident with a runaway horse and rig, or even drowning! They were all suppositions, Adry explained, but Harry was losing patience with his brother and eventually gave up on him and his so-called experiment.

Adry was getting very angry. He told Morrissey that Harry had threatened him and in recent months, Harry treated him with more contempt than ever. Still, there was no mention of Kitty Ging. Then there was a long pause in the questioning and Adry, who was leaning forward in his chair and rubbing his hands together nervously, looked up at Morrissey. There was a quiet tone in his voice.

"I tried to tell him that he couldn't carry out such terrible plans to get rid of the girl. He'd get caught—and hang for it." He rubbed his hands some more. "But all he did was get mad and yell at me."

"What about Catherine Ging?" John Morrissey asked quietly.

Adry looked out the frosted window as if he hadn't even heard the question. "Even now, I don't think he knows what the consequences are." He looked up at the detective again. "He's upstairs, talking of somebody writing a novel about this whole thing!"

John Morrissey now decided he had just about everything he was going to get by himself from Adry Hayward. He asked the court stenographer to step out in the hall and turned to Adry.

"Adry, there's someone here who would like to talk to you. You relax for a minute and I'll be back." With that, Morrissey stepped into the hall.

Within a matter of seconds, another visitor came into the little room where Adry was still sitting. It was Levi Stewart. The grey-haired little man with the heavy mustache and short beard, was dressed in a dark suit, carried a grey winter coat over his arm and held a hat. He looked like a gentle man and his face showed great compassion for Adry. Adry was dumbfounded to see his old family friend.

"Adry! How are you?" questioned the old friend.

"Mr. Stewart. I didn't expect to see you here."

"I had to come when I read about what happened. Adry, what are you doing here? Have you told the police what you told me the other night when you stopped at my place?"

Adry looked guilty. He shook his head. "No, I haven't told anyone anything."

"My God, boy, what are you waiting for," Levi pleaded. "You surely know right from wrong. I admire what you're doing. But this is no time for that kind of loyalty. It's time to tell the truth!"

Seeing his old family friend under these circumstances was too much for Adry Hayward. Tears began streaming down his cheeks and he could no longer control his emotions. He began to cry aloud.

"It's no use, Adry," Levi Stewart told him compassionately. "This quibbling will be of no avail. You'll be much better off if you'll only tell the truth—just as you told it to me the other night."

It was no use delaying it any longer. Adry knew his old friend was right. "You're right," he told Levi Stewart. "You're so right." He sat there with his legs spread apart, holding his head in his hands.

"Levi Stewart went to the door and stepped into the hallway where Detective Morrissey and the stenographer were waiting. "Lieutenant," he said, "I think that Adry has something to tell you."

The main dining room of the West Hotel was particularly busy at lunchtime on this Christmas Eve. Bright green napkins had been added to white tablecloths and there were some Christmas trees placed in the corners of the elegant room. One large decorated tree dominated the very middle of the dining area. Although the hotel would be nearly empty because of the holiday, there was a line of people waiting to be seated for lunch today. Hillary had met Rex Barnett in the Exchange on the first floor and they had purposely met early so they could be seated for an early lunch. Hillary would have to catch a streetcar to the depot by 2:15 to meet her family coming in from St. Louis. Less than an hour later they would be on a train for Excelsior—and home!

Dining in the elegant West Hotel was not a routine event for a city detective. He was glad to be here with Hillary, but he would have been more comfortable back in a booth at the New York Cafe. He realized he was now on her home ground and even though he was at ease with it, he knew this wasn't for him. It was perfect for Hillary, however. She was beautiful! And she belonged in this setting. Rex ordered wine for them and the waiter left menus. Rex looked at the menu but his mind was whizzing through his relationship with Hillary over these past few days—when he first saw her, their first luncheon, and the night at the Ozark Flats. As he looked at her, he was aware that all of those walls he had placed between himself and women over these past few years were crumbling. Those old feelings, which he hadn't experienced in years, were creeping back into his inner-self. What surprised him was that he didn't seem to be afraid anymore. He knew this whole thing with Hillary was impossible, but he did not fear what he knew was inevitable.

The two of them decided on a selection from the menu and Rex ordered Coquilles St. Jacques for both of them. He was proud of himself. He hadn't forgotten what little French he had learned in college, or how to pronounce it. The two of them chatted over wine and Rex brought her up to date on the Ging case—the arrest of Harry and Adry and what had happened to them this morning. He told her Harry was not cooperating at all, and although Adry had not told the police anything, they felt that he was struggling to hold something back and that John Morrissey was back at the county jail at this hour, questioning the older brother again. He said he was sure there was at least one more person involved—maybe two. Rex could no longer talk about the murder, however, and he touched his napkin, nervously, to his lips and then began twisting it in his lap.

"I have something to tell you, Hillary," he said hesitantly.

"What is it, Rex? Is something wrong?" she asked with some concern.

"No, nothing like that," he assured her. "But I have been thinking that I have only known you a few days—and not under the best of circumstances. And I know you're married and have a family—and what a good man Emmett is. And yet, I must tell you—" He paused for a moment. He was having difficulty with the words. He had not said them in a very long time. It was too hard for him. He was about to give up. The silence was embarrassing to him. His eyes were downcast. Then he knew he must go on. He was almost apologizing as he spoke. "I haven't said words like these since Josie left." Then he looked up at Hillary.

"I love you, Hillary!" She started to speak, but Rex went right on.

"I'm not just saying that—not like some friends say it casually, without meaning. I really love you. I'm physically attracted to you and I feel good when I'm around you. I can't help it, Hillary. I just love you."

"Rex, I—"

"And I know this whole thing is impossible, and we may never see each other again. But I have to tell you this. Because of you, I know now that I need other people in my life. You have brought so many memories of Josie back to me, and I've found I can think about her now, and it doesn't hurt anymore. Please don't leave. I just had to tell you, that's all."

"Oh, Rex," she smiled. "I'm not leaving. I—" The smile broke down, just a little, and tears came down her pretty cheeks. There was a little sadness in her face, now, and a look of relief. "Oh, God! I love you, too, Rex." She took a deep breath. "I was going to tell you that today. And you're right, this is all so impossible. I'm married, I love my husband, my family is coming, I'm going home for Christmas! And my God, it's my wedding anniversary!" She reached across the table and touched Rex's hand.

"It's true, Rex, about needing other people in your life. I know that I do. As much as I love Emmett, and as fine a man as he is, there is no way that he can be all things to me. There are times when each of us shares joys or sorrows or close secrets with a friend we love. And the friend doesn't always have to be of the same sex—or even the same age. I needed you. I need you now. And I do hope you've needed me, too. I've been thinking about us these past few days, Rex, and all kinds of thoughts and possibilities passed through my mind. I

know now that I want to be with my husband. My love for Emmett transcends any love which I have for you or anyone else. But I do love you. And although we can't go back, I cherish what few little innocent intimacies we have had." She was crying now, and Rex reached across the table to hand her his handkerchief, just as the waiter brought their lunch.

When John Morrissey came out of the second-floor room in the county jail, he told the jailer standing outside the door that he could have Adry Hayward back to take up to the third-floor cage. John thanked the stenographer for her help, and didn't even stop to make a phone call. Instead, he left the old brick building and headed directly back to the Central Police Station a few blocks away. When he arrived at Lock-up Alley, he went straight to Chief Vern Smith's office and told him about his interrogation of Adry Hayward. He had hardly finished when the chief reached for the phone and called Mayor Eustis.

With the arrest of the two Hayward brothers and this morning's arraignment, Bill Eustis had found his morning dominated by the Ging murder case. There were still reporters downstairs and even with two prime suspects in custody, they still didn't have a confession. The newspapers had enough to chew on for the time being, but the mayor knew there had to be more before this case could be resolved. When Vern Smith called him from the police station, Bill Eustis was both relieved and anxious.

"You go ahead and pick him up, Vern," but don't bring him into the police station. There's just too damn many reporters and others around there—and here. I'll have my office reserve a room over at the West Hotel and you have your people bring him up the back way." The mayor added, "But bring him in—and NOW!"

Neither Hillary nor Rex spoke much while they were eating lunch. Oh, Rex told her about the investigation and that things were winding down. Hillary looked forward to seeing her parents and younger brothers for the first time since last summer when her father had come to Excelsior for the M. and St. L. to check out their hotel properties. But as they finished their lunch, they looked at each other and smiled.

"It's Christmas Eve," Hillary said, "and I have a present for you." Rex looked astonished, but Hillary went right on. "Here, Rex, this is for you. Merry Christmas!" She handed a gift box across the table to Rex and she urged him to go ahead and open it. The small package was wrapped in white tissue paper with thin red ribbon, and the handsome detective opened it carefully.

"It's my first Christmas present this year," Rex said as he carefully opened the small white box. Then he took the cover off and removed some cotton filling. He smiled as he lifted a small gold cross out of the box.

"It's a watch fob," she said excitedly!

"It's beautiful," he said, as he held it up to the light. "Thank you, Hillary. This means an awful lot to me. My father wore one like this." Then, as if he had been in a trance and just remembered where he was, he reached into his pocket. "I have a gift for you, too." Rex handed the small dark box across the table. It was not wrapped, and had no ribbon.

Hillary quickly opened it. Then she began to cry. It was a gold cross. "Oh, Rex, it's lovely. It's just beautiful. I have just the chain for it. It's beautiful." She reached across the table and took his hand. "I love you Rex Barnett."

The waiter came with the check and the two of them left the dining room and came down the stairs to the expansive lobby area of the West Hotel. They left the hotel through the side entrance on Fifth because Rex had decided they should take a hack to the depot. Hillary had already been to the depot before lunch to leave her bags, so the two of them stepped up into the buggy with side-curtains to protect them from the brisk day, and the hackie started off for the depot. The ride was silent. The two spoke only briefly and when they arrived at the foot of Hennepin, the rig pulled up in front of the depot.

"You don't have to come in, Rex. I'll find my way. I've plenty of time," she told him.

"All right, Hillary. I'll say goodbye here. Then I'm off to the station."

The two stood on the walk in front of the great depot as horses and buggies and streetcars noisily rolled by. Neither of them spoke for a long time.

"I've got to go in, now." Hillary looked up at him and her eyes were filled with tears.

"I know," he told her. "I can't thank you enough for the gift."

"I'll wear it to church tonight," she promised him. There was another moment of silence. He put his arms around her waist.

"I love you, Hillary. Merry Christmas!" Then he kissed her gently.

"Merry Christmas," she said.

Rex turned away and climbed back up into the cab. The rig pulled away and started back down Hennepin avenue. Rex turned to look through the small isinglass window of the rear curtains on the rig. He could see Hillary standing there. She waved, hesitantly.

Hillary watched the cab as it faded into the traffic along Hennepin avenue. She had the same feeling she had known when she looked back at Kitty Ging as the streetcar pulled away. "Merry Christmas, Rex," she whispered. Then she turned and started toward the front doors of the depot.

A doorman opened one of the large glass doors for the lovely blonde woman as she entered the depot. He noticed she was crying.

22

EMMETT MARKHAM was satisfied *The Minneapolis Journal* would carry the best story about the Hayward brothers being arrested and about the ensuing proceedings at the jail in court today. Even though tomorrow's Christmas edition would be light, Emmett was confident the latest developments were being monitored by Journal reporters at the mayor's office, at the Central Police Station, and over at the county jail where the Hayward brothers were now being held. Emmett felt his involvement in the Ging case yesterday and his investigation with Rex Barnett last night were helpful in *The Journal's* coverage, and even Mr. McLain offered his congratulations to Emmett for his part in reporting last night's arrests. His friend and co-worker, Charlie Strong, had volunteered to stay close to the situation for Emmett on this Christmas Eve and again tomorrow on Christmas Day while Emmett took the weekend off to return to his home at Excelsior.

The Journal would also carry a story of a fire in the Stillwater community where the A.G. Schuttinger Dry Goods and Millinery suffered a loss of twenty-thousand dollars. There was a piece on a race war in Georgia, and there would also be a three-column drawing of old Santa Claus taking a rest with his feet up near the fireplace, reading *The Journal*.

It was mid-afternoon when Emmett stepped from the streetcar at Thirteenth and Hennepin and started up the steps to the Ozark Flats. He would have time now to pack a small bag, gather some last minute Christmas presents together which he had purchased and wrapped, and be off for the late afternoon train for Excelsior. He knew Hillary was already at the depot to meet her family and they would preceed him out to the lake by a couple of hours. She would have time to keep her appointment with Doc Perkins, and they would all be settled in at home by the time Emmett arrived in the early evening. It was the first time this year that Emmett had begun to feel the Christmas spirit. Maybe it was because the Ging case was coming to its completion, or maybe it was getting away from the office for a few days and getting back to Excelsior again. Perhaps it was just the thought of being together with Hillary for a couple of days—at home! Whatever the reason, Emmett could sense the excitement of Christmas as he moved through the massive front doors and the foyer of the Ozark Flats and waited for the elevator at the end of the hallway. Young Joey was on duty and promptly took Emmett to the fifth floor.

He had no more than let himself in the front door of the apartment and closed the door behind him when he heard a noise in the bedroom. Surely Hillary couldn't still be here, he thought. If she is, she's going to be late and miss her parents at the depot. He was about to call to Hillary when a man came out of the bedroom, obviously unaware that Emmett was in the apartment. It was the janitor, Claus Blixt. He was as surprised to see Emmett as Emmett was to see him.

"What the hell are you doing here?" Emmett asked angrily.

"I just let myself in to fix the sink," Blixt answered, somewhat nervously. "I told Mrs. Markham that I'd be up to fix the leak." Blixt began to back away from Emmett towards the dining room door which led to the kitchen.

"In the bedroom?" Emmett asked in an incredulous tone of voice.

"I thought I heard something in the bedroom," Blixt replied awkwardly. "I just went into make sure there was no one here."

"There was no one, was there, Claus?"

Ozark Flats

"No—"

"Because you didn't hear any noise in there at all, did you?" Emmett sounded angry and Blixt backed into the door to the kitchen with Emmett following. "What do you have in your left hand?" Emmett pointed to Blixt's hand which held a crumpled piece of paper. In his right hand the janitor held on tightly to a large wrench.

"It's nothing," Blixt answered. But the guilty look in his face betrayed his voice.

"Let me see it," Emmett demanded. "Give it to me." He reached out to take the paper and Blixt whirled and started to dash through the kitchen toward the back door with Emmett running after him. Emmett grabbed him from behind and spun him around, grabbing the paper from his hand and backing Blixt up against the kitchen counter. The janitor stood, frozen, while Emmett opened up the note. It was for Emmett—from Hillary! "What the hell are you doing with this?" Emmett demanded. Before Blixt could answer, it dawned on Emmett.

"You were snooping, weren't you? You were looking for the money!" Then Emmett realized that it must have been Blixt who was here the other night when Hillary was alone. "It was you!" He pointed a finger at Blixt. "It was you all the time!"

"No—it wasn't me," Blixt shook his head. "Err . . . what I mean was—well . . . ." He looked terribly frightened now as Emmett faced him. "Yes . . . . it was me . . . . but I didn't kill her, I didn't realize . . . ." Blixt's voice rattled on, in a mixture of English and Swedish, uncontrollably, and Emmett realized that Blixt had misunderstood. Emmett was talking about the break-in. Blixt was talking about the murder. My God! Emmett was grasping the seriousness of the situation. Not only was Blixt the intruder the other night, he was the murderer! He had killed Kitty Ging!"

"You killed her!" Emmett shouted! Then there was silence. Blixt looked more frightened than ever and he clenched the wrench in his right hand a little tighter. In a quiet voice, Emmett spoke again. "you killed her, didn't you, Claus?" There was more silence as Blixt blinked at Emmett. "Didn't you?"

"No," Blixt replied. Then he shouted, "Noooooooooooooo!" As he screamed his defiance, he swung the heavy plumber's wrench at Emmett. Emmett ducked and the wrench slipped out of Blixt's hand

and sailed across the room, crashing through the glass in the back door of the kitchen. The flying wrench whistled by John Stavlo's ear, just as he came up the back outside stairway and reached the back door of the apartment. The stocky detective quickly burst through the back door and he and Emmett wrestled Blixt to the floor.

"How did you know to come here?" Emmett asked as he gasped for breath.

"We were sent out here to pick up Blixt and when we got to his apartment, Mrs. Blixt told us that her husband was up here fixing a leaky sink. The elevator boy told us that you had just come home," Stavlo explained. Then he remembered and asked Emmett to let Michael Hoy in the front door of the apartment. In seconds, they were both back in the kitchen to help Stavlo with Blixt.

"I think he killed Kitty Ging," Emmett said.

"We'll know soon enough," Stavlo said. We're taking him down to the West Hotel now."

"Why the West Hotel?" Emmett asked. "What's the matter with the city jail?"

"Morrissey told us to bring in Blixt but to take him to the West Hotel. I guess we're gonna meet Morissey and the mayor and the county attorney down there."

Emmett said he'd like to go along and quickly gathered the things he needed for his trip to Excelsior and followed the two detectives and Blixt out to the elevator. When Joey opened the door to the elevator, all four men stepped inside and young Joey looked frightened. As the elevator began to descend, Stavlo looked at Michael Hoy and remarked, "It's a hell of a way to spend a Christmas Eve, isn't it?"

Minnie Jacobs had just about completed the grocery shopping for the Markham's Christmas weekend and had left A.B. Show's Grocery Store. The store always advertised in the local newspaper that "If it's Good, it came from A.B. Show," which was known throughout the area for its "fancy groceries" and "special teas and coffees." It had been Hillary's favorite place to do her marketing and Minnie Jacobs

Ozark Flats

simply ordered all the things on her shopping list. Mr. Show himself, gathered the large order on the low, wide counter. Then he rung it all up on his new cash register which he bought last summer, and put the sales slip in the cash drawer to be entered later on Markhams' account at the store. Then he unfolded the special, slatted wood delivery boxes with the store's name burned into the side, and began to pack the grocery order which would be delivered by horse and sleigh to the Markham residence this afternoon. He even offered to stop down the street at the Excelsior Butcher Shop and pick up the fresh turkey which Minnie had ordered.

Minnnie left the store and crossed the street to the Excelsior post office to pick up the mail and then she would make one last stop at Newell's Drug Store before walking back to the Markham home located on the large bluff overlooking the lake, just three blocks away. The post office lobby was quite empty this hour as Minnie walked in. She went directly to the rows of small metal and glass postal boxes which lined the whole wall next to the service windows. There she found box number twenty-four, halfway up the wall, and she stooped over to work the combination, right to three o'clock, then left to six, and back to eleven o'clock on the dial.

There were two envelopes in the box—one from Hillary's older brother, Bob, now in New York, and one postmarked Wayzata, Minnesota. The return address included the name, Mr. and Mrs. George D. Wolfe. Minnie recognized the name. It's the gambler, she thought. Minnie and Madge Phelps had been the head housekeepers each summer at the White House Hotel for years and Pinky Wolfe had made the hotel his headquarters back in his gambling days. Minnie smiled. She always liked him and she had missed him these past summers since he married that Mrs. Chase. Minnie turned to leave the postoffice when Mr. Dickinson called to her.

"Got a package for Mrs. Markham, Minnie." The small man in the white shirt and the coat sweater shoved the package through the service window. Minnie thanked him for it, checked the address, and tucked it under her arm. It was for Mrs. Markham, all right—from some dressmaking shop in Minneapolis. Minnie left the post office and started down the snowy main street toward Newell's Drug Store.

23

THE ST. PAUL AND PACIFIC RAILROAD had brought the first train to Minnesota in 1862 with the inaugural trip running from St. Paul to St. Anthony. The first two locomotives in the state were the *William Crooks* and the *Edmund Rice* named for the chief engineer and the president of the railroad. After the Civil War, there was a railroad boom with a long list of lines organized and reorganized within the state. In the 1870s, the Minneapolis and St. Louis, the Chicago, Milwaukee, and St. Paul, and the Northern Pacific were established. And the Northern Pacific was extended to the Pacific in 1883.

James J. Hill, the Empire Builder, reorganized the St. Paul and Pacific as the St. Paul, Minneapolis, and Manitoba in 1879. He also founded the Minneapolis Union Railway in 1881 to run a line from the Union Stockyards in the midway district to Minneapolis' warehouse and milling district. To this end he built the Union Depot at the foot of Hennepin avenue just downstream from the suspension bridge and the great stone arch bridge which became his monument and the symbol of Minneapolis industry for generations.

In 1889, Hill established the Great Northern Railway Company to finance the construction of the Manitoba to Seattle and, eventually, to operate all his railroads. The Pacific extension was completed only last year.

Earlier in this very year, the famous Pullman strike had caused a furor and a general strike that brought in Federal troops and countless court proceedings. The Pullman cars had been named after their founder and inventor, George M. Pullman, who had formed the Pullman Palace Car Company in 1867 and had a virtual monopoly on sleeping cars being leased to the railroads. The *Pioneer* was the first of the sleeping cars known as *Pullmans* in 1863 and by 1868, George Pullman had developed the dining car and then the vestibule car.

The train from St. Louis, which included those famous Pullman sleepers, arrived in Minneapolis almost an hour behind schedule and Hillary waited quietly in the crowded lobby of the spacious Union Station as passengers arrived on other incoming trains for Christmas. The depot was also filled with businessmen, couples and families, departing for small towns outside of Minneapolis for the holiday weekend. The lovely Mrs. Markham had regained her composure after saying goodbye to Rex Barnett. She knew it would be difficult to tell him how she felt about him, but she also knew what she was doing was right. Now that it was over, she hoped to keep Rex Barnett as a good friend, a close friend. And although she knew she still loved him, the romantic feelings she had discovered for him over these past few days would now be put in proper perspective.

She looked up at the big clock on the wall of the depot behind the reservations counters. She didn't realize the time had gone by so quickly and now it was time to greet her family. She crossed the lobby floor and passed through the doors at the far end of the depot and down a short stairway to the train docks. Arrangements had already been made to have her luggage and Christmas packages placed aboard the train when it arrived in Minneapolis. A half-hour later, it would be pulling out of the Minneapolis depot and heading west, through Excelsior and on to South Dakota.

It was cold down on the train docks and Hillary found herself moving against the flow of people who had just got off the five-car passenger train from St. Louis and were now crowding toward the depot. Hillary pushed through the crowd and kept a lookout for the

Ozark Flats

Pullman car with the title, "Hiawatha" on the side. Even before she saw the lettering, she looked up and saw her two brothers' faces pressed up against the glass window. She shouted a greeting to them and they smiled, excitedly, and waved back to their older sister. At the far end of the car, a porter helped Hillary up the small portable step and then on to the steps of the Pullman car. Hillary hadn't realized how noisy—and cold—it was until she opened the door and went inside the long railroad car. The minute the door shut behind her, it was quiet—and warm. That same peace had now come over Hillary and she had no more than got through the door when she saw Frances Blair.

"Oh, Mom. I can't tell you how glad I am to see you." She could see the rest of her family coming down the aisle now, too, and she rushed to put her arms around her mother.

"Merry Christmas, dear," Frances whispered in Hillary's ear.

When Rex Barnett returned to the Central Police Station after taking Hillary to the train depot, he found John Morrissey at his desk. Morrissey quickly filled Rex in on what had happened since Morrissey went to visit Adry Hayward a second time this morning and told Rex of Levi Stewart's visit to the County Court House to confront the elder Hayward brother.

"When I got back here, Vern called the mayor over at the City Hall and he told us to pick up Claus Blixt and take him over to the West Hotel where we could interrogate him without a lot of reporters around." Morrissey went on. "So I sent Stavlo and Hoy out to the Ozark Flats and wouldn't you know they'd find Emmett Markham confronting Blixt up in the Markhams' apartment."

"What the hell was Blixt doing up there?" Rex asked.

"Seems like he went up to the fifth floor to fix a leaky sink but thought he'd look around for Kitty Ging's money. That's when Emmett Markham walked in on him."

"Then it was Blixt who broke into Hillary's"—Rex caught

himself—"I mean, into the Markham apartment the other night, then, wasn't it?"

"That's exactly what Markham thought," Morrissey continued. "But Blixt wasn't having any of it and he swung a plumber's wrench at Markham! It flew out of his hands, fortunately missing Markham, and crashed through the kitchen door, just as Stavlo arrived."

Rex smiled. "That would have been more than John could take after getting the wind knocked out of him yesterday."

"Anyway, they've taken Blixt over to the West Hotel and that's where I'm headed right now. Vern just called to tell me that he had sent Stavlo and Hoy back to the Ozark Flats. This time Hoy is gong to bring Mrs. Blixt down to the West Hotel, and Stavlo is going to make another arrest out there—this time an Ole Erickson."

"Who the hell is Ole Erickson?" Rex asked, unbelievingly.

"I guess he's a former workhouse prisoner who needed a place to stay and Blixt put him up in the furnace room in the basement of the Ozark Flats. I won't know any more until I get over to the West Hotel. They're all up there on the top floor now, quesioning Blixt."

"Do you want me to go with you?" Rex asked.

"No—I think it would be better if you'd stay here at the station. We'll need to question this Erickson when they bring him in, and I'd like to have you here for that."

John Morrissey put on his overcoat and started for the front entrance of the station. Just as he was about to leave, however, he turned back to Rex and smiled.

"You can call it Hillary's apartment if you want to. I don't mind." Then he smiled again and left.

As the M. and St. L. train bound for South Dakota was pulling out of the Union Station, Hillary looked out the window of the Pullman suite in which the Blair family had travelled on their trip from St. Louis. Being a vice president of a railroad had its advantages—particularly when it came to travel accomodations. Tom and Frances Blair had been visiting with their daughter while the boys were somewhere out in the car or in the next car, watching the excitement of the train leaving the Minneapolis station. As the train began to move, Hillary could see another passenger train loading on the next track, just across the train dock. She could see lights and forms but could not distinguish faces. She hoped that wherever their destinations, the passengers would not have to go too far so they could be home for Christmas. Riding the train was no way to spend Christmas, she thought.

In the third passenger car of the Great Northern's afternoon train to Chicago, two men had just been shown to their Pullman compartment. The porter hauled in their luggage—four large suitcases—and was awarded with a generous tip. The bill would pass through four sets of hands before the bank would finally discover that it was counterfeit.

"Thank you Sirrrr," the porter said, gratefully acknowledging the gratuity. The two men hardly noticed him but went about taking off their coats and getting settled for the trip to Chicago. The larger man finally sat down and pulled out a cigar as he looked out of the window of the Pullman car. It had been a trying day for him. In fact, it had been a bad week for him and he was glad to get settled in for the train ride.

The smaller man neatly folded his overcoat and placed it in the corner of the seat across from his cigar-smoking companion. Then he sat down to read the afternoon papers which he had carried on board.

The large man finally spoke, just as the railroad car lurched and then started to slowly move. They were on their way.

"Well, Walter," he said between puffs, "I don't know where that Kitty Ging put the money, but if our friend Harry has it, I have a feeling that he's never gonna get a chance to spend it."

The little man nodded in agreement and started to read *The Minneapolis Journal*. He still had his bowler hat on. It was brand new.

24

WHEN JOHN MORRISSEY arrived at the West Hotel on the afternoon of Christmas Eve, he took the elevator to the eighth floor where a uniformed patrolman met him and escorted him down the hall to room number 831. There he found his chief, Vern Smith, along with the County Attorney, Frank Nye, and a court stenographer. Sitting in an overstuffed chair in the middle of the room was Claus A. Blixt, the janitor of the Ozark Flats. He wore a coat and pants that didn't match. His shirt was buttoned at the neck, and he wore no tie. In addition to his mustache, his face was covered with a stubble of a beard. He was brought to the West Hotel directly from the apartment where he had been subdued by John Stavlo and Emmett Markham. Both Stavlo and Hoy had been dispatched again, this time to bring Mrs. Blixt back to the hotel, and to pick up one Ole Erickson and take him down to the Central Police Station.

Morrissey was tired. He had been on the go since last night and seemed to pick up momentum as he went along today—with the arrests, court appearances, and his visit with Adry Hayward late this morning at the county jail. His idea of bringing the distinguished Levi M. Stewart down to confront Adry had been brilliant, and Adry had finally told the detective what he could about the murder.

Adry's story took him back to last summer when Harry had tried to hire a hackie to drive his buggy—and Catherine Ging—into Lake Calhoun. When that plan didn't work out, Harry approached Adry with other plans to take Kitty Ging's life. Just to test his older brother, Harry even offered Adry a hundred dollars to simply shoot someone—anyone! Adry apparently turned down the challenge, but Harry was persistent. He told his brother "there was big money to be made" and then upped the ante to two thousand dollars if Adry would kill Kitty Ging. Harry even offered suggestions as to how Adry could do the deed, including taking Kitty for a ride and faking an accident with the buggy; or getting her tangled in the reins and staging a runaway accident; or just plain taking her out in a rig and shooting her.

Despite Adry's loyalty to his brother, he could not bring himself to do what Harry was asking of him, and even though Harry gave up on Adry as the means to carry out the murder, Harry continued to talk unguardedly in front of Adry of his plans for Kitty's death, as though Adry was not fully capable of understanding what was going on. Adry told John Morrissey that just a week ago, Harry had taken Kitty for a buggy ride in a rig from Goosman's Palace Livery Stable. He intended to bludgeon her to death while they were out for their ride and then use the runaway horse ruse and overturn the buggy to make it all look like an accident. But the Saturday night crowds spoiled Harry's plans. There was just no opportunity to kill her, and Kitty and Harry returned to the Ozark Flats.

Vern Smith and the county attorney were both glad to see John Morrissey. He had been involved with the case from the very beginning and after all of the false alarms and dead ends, Morrissey had been persistent in seeking a solution to the notorious murder. The confession Adry made to him had brought them to where they were now, here on the top floor of the West Hotel. Vern asked the detective if he would take over the questioning for awhile and John removed his overcoat and hat and finally confronted Claus Blixt.

"Tell me, Mr. Blixt," the detective started out, "just what were you doing up in the Markhams' apartment when Mr. Markham happened to come home?"

"I went up to fix the sink," Blixt replied.

"In the bedroom?"

"Well, no. I thought I heard a noise in there so I went to see what it was."

"You did not hear any noise in there, Mr. Blixt," Morrissey corrected the janitor. "You were snooping around, weren't you? You were looking for the money."

"Well——, I——"

"You were looking for the money the other night, too, weren't you, when you let yourself in the back of the Markhams' apartment."

"I didn't take anything," Blixt apologized. "I was just looking around."

"Why did you kill Catherine Ging?" Morrissey snapped.

The question took Blixt by surprise. He sat still and didn't move. He looked as if he were trying to find the right answer to a quiz. "I didn't ki———"

"You know that your wife is on her way down here to tell us that, in fact, you weren't home all evening long on the night of the murder. That in fact, you were gone for some time. Isn't that right, Mr. Blixt?"

The janitor began to squirm a little. He hadn't planned on his wife being questioned again. The thought of Julia being questioned made him feel guilty again. She had already lied for him, telling the police he had been home all evening on the night of the murder.

"As a matter of fact, Mr. Blixt," we've also picked up a Mr. Ole Erickson and taken him down to the Central Police Station. He's either going to tell us what he knows about all of this, or, he too, will be charged with murder."

With the mention of Ole Erickson, Claus Blixt seemed to turn pale. He was about to speak when John Morrissey spoke to him again.

"You might as well tell us what happened. Adry Hayward has already told us everything he knows about this, and we know that Harry didn't kill her. He was seen at the Grand Opera House that night. It looks as if you may take all the blame, Mr. Blixt."

The thought that Harry Hayward might not be blamed for the murder was more than Blixt could bear. Everything had finally caught up with him and there was no place to hide, no Harry Hayward to talk everyone out of this, and no whiskey to help him forget.

He buried his head in his hands and began to cry. It was all over. "He made me do it," he sobbed.

What followed seemed like a repeat of Adry Hayward's encounters with his brother. It had started last June when Harry Hayward hired Blixt to hold up the buggy in which Kitty and Miss Veters were riding. It was Blixt and a friend who had taken what little money and jewelry the women had that night. Later he turned it all over to Harry Hayward. Then it was another of Harry Hayward's schemes—this time a test for Blixt who was provoked into going out and setting fire to a barn. After that, Harry pronounced that Claus Blixt was ready to put Kitty Ging away. Harry explained it all to the not-too-bright janitor—the counterfeit money, the loans, and most important of all, the insurance policies. Blixt, too, told of Harry's aborted attempt to kill Kitty himself, just a week ago.

"When he came to me on Tuesday he told me that I had to kill her that night." Blixt rubbed his hands together, nervously, and went on. "I told him I didn't think I could do it, but Mr. Hayward said he'd kill me—and Julia—if I didn't go through with it. Then he gave me a bottle of whiskey and told me to drink it all. And when he looked at me with those cold eyes, I knew I had to go through with it."

Then Blixt led John Morrissey and the rest of those in the eighth-floor room through the fateful evening. "We left the apartment and walked over to Kenwood—Mr. Hayward followed me—and we met Miss Ging, waiting in her rig. Then he told her that my working as a janitor at the Ozark Flats was only a dodge and that I was part of the counterfeit gang, and that we would meet some others over by Lake Calhoun. He said it was too dangerous to be seen with her, so he'd meet us there and switch rigs—just in case anyone was following us. Then I got into Miss Ging's buggy and drove off.

Blixt was sweating as he continued the steady stream of confession. Once he got started, the words just kept on pouring out. "I drove her down Hennepin to Lake street and then headed for Lake Calhoun. When we got to the lake, she keep lookin' around for Mr. Hayward. I could have killed her ten times, but I just couldn't. Then she looked out of those side-curtains just one last time. And I shot her!"

The room was silent. No one said a word. Then Blixt whispered. "She lurched toward me and I got scared and gave her a few whacks with the gun. After that I put the carriage robe around her, pressed it up over her face, and drove a little further. Then I pushed her out of the buggy. A front wheel rolled over her and I pulled the Buckskin mare up and got out and laid the carriage robe down on the ground and rolled her body on to the robe. Then I got back in the rig and drove like hell for a few blocks. After that, I got out and slapped the mare on the ass and sent her on her way. I knew she'd go back to the livery stable. Jag ar dumte. I had to walk." Again the room was silent. Blixt shook his head. "Himmle, but I remember her eyes!"

John Morrissey's voice was more sympathetic now. "What did you do with the gun?"

Blixt replied that after the murder, he walked to Hastings and Dakota on the railroad tracks and stopped at a switchman's shanty to see an old friend. But the friend wasn't there, so he walked down the tracks to Twenty-seventh street and took a streetcar down Lyndale to Washington avenue. Then he walked a few blocks and took another streetcar to Franklin avenue to visit another friend and found no one home. That sent him back to Washington avenue again—to Swanson's bar—where he shook dice for awhile and eventually walked up Hennepin to the Ozark Flats. When he got back to the apartment house, he took the gun to Harry Hayward's apartment, cleaned it, and put it under Harry's pillow in the bedroom, just as he had been instructed to do. Then Blixt went downstairs to his own basement apartment.

"What did you do with the money?" Morrissey asked quietly.

"She didn't have any. I took her purse but there wasn't anything in it."

"You'd better tell us the truth. We'll find it, you know," he said firmly. Then he almost whispered in Blixt's ear. "Your future depends on your cooperation with us."

"She didn't have any!" he said in frustrated tones. "I would have left town if I had the money." He paused. "Mr. Hayward thought she might have hidden the money close by—across the hall, maybe, in Markham's apartment. He told me to look there."

John Morrissey turned to Vern Smith and the county attorney, Frank Nye. "I think we have enough for now," he said in matter-of-fact tones. "I suggest we take him over and lock him up for the night."

The police chief agreed and Claus Blixt was taken from the room by Michael Hoy who had been waiting outside. Hoy took Blixt downstairs, through the billiard room of the hotel and out the side entrance to a hack, and they were off for the Central Police Station. Vern Smith and the county attorney spoke in quiet tones in the corner of the room for a few minutes and then Frank Nye left. Mayor Eustis was dumbfounded. He had watched the entire proceedings without saying a word. Up to now he had been leading the investigation and had personally taken charge of the case over these past few days. But he had sat by in silence, watching John Morrissey question Claus Blixt, and the mayor realized that Vern Smith and his men knew what they were doing. They didn't need the mayor to get in their way. John Morrissey was a real professional, Bill Eustis told himself. And he was glad it was over.

Morrissey talked to Mrs. Blixt for a short time and then had her taken back to the Ozark Flats. Before he left the hotel, he also took time to visit with Emmett Markham. There had been no other reporters at the hotel, but there would be plenty of newsmen over at the Central Station and they'd all have the story for tomorrow's editions. Yet Morrissey felt some obligation to Emmett Markham. After all, Emmett did discover Blixt in his apartment, and he had made the first accusation about the murder. He had also helped subdue Blixt when Stavlo arrived at the Ozark Flats. So John Morrissey spent a little additional time answering Emmett's questions. Then he headed back to Lockup Alley.

Emmett Markham simply had too much material, too many notes, and too many personal experiences to turn over the story of Blixt and the murder of Kitty Ging to anyone else. So he went back to Newspaper Row to write the story himself for tomorrow's *Minneapolis Journal*. When he got back to his office, he found Charlie Strong and asked for his help with the re-write, and then he placed a call to the police station where he finally reached Rex Barnett.

Rex filled the newspaperman in on what had happened while Claus Blixt was being questioned. Detective John Stavlo had brought

Ozark Flats

Ole Erickson into the station and it hadn't taken long for Erickson to tell the police about his small part in the crime.

"It seems that Erickson had made some money shovelling snow, left town the morning after the murder and took some of Blixt's bloody clothes with him to Iowa," Rex told Emmett over the phone. Then he went on, explaining that Erickson's wife worked in a hotel at Iowa Falls and that his wife and his sister washed a bundle of clothes for him before he returned to Minneapolis.

"He just told us that he hocked the clothes over on Washington avenue and we probably won't be able to get in there until sometime tomorrow," Rex explained on the phone. "I guess the rest of the clothing was burned in the furnace at the Ozark Flats."

Emmett checked out a few more details with the detective and thanked him for his help. "I'm supposed to be on the train for Excelsior right now," Emmett explained, "but I've got to finish this story for tomorrow's edition before I can get away." Then he added, "Thanks again, Rex, and have a Merry Christmas."

"Merry Christmas to you, too," Rex replied, "——and have a happy anniversary!" Then he hung up.

Emmett and Charlie Strong started work on the story and Charlie took time to dig out the pictures of Catherine Ging, the Hayward brothers, and one of Claus Blixt. *The Journal* had pictures of just about everyone living in the Ozark Flats or connected with the murder case. Now was the time to use them. When they finished, Emmett went over the material with Charlie again. Some preliminary headlines were also written to accompany the murder story. Emmett was satisfied. So was J.S. McLain who had gone home early in the afternoon to enjoy Christmas Eve, and who had come back to help out.

Tomorrow's headlines in *The Journal* would read:

MURDER WILL OUT

**And the Mystery of How Poor Catherine Was
Killed is Solved at Last.**

Ozark Flats

A Most Hellish Conspiracy—Harry Hayward
Sought Medical Advice on How to Kill.

Adry A. Hayward, the Least Guilty, Breaks
Down Under the Load and Confesses.

Blixt, the Janitor, Fired the Fatal Shot—A
Bloody Handkerchief Found.

Ole Erickson, an Ex-Workhouse Prisoner,
Arrested with Blixt as Accomplice.

Emmett took one last look at his story for *The Journal* tomorrow. Then he'd leave for the station to catch the last train to Excelsior.

The murderous combine that did Catherine Ging to death on Tuesday night is broken.

Adry Hayward, the least guilty of this bloody band of assassins, was helped last night on being confronted with strong evidence of guilt, and gave up the story.

The confession makes it evident that Harry T. Hayward is the coldest-blooded murderer in criminal history. It was he who deliberately planned the murder in order that he might realize Miss Ging's insurance.

Claus A. Blixt, engineer of the Ozark Flats, was the actual murderer. Ole Erickson, and ex-workhouse prisoner, and his assistant at the Ozark was his accomplice.

Hayward instructed his accomplice as to where the shot would be fired and in what manner the revolver should be held so that the shot might be surely fatal.

The testimony of a physician will be produced by the prosecution that Hayward, recently, in conversation questioned him very closely as to the vital points of the human body. The conversation on this topic was persisted in by Hayward in such a degree that it excited the doctor's curiosity. Before the interview closed, Hayward asked the doctor direct:

"Now if you were going to shoot me, for instance, how would you proceed in order to make my death certain and instantaneous?"

Blixt was arrested yesterday and is now in jail. A workhouse prisoner named Ole Erickson, an accomplice in the affair, and the man who disposed of the bloody clothes worn by Blixt, is also under arrest. Erickson took the clothes to Iowa Falls the morning after the murder and returned yesterday morning. He had the bloody clothes washed while in Iowa where his wife is employed in a hotel. On his return he sold a portion of the clothes to an old clothing dealer on Washington avenue. It has been discovered that some of the garments were burned in the Ozark Flats furnace.

Blixt was taken in charge by detectives yesterday afternoon. He was questioned by the police and Mayor Eustis in a room on the top floor of the West Hotel to avoid attracting public attention. After a part of the afternoon had elapsed, it was believed that a strong case had been made out against Blixt and Erickson.

Blixt's wife was also brought in. There was no cessation of questioning until the announcement was made that the real murderer of Kitty Ging had been found. Blixt was the man. At the time this announcement was made, Blixt was already under arrest and on his way to the lockup. Ole Erickson, Blixt's accomplice, was also jailed. The later was searched at the station and a key was taken from him. Mrs. Blixt was compelled to accompany a detective to the Ozark Flats in search of evidence.

Blixt, the murderer, was formerly a streetcar driver in Minneapolis. The coat he wore when a driver was the one in which he committed the murder. This garment was handed over to Erickson after the crime and he took it to Iowa Falls where the blood was washed off and he wore the coat back.

When confronted with the evidence that had been secured, Adry Hayward weakened and made a confession yesterday. He declared that he had been forced into whatever complicity he has had in the crime by his brother Harry. He declares that Harry planned the affair with great deliberateness and fixed everything so that both he and Adry would be able to prove their whereabouts on the night of the crime. Adry declares that he fought desperately with his brother to prevent the commission of such a crime, but admits that he was so strongly influenced by his brother that the influence almost amounted to hypnotic control. Harry Hayward threatened to kill his brother if he refused assistance in the plot and the brother feared him.

Before the murder Adry went to Levi M. Stewart and made the statement that he believed his brother was going to commit a terrible crime. He detailed the story of Miss Ging's life insurance and went into details that pointed strongly to a plot of some kind, but Mr. Stewart could not believe that there was such a monstrous conspiracy against Miss Ging, and told Adry that while he considered Harry Hayward a rogue, he did not believe him a fool, and that it was not possible he would entangle himself in such an affair.

Adry remained convinced that his brother intended committing the murder, and he endeavored by threats, exploitation and entreaty to dissuade him from such a course. The threats made by Harry Hayward toward his brother were indeed earnest, and the man making this confession feared for his own life. Adry Hayward declares that his brother exercised a perfect control of the actions of the murdered girl. It was a sort of mental subjection, in which both Adry and the young woman were included. The brother believes that his control extended in part to other persons implicated in the affair.

Adry Hayward's confession in full will not come out intil it has been submitted to the grand jury. It tells the story of this crime from its inception by Harry Hayward, and points out how the girl herself unwittingly aided the murderers in their design at every step.

Julia Blixt, the wife of the murderer, gave up sufficient evidence in her examination at the West Hotel to warrant the arrest of the man Erickson. He put on the air of bravado when pulled out of bed at the Ozark Flats but was overwhelmed when he learned how much of the plot had been unearthed. A few articles of clothing were confiscated and spots of blood were found in a clothes closet in Harry Hayward's room.

In the bedroom, a Detective Howard found two revolvers belonging to Harry Hayward. One was a double-barreled Derringer and the other a 38-caliber Colt revolver. Several cases of cartridges were also taken. In the examination of Harry's clothes, nothing incriminating was discovered. There were a half-dozen letters from young ladies in the city but none bearing the handwriting of the murdered woman.

No one is permitted to see the Hayward boys except their attorneys and relatives. W.E. Hale was an early caller at the county jail and remained in their cell for a long time. It is reported that Harry Hayward has admitted that Adry may be sincere in his confession, in view of the information in his possession. Harry, however, still stoutly denies all connection with the crime.

Christmas Eve

25

WHEN HILLARY MARKHAM and her family arrived in Excelsior, it was late afternoon. Tom Blair had already made arrangements through the M. and St. L. to have a rig—a sleigh—from the Bennett Livery Stable waiting at the Excelsior Depot to take all of them and their luggage to the Markham home. The sleigh pulled away from the depot where depot agent Herb Johnson had to wait for one more train to arrive before he could close things up for Christmas Eve. The jingle of the sleigh-bells on the Bennett team gave Hillary and the Blairs a real feeling of Christmas as the horses jogged down Excelsior's Water street, the main street of the small town. The rig stopped at the far end of Water street and Hillary climbed out of the sleigh and told her parents that she would meet them at home in a little while. Minnie Jacobs was at the house fixing supper and she would help the Blairs get settled. In the meantime, Hillary kept her appointment with Doc Perkins who had served as the Markham's family doctor over the past seven years. Hillary didn't get out to Excelsior very often and although this was not the most convenient time, she had made the appointment some time ago.

When she left Doc Perkins' office on the second floor over Newell's Drug Store, she started up the hill on Second street toward home. It was not easy walking, she thought, as she trudged through the snow. There hadn't been much plowing in Excelsior and she followed the tracks left by the wagons and sleighs in the middle of the street. The hill seemed steeper than Hillary remembered. She laughed at herself. It had to be the deep snow. At the top of the hill she paused. Home was only a couple blocks away now—just down the hill and over a half-block to the big two-story house that overlooked Excelsior Bay. But something made her stop. Instead of turning right towards the lake, Hillary swung off to the left and walked a long block to the next corner, then turned left again and stopped halfway down the block. She was in front of Trinity Episcopal Chapel.

The beautiful little church was the home parish for the Markham family. It also held many memories for her. She had attended summer services there with her family even before she had met Emmett. She and Emmett had gone to church there before they were married. Jamie had been baptised there and would be confirmed there. Hillary felt a quiet, inner surge of faith. She had been eager to get home. Their home in Excelsior had been uppermost in her mind for a long time now, and especially during these past few days. And she had something important to tell her mother. Yet something had drawn her to Trinity Chapel and she stood there in the dusk, just looking at the church. It would be good to be back here tonight at the Christmas Eve service near midnight. She could visualize the chancel decorated with Christmas trees and poinsettias, the priest, the processional with the vested choir and the acolytes in their bright red cassocks and white cottas, the familiar Christmas hymns and carols, and the liturgy which she loved. Though the parish wasn't that large, the church would be full tonight. No other church in Excelsior would be holding midnight services tonight and there would be lots of visitors and members of other congregations. She realized it was getting late, but she stood there in the middle of the street for just a minute longer. "Thank you God," she whispered. Then she started back up the street. Somehow the walking seemed a little easier. It was starting to snow. It would be a white Christmas!

Ozark Flats

The gas lights out in front of the entrance to The Fountainhead were dark, and early on this Christmas Eve, the street was deserted. Inside, the main bar on the first floor was closed and only a few lights were on in the lounge. Upstairs, however, it was a different story. The lights in the main dining room were bright and the Christmas decorations glistened. A portable bar had been opened, some musicians were standing in the middle of the room playing Christmas Carols, and eight or nine round tables had each been set for six to eight places with fresh white cloths, red and green napkins, fresh candles, and place cards. At each table setting was a small gift box, beautifully wrapped, with either green or gold ribbon and bows. The music was almost drowned out by the conversations of the small groups of well-dressed people huddled in small clusters of conversation, and all in a festive mood.

It was Big Glady's Christmas Eve Dinner for her employees, mostly dancing girls. Gone were the skimpy corsets and black opera hose. All of the young women were in evening gowns of the latest styles, in satin and taffeta and velvet, and in all the colors of the rainbow. The bartenders, the bouncers, waiters, busboys—everyone who worked for Big Glady—were dressed in their fine clothes, at least the finest they had. The Christmas wine was flowing and they would all sit down soon to Glady's traditional Christmas Eve Dinner. This night it would be prime rib. After dinner, they would all go their separate ways. Some would go home to their parents, or to apartments or rooming houses which they shared or lived in alone. A few girls had brought their husbands or boyfriends, and two or three women even brought along their small children. The guests began to find places to sit, and the wine at the table was poured. Then Glady, dressed in a bright green satin gown, her hair piled atop her head with a sparkling diamond comb holding it in place, tapped on a glass with a piece of silverware, and the room became quiet.

"We thank God for this chance to celebrate part of our Christmas

together, and for the food which we are about to have." Then she raised her wine glass in a toast. "I love you all! Have a Merry Christmas!"

Christmas Eve supper in the county jail was not the kind of meal that Harry Hayward nor his brother Adry were used to. It had consisted of liver and onions and black coffee, served on tin trays. Though the brothers were in separate cells, they were allowed to eat together. William Hayward had come to visit his sons late in the afternoon, and he and Mrs. Hayward would be back tomorrow. The brothers hardly spoke during the supper and Adry was taken back to his own cell after the meal. In four days, Harry Hayward had become the archcriminal of Minneapolis. In the quietness of the third-floor cell, he was at least thankful for one thing. He didn't have to worry about Hudson and Farber anymore. Not for awhile, anyway.

Julia Blixt had been busy. She was questioned at the West Hotel and then went back to the Ozark Flats so that a city detective could look around the Blixt's basement apartment. Afterwards, she had called the Rev. Mr. Folk and the two of them came to visit Claus Blixt. The minister had also made a call for Mrs. Blixt to Cannon Falls to Sheriff Anderson and another friend of theirs to ask them to visit Claus as soon as they could and to help him if at all possible. The frightened Claus Blixt and his tearful wife had prayed together before she left his cell on this Christmas Eve.

Ozark Flats

At the Ozark Flats, Roger and Florence Wilhelm had invited Francis Gordon Kelly from across the hall to their apartment for a glass of wine. The Wilhelms had attended the funeral of Catherine Ging yesterday afternoon and admired the young lawyer for volunteering as a pallbearer to represent the residents of the Ozark Flats. Later, the young red-head would leave to spend Christmas with his finace and her parents in south Minneapolis.

The apartment of Adry Hayward was dark. Charlotte had spent some time with the senior Haywards and had visited her husband at the county jail. She would spend Christmas with her parents.

Up in their fourth-floor apartment, the Goosman's were hosting a quiet dinner for some members of Mr. Goosman's family.

Mr. and Mrs. William Hayward would spend a sad Christmas Eve. Their old friend, Levi Stewart, had stopped by for a short visit with the Haywards and brought with him a holiday gift, a basket of walnuts and some fruit. He did not mention his letter to Mayor Eustis but told the Haywards that he was sorry for what had happened and that he was proud of Adry and the way he had told the truth. When he left the Ozark Flats and climbed back into his carriage, he sat there for a moment in the quietness of Christmas Eve and wept.

Mayor William H. Eustis and Police Chief Vern Smith had left the West Hotel and would be off for their own homes to celebrate Christmas with their own families. They had stood outside of the West Hotel and congratulated each other on getting through these past few days and bringing the investigation of the Ging murder to a conclusion. As one writer would later record, "without recourse to fingerprints, instruments of scientific analysis, or crime laboratories, the Minneapolis police found their murderer in four days." Vern Smith agreed that there would be busy times ahead at the coming trials, and Bill Eustis admitted that he would have some peace of mind and a great deal of satisfaction when he completed his term of office as mayor at the end of next week. In the meantime, they could all rest a little easier over this holiday.

Ozark Flats

Detective John Morrissey was already at home for Christmas Eve with his wife and five children. John Stavlo and his wife would spend Christmas Eve with her brother's family, and Michael Hoy was the last to leave the deserted Central Police Station to go home for Christmas Eve and the holiday weekend. Only the bachelor officers would draw the holiday duty.

Hillary arrived home to find Frances Blair already busy in the kitchen helping Minnie Jacobs with the Christmas Eve dinner. Tom Blair and the boys were unpacking and Minnie told Hillary that a couple of letters had come in the mail today.
"And, oh yes, there's a package for you from some dress shop in Minneapolis," Minnie told her.
"I wonder what that could be." Hillary frowned. She couldn't remember buying any dresses that would have been sent out here to Excelsior.
"The letters are on the mantle in the living room," Minnie said, "and I put the package under the Christmas Tree." Then she added. "It seemed the thing to do."
Hillary went through the short hallway that led from the kitchen past the dining room and into the large living room. The room featured mahogany wall panelling and large dark beams across the ceiling. A huge fireplace with a roaring fire took up most of one side of the room, and oversized windows looked out on Excelsior Bay and the lower lake of Minnetonka from the high bluff. In the far corner of the room was a Christmas tree—about an eight-foot pine—but it had not yet been decorated. It was held in place by a wood frame base which had been fashioned by Mr. Aldritt when he brought the tree in from out in the country west of town. Hillary found the letters and opened them immediately. The first brought Christmas greetings from her brother Bob in New York. The second was an invitation from George and Jenny Wolfe to spend the New Year's weekend with them at Fairmont, their family estate over on Smith's Bay. Then Hillary found the lone package under the tree, wrapped in brown

paper and addressed to her. The return address read, "309 Syndicate Building, Minneapolis, Minnesota."

Hillary sat down in a loveseat near the fireplace and carefully removed the wrapping paper and opened the package which looked to be about large enough for a jacket or sweater. On the top of some white tissue paper was an envelope with "Hillary" written across the front. Inside was a short note which Hillary held up to the light from the fire and read.

> *Dear Hillary,*
> *I have enjoyed this afternoon with you more than you can imagine. My life has been filled with business and dealings and our lunch and little shopping spree reminded me of what nice people there are in the world and what a family can mean. I just realized that I haven't had a close friend since my sister, Julia, and I were youngsters back home in Auburn, New York. I feel that I have found a new friend today. I have new business ventures to explore, and I must entrust this box to our new friendship for a few days. Please keep it in a safe place for me. When the Christmas holidays are over, you and Emmett will have to come to dinner and tell me more about your home. Excelsior sounds like a lovely place.*
>
> *Your friend,*
> *Kitty*

Hillary was touched by the contents of the note. Then she opened the tissue paper in the box and gasped. It was filled with bundles of money!

26

THE 6:14 TO EXCELSIOR was just a little late in getting out of Minneapolis and Emmett Markham was grateful. It had taken him a little longer to finish up part of tomorrow's work at *The Journal* for Charlie Strong's holiday skeleton crew, and he almost missed the train, even though it was behind schedule. It was a pleasant surprise to run into Andy Ross at the ticket counter in the Minneapolis Union depot. Andy's plans had changed since they last talked and now the young hotel man was off to Excelsior to spend Christmas Eve with Rose Fortier Stark and her two sons. Andy had just come from visiting with his parents at the Nicollet House and on the trip out from the city, Emmett told Andy about the latest developments in the Ging murder case. Then they talked with anticipation about getting together tomorrow.

Excelsior's Water street was quiet and lonely when the last of passengers stepped off the train at the Excelsior depot.

"Herb Johnson can go home now," Emmett jokingly referred to the depot agent. Andy Ross laughed.

Ozark Flats

The two of them walked down the main street in the dark. The stores were closed. The newspaper office was dark. Even the street lights looked dim as they reflected off the light snow falling. At the corner of Water street and Second street, Andy looked off to his right and noticed that up in the next block the long front porch of the Sampson House Hotel was still ablaze with lights. The only other place open was Newell's Drug Store, and E.L. Newell would be closing his doors shortly, only to be open again for a short while on Christmas morning.

The two men stood there in the intersection for a moment before they went their separate ways.

"Wish Rose a Merry Christmas for me," Emmett told Andy.

"I'll do that, Emmett." He paused. He wished Emmett a Merry Christmas and then added, "It's nice to be home again, isn't it?"

Emmett hiked up the hill and then down towards the lake to his own house on the bluff. To save time, he went up the back alley and entered the house through the back door where cordwood was stacked on the back porch. When he opened the door to the kitchen, Frances was there and they embraced as they greeted each other. There were tears in Frances' eyes as she stepped back from Emmett. He wasn't sure just what she meant when she told him that she and her daughter had had a good visit and that "everything's going to be all right now."

Frances told Emmett that Tom Blair and the two Blair boys had taken Jamie for a hike down by the Excelsior Commons and the lake.

"They'll be back soon for supper. Hillary's in the living room."

Emmett shouted, "Merry Christmas!" to Minnie who was busy at the large kitchen range, and he moved through the hallway to the living room. There was Hillary. She looked radiant in the firelight. The two embraced. Then Hillary stepped back and reached down to pick up the package and the note under the tree.

"Here, dear." She handed him the note. "This came in the mail today."

Emmett read Kitty's letter. Then he looked to the package as Hillary opened it.

"My God!" Emmett blinked. "It's the money! It's the counterfeit money! Thousands of dollars of counterfeit money!"

"Green Goods!" Hillary exclaimed without even thinking. "Of course! That's what Harry Hayward called it that day at lunch!"

"It's what everybody has been looking for!" Emmett said. "I'll call Rex Barnett. He and Morrissey will be glad to know where it is—and that it will be safe over the weekend." Emmett set the package back under the tree and turned to Hillary again.

"You look beautiful," he told her as the two embraced again.

Hillary whispered in his ear. "I have another surprise—a special anniversary gift for you." She held on tight. Then smiled. "We're going to have a baby! I just came from Doc Perkins' office a little while ago. Near the end of June."

Emmett hugged her again. "I've got an anniversary gift for you, too, dear." He reached into his suitcoat pocket and gave her a small gift box with Christmas ribbon. She stood in front of the fireplace and opened it. Then she began to cry and threw her arms around her husband's neck. In her hand was the gift—a small gold cross and chain.

Through the tears she whispered, "Happy Anniversary, dear. I love you!"

Emmett held her tight. "Merry Christmas!"

St. Mark's Episcopal Church was located in the heart of downtown Minneapolis on the south side of Sixth street between Hennepin and Nicollet, and the church was filled for the midnight Christmas Eve service. The organ began the processional and the choir, acolytes and the priest started down the center aisle toward the chancel. Everyone stood and opened small hymnals to sing the opening hymn, including Gertie Lewis and her companion. The hand she was holding belonged to Rex Barnett. With his right hand he pulled out his watch from his vest pocket to check the time. Hanging from the watch chain was a bright new gold cross. The service had started right on time. It was the first time he had been in church in years.

O come, all ye faithful,
Joyful and triumphant,
O come ye, O come ye to Bethlehem;
Come and behold him,
Born the King of angels
O come, let us adore him,
O come, let us adore him,
O come, let us adore him,
Christ the Lord.

THE END

Epilogue

DURING THE GRAND JURY proceedings, Harry Hayward's suave and controlled demeanor did not falter. He told jailers that because of their kind treatment to him and his brother, "I'll have you all for a wine supper next week."

Both Harry Hayward and Claus Blixt were indicted for murder by the Grand Jury and Harry's trial began on January 21, 1895. Julia Ging, Kitty's twin sister, had come to Minneapolis and on the morning of the trial, she dressed to resemble her dead sister and was taken to face Harry Hayward in his cell. Harry was not moved by the ruse and recognized Julia, greeting her by name.

Thousands of spectators stood in the streets, unable to get seating in the overcrowded Labor Temple courtroom where the Honorable Judge Seagram Smith presided. The respected Judge Smith, bold, in his fifties, and an impressive figure with his beard and large ears, ruled the trial with an iron hand. Almost immediately, he had to settle a controversy between *The Minneapolis Journal* and *The Minneapolis Tribune* over the reporting of the trial, as well as scolding *The Minneapolis Times* for stolen stories involving confidential material about the trial. It took nine tedious days to select a jury of twelve from some two hundred men who were examined amidst long arguments between the attorneys. Mrs. Hayward senior sat cold and unmoved through the first day's proceedings while Harry's father was in tears.

The trial lasted forty-six days, turning brother against brother as the defense moved to make Adry and Blixt the guilty ones. News coverage of the final days of the trial included banner headlines, and the front pages were almost completely devoted to the summations of the attorneys.

A DEFENSE OF SHREDS AND PATCHES

County Attorney Frank M. Nye, worn out by his arduous labors, and trembling with sickness, closed the Hayward case with one of the most brilliant and powerful arguments in the history of American criminal prosecution!

In his closing words, the county attorney charged the jury:

Gentlemen of the jury, take this case. If a sinful publican might at this moment invoke the guidance of the divine, if a frail and erring child on this life's stormy voyage may be heard, if my broken and feeble words may rise above the roaring waves to the loving Master who stills the tempest and the angry sea, I pray Him guide you in the sacred way of truth and justice!

Frank Nye's closing address had taken five hours, and when he sat down, there was a spontaneous outburst of applause in the courtroom. The chief attorney for the defense, the well-known W.W. Erwin, was so moved that he congratulated his adversary on his summation. The next day the banner headlines read MR. ERWIN'S EFFORT TO SAVE A LIFE. The handsome, clean-shaven lawyer addressed the jury for eleven hours over a two-day period.

When the jury retired to seek a verdict, Harry Hayward was still confident and said, "In two hours I will be a free man." The jury deliberated for three hours but was in agreement on the first ballot. Then the decision was announced.

We, the jury in the above entitled cause, find the defendant— there was a pause—*guilty as charged in the indictment.*

On March 11, 1895, Judge Seagram Smith, who opposed capital punishment, sentenced the defendant. The judge, known for "his large, tender heart," revealed his compassion as his voice faltered. Minutes passed. Finally, he spoke.

> *It is considered and adjudged that you, Harry T. Hayward, as punishment for the crime of murder in the first degree of which you have been convicted, be taken from here hence to the common jail of Hennepin County and there be confined. And that after a period of three calender months from this day, and at a time fixed by the governor of the State of Minnesota, and designated by his warrant, you be taken to the place of execution and there be hanged by the neck until you are dead.*

Appeals and stays of execution by the Minnesota Supreme Court delayed the execution. Harry Hayward maintained his debonair personality as he waited in his jail cell through most of the year. The last attempt to save Harry's life came in early December when his parents asked Governor David M. Clough for mercy—and were refused. Harry finally confessed to the crime and, in discussing the date of his execution, reflected that it was "a long time to wait for a train."

Harry became Minneapolis' number one tourist attraction. Newspapers compiled the proceedings of the protracted trial into book form and advertised them for sale. Photographers sold postcard-style photos of Harry, Kitty Ging, Claus Blixt, and, even the horse and buggy. Harry had numerous visitors. Someone actually smuggled an Edison recording machine into his cell and made a cylinder of a conversation with Harry. Transcriptions were made and circulated. One unknown person put pen to paper and composed the

Ozark Flats

Ballad of Harry Hayward:

Minneapolis was excited,
And for many miles around,
For a terrible crime committed
Just a mile or so from town.
It was a cold and winter's eve,
The moon was passed away,
The road was dark and lonely
When found dead where she lay.

He was at heart a criminal
But a coward of a man!
And so he sought another
To execute his 'plan.'
The bargain it was struck,
The villain did reply,
'Tonight she takes that fatal ride
Yes, she will have to die!'

When for pleasure she went riding
Little did she know her fate,
That was to take place on
        that lonely night
On the road near Calhoun Lake.
She was shot while in the buggy,
And beaten ('Tis true to speak!)
Until all life had vanquished,
Then was cast into the street.

Oh, how could he have done that deed,
So terrible to do?
Or how could he have killed a girl
With heart so pure and true,
It was a cold and bloody plot
Likewise a terrible sin
To take a life so kind and true
As she was then to him.

        CHORUS

The stars were shining bright
And the moon had passed away,
The road was dark and lonely
Where her form had turned to clay,
Then tell the tale of a criminal.
Kit was his promised bride,
Just another sin to answer for,
Just another fatal ride.

It never caught on.

On December 8, Harry was moved into Cell Number Three on the second tier of the county jail, and wrote to his brother.

>*My Dear Brother Adry,*
>   *Adry, my days are numbered and I sincerly hope and trust that you will grant me this one last request to you. It is for you to come to me immediately upon*

receipt of this, and forgive me for the wrong I have done you, and in order that I may forgive you for any wrong your imagination may have led you to think you have done me. Trusting and believing that you will come, I am your sincere and loving brother.

Harry T. Hayward

Adry came to say goodbye.

On December 11, Harry T. Hayward had his last meal which he called his "wedding breakfast." He was hanged in the early morning and died of strangulation. Doctors said his heart had continued to beat for thirteen minutes after he dropped through the gallows. A newspaper headline read, HIS LIFE FOR CATHERINE GING'S.

Claus Blixt was sentenced to life imprisonment. He told newsmen, "That horror has never left me. Deep in my breast is the sore, but God in heaven has wiped the feeling away." He spent thirty years in the state prison at Stillwater and was termed "insane" when he died in August of 1925.

Adry Hayward left the Ozark Flats to live in south Minneapolis. He lived in several different places and held various jobs—bookkeeper, clerk, salesman, travel agent—before dying in 1920 at the age of fifty-eight.

Mayor William H. Eustis, whose memoirs were published in *The Minneapolis Journal* in 1930, felt that he had done all he could for Minneapolis under the system of city government at that time. He chose not to run for re-election and his successor, Robert Pratt, won easily and kept Vernon Smith on as Superintendent of the Police Department. William Eustis ran, unsuccessfully, for governor in 1898.

The Ozark Flats was disposed of by William W. Hayward for one hundred and ten thousand dollars. As the Bellevue Hotel, it gradually deteriorated into an inner city rooming-house. Recently, it was superbly restored to its former elegance without, however, its former name.

The West Hotel, originally billed as fireproof, was the scene of a fire, starting in the elevator shaft, in 1906. It lost ground to newer hotels in the central business district—the Radisson, the Dyckman (built on the site of St. Mark's Church), and the new Nicollet. The West was torn down in 1940 and is now a parking lot.

Rex Barnett and Gert Lewis were married in 1895. Emmett and Hillary attended the wedding and John Morrissey served as best man. The marriage produced twin boys the following year. Rex served with military intelligence in the Spanish-American War, stationed at Key West. He retired from the Minneapolis Police Department in 1912 and moved to Key West permanently.

The Markhams returned to their home in Excelsior in the spring of 1895. Emmett resigned from his post with the *Minneapolis Journal* to return to the weekly newspaper field. Hillary gave birth to a baby girl, Catherine Frances, on July 13, 1895. Emmett rededicated himself to his family but his enormous energy could not be contained. Over the years he acquired three more weekly newspapers and two small daily newspaper plants in Minnesota. The Markhams spent their following Christmases in St. Louis and the Blairs returned to Excelsior each summer. In 1904, Hillary and the children spent the summer with her parents in order to attend the Louisiana Purchase Exposition. Emmett joined them late in August. Both families spent Christmas that year in Excelsior—ten years after Ozark Flats.